THE
PALAZZO

Also by Kayte Nunn

Rose's Vintage
Angel's Share
The Botanist's Daughter
The Forgotten Letters of Esther Durrant
The Silk House
The Last Reunion
The Only Child

THE PALAZZO

KAYTE NUNN

NO EXIT PRESS

First published in Australia in 2025 by HarperCollins
First published in the UK in 2025 by No Exit Press,
an imprint of Bedford Square Publishers Ltd,
London, UK

noexit.co.uk
@noexitpress

© Kayte Nunn, 2025

The right of Kayte Nunn to be identified as the author of this work has been asserted in accordance with the Copyright, Designs and Patents Act 1988. All rights reserved. No part of this book may be reproduced, stored in or introduced into a retrieval system, or transmitted, in any form or by any means (electronic, mechanical, photocopying, recording or otherwise) without the written permission of the publishers.

Any person who does any unauthorised act in relation to this publication may be liable to criminal prosecution and civil claims for damages.
A CIP catalogue record for this book is available from the British Library.
This is a work of fiction. Names, characters, places, and incidents either are the product of the author's imagination or are used fictitiously, and any resemblance to actual persons, living or dead, businesses, companies, events or locales is entirely coincidental.

ISBN
978-1-83501-149-2 (Paperback)
978-1-83501-150-8 (eBook)

2 4 6 8 10 9 7 5 3 1

Printed in Great Britain by CPI Group (UK) Ltd, Croydon CR0 4YY

The manufacturer's authorised representative in the EU for product safety is Easy Access System Europe, Mustamäe tee 50, 10621 Tallinn, Estonia
gpsr.requests@easproject.com

Evil is unspectacular and always human.
And shares our bed and eats at our own table.

Herman Melville, **WH Auden**

The morning after

Delfina rests her bicycle against the palazzo's crumbling stone wall, the half-open gate the first sign that something is amiss. Later, she will wish she had chosen to stay in bed, in her tiny room in the village far below, but in this moment she is eager for the silky feel of the water as it flows across her body. Though the air will be insufferably hot in the middle of the day, for now it is cool enough to raise goosebumps – *pelle d'oca* – on her skin, and she shivers involuntarily.

The gate slams shut behind her as she hurries up the stone steps. At the top, she ducks to avoid fairy lights strung between the trees, her feet flying along the gravel path. Unbuttoning her blouse with one hand, she pulls a pair of goggles from the pocket of her skirt with the other without missing a step.

It is the most beautiful swimming pool she has ever seen, the water a pale turquoise, surrounded by cypress trees, fragrant flowering shrubs and winding sand-coloured gravel paths. Every morning for the past two months, she has ploughed through forty laps, breathing to each side, noticing the flutter of her feet, the shape of her hand as it breaks the surface, her mind blissfully free of all other thoughts. She savours the precious half-hour that offers the chance to disappear into herself, to be nothing but breath and movement, muscle sliding and stretching over bone, lungs ready to burst as she slices through the water.

She is getting faster.

Afterwards, as she dries off, the first rays of sun on her skin, she will often find a peach nestled on her towel, a couple of ripe figs, or a small bunch of grapes, still cool from the night air. She never sees Marco leave them – he slips onto the terrace like a shadow, and besides, she's too busy counting her strokes to watch for him. The gifts make her smile, though she still cannot decide if it is a deliberate courtship or merely a simple kindness.

Designed as a lap pool with a semi-circular bulge, the pool's straight side is bordered by wide-planked decking furnished with a handful of sun-bleached wooden loungers. The other offers an infinity edge and a jaw-dropping view of the valley below.

Several private, curtained cabanas are tucked away among trees and shrubs, and there is a partially restored outbuilding a short distance away, its rough stone warmed to gold by the first rays of the rising sun. Campari-coloured market umbrellas have been left up from the night before, and wet towels are clumped on the ground like sleeping dogs. An empty wine bottle has rolled under a sun lounger, a small table is crowded with stained glasses, and a cylinder of pills – headache tablets? – lies abandoned next to a tangled puddle of bikinis. A heavy, wrought-iron chair has been knocked on its side, the cushion appearing to have soaked up a puddle of spilled red wine.

Delfina sighs. It's not the first time she's found things like this. She will clear everything away after her swim, but it will make her late for breakfast service.

She reaches the pool, comes to a halt and dips a toe in, frowning. A dark shape at the other end is in stark contrast to the turquoise tiles. Has someone thrown a towel in the water? It's hard to tell in the dawn light.

As she skirts the mess, the shape begins to take a distinctly human form, and she wonders if it is an early riser attempting to rid themselves of a hangover. Plenty of the guests drink too much. Marco keeps the alcohol flowing — as he has explained, the mark-up helps to keep the palazzo afloat.

Disappointment tightens her chest at the thought that she might miss her swim this morning, that someone else has beaten her to it. She nurses the faint hope that the guest might not linger.

A few more steps towards the far end, and the first inkling that something is wrong snakes along her spine.

The person should be moving, even if only a little. Instead, they're floating face-down, hair fanned like a halo of seaweed.

CHAPTER ONE

Five days earlier

Knapsacks of yellow pollen weighting its hind legs, the bee lands with the precision of a military helicopter on the woman as she lies draped across the sun lounger. Her foot twitches briefly as the bee tickles the smooth skin of her inner thigh, and her toes dance to a jittery rhythm, a nervous tic, but she remains asleep, lulled by the drone of insects and the searing noon heat.

She could be anywhere from her late twenties to mid-thirties, though in fact she is about to turn forty. Her glossy chestnut hair is smoothed back from an unlined forehead (botoxed or not, it's hard to tell, even up close), and an expensively cut swimsuit accentuates her hourglass curves and legs toned by a near-daily Pilates habit. Her pedicure (Blood Oath, part of a new line of super-charged, vitamin-enriched red nail polishes that she hopes will be popular come Halloween) is echoed by the gloss on her lips.

Though she is shaded by an umbrella, her eyes shielded by her oversized sunglasses and her skin slathered in fifty-plus sun lotion, her face is beginning to flush. The sun is stronger than she's used to, and she doesn't generally expose herself like this. If she lies there much longer, she will suffer the consequences. She knows exactly how much damage the sun can do. It's a professional requirement that her skin always look good, and she generally opts for fake tan rather than risking the real thing.

An unopened paperback – the latest bestseller, picked up on impulse at the airport – sits abandoned on a small table next to her phone and a glass in which the ice has long melted. She last had time to read a novel sometime in the noughties but felt a surge of optimism when making the purchase earlier that morning.

A few feet from her outstretched body, the pool ripples turquoise, glinting an invitation, though she is yet to dip so much as a polished toe in the water. At her back, past a stand of cypress trees, along a winding path lies the palazzo, its entrance opening to a stone fountain in the centre of a turning circle. A track leads from this circle, unspooling until it reaches a pair of locked wrought-iron gates.

The palazzo is perfectly isolated, a fortress nestled into the foothills of the mountains.

Beyond the water, a dirt road offers a switchback of tight bends descending several hundred feet to the valley. There, grapevines heavy with fruit, their leaves wilting in the heat, run perpendicular to the road. It's a scene that wouldn't look out of place on the cover of the book she bought but probably won't finish.

A cloud of dust rises in the distance, hazing the horizon, and it's followed slow, languorous minutes later by the throaty buzz of an engine that momentarily drowns out the cicadas. The change in atmosphere pierces the woman's consciousness, and as Vivienne Savidge opens her eyes, for a moment she cannot remember where on earth she is.

'I think someone's here,' says her assistant, Jade, sitting on a lounger in the shade a short distance away.

'Oh good!' Vivi takes another look at Jade, who has taken off the shirt she was wearing earlier. 'Nice suit.'

'Thank you.'

'Is it Eres?' Vivi looks down at her own swimsuit, almost identical to the one her assistant is wearing.

Jade begins to put her shirt back on, threading her arms awkwardly through the sleeves. 'I didn't think you'd mind. It's such lovely fabric. I ordered one for myself when I was finalising your Net-a-Porter delivery. I got a different colour.' She swallows audibly. 'Of course.'

'Hmm. It looks better on you.' It's not the first time her assistant has copied her look.

The honk of a horn interrupts Vivi's thoughts, and as she rises to go and see who it is, her phone buzzes with a notification. Her hand is slippery with sun cream and sweat, and she almost loses her grasp as she flips the phone over to check the screen, angling it away from the glare of the sun so she can see.

The words send a jolt of alarm through her, and her hand jerks as she reads the message again, gripping the phone tightly now.

Soon everyone Will know.

The number has been withheld. As she struggles to process the meaning of the words, her phone buzzes with another message, again anonymous.

Enjoy your holiday :)

'Everything okay?' Jade asks, lowering her sunglasses and regarding Vivi with concern.

Vivi's been subjected to a cesspit of trolling over the years: insults so vicious they feel like a knife to the guts, jibes about her personal life that bear no resemblance to reality, and once, a cruel newspaper caricature that was in no way amusing. She realised long ago that it came with the territory, but that doesn't mean it ever stops stinging. Haters gonna hate, right? It's the price of being visible in a connected world. As Will always said when a particular comment or criticism got her down, 'Darling, opinions are like arseholes – everyone's got one.'

Visibility as a woman in business, particularly in the notoriously fickle beauty industry, comes with the impossible expectation that you should, above all else, be likeable. You must never put a foot wrong, you must be aspirational but also relatable. A kind of elevated girl-next-door. People either want to be your friend or they hate you – sometimes both at the same time. It's exhausting.

The threats to her company she takes more seriously; those are referred to the IT and legal teams, who take almost visceral delight in uncovering the grubs cowering behind their keyboards. A cease-and-desist notice on official letterhead from her solicitors usually shuts them up.

Spam filters mostly corral the emails before they get to her these days, and she no longer reads product reviews, leaving that to Vivid's marketing team. More personal reviews, on the other hand …

But a text message? This is a new invasion, and she feels a prickle of disquiet. Only a small circle of close friends and colleagues have her number. She sighs, thinking more clearly now. Nothing's entirely private these days, and if you're determined enough, you can probably uncover almost anything, including a personal phone number.

Thanks to YouTube, her face is well-known enough that someone could have recognised her at the airport. Then it hits her – she'd posted a photo while she was packing of 'travel beauty essentials'. All Vivid products, of course. It's the end of July, so no big stretch to deduce that she was going on holiday. Plus, she'd followed it up with an artistic shot of the pool at the palazzo when she arrived. For God's sake, she'd even tagged it #bellaitalia and #palazzostellina. Like she was exactly the kind of jaunty person who heads off for a break without a care in the world, unafraid to subtly brag about where she was holidaying.

She had been stalked briefly once: someone sending her cryptic messages about places she'd recently been, especially at night. She'd changed her number, and it's been three years since the last message. Until now, she'd almost managed to wipe it from her memory, though she still doesn't like to be out on her own after dark.

Her skin prickles despite the heat, and the feeling of impending doom that's been her almost constant companion for the past few months returns, clouding the glorious day. What do they know? She can think of a couple of things that must never be allowed to come to light. Ever.

Deciding to ignore the messages, for now at least, she marks them as junk, deletes them, and then slips on a sheer cover-up over her swimsuit. The others are due to arrive any minute, and that car horn is more than likely one or several of them.

'Would you like me to go and see who it is?' Jade asks, putting down her book, but Vivi's already on her feet.

'Absolutely not! After the shitshow of a year we've had, this is the only thing I've been able to look forward to for months.' She pushes her feet into a pair of Hermes Oran leather sandals (bought on sale – she might be wealthy by most people's standards but that doesn't mean she throws her money around) and walks quickly along the path to the palazzo.

CHAPTER TWO

'Taking it to extremes, isn't she? Running away to a convent.' A tall, fair woman in a crumpled oversized cotton shirt, striped track pants and dirty white sneakers steps out of the car that has pulled up at the front. She surveys the buildings before her, shading her eyes against the glare of the sun as she takes in the razor-sharp mountain peaks beyond. 'Jesus, it's hot.'

'Alice! I'm so glad you made it!' Vivi peers over the balustrade, her face alight with pleasure, although if someone were to look carefully, they would see wariness etched into the fine lines around her eyes. '*Former* convent,' she stresses, then straightens and throws her arms wide, as if she is the proprietor of this magnificently crumbling mansion when in fact she has merely rented it for the week. 'Welcome to the Palazzo Stellina!'

Two teenage girls emerge from the back of the tiny car, unfolding their limbs like baby giraffes. Younger versions of their mother, they're almost identical, with long, poker-straight fine blonde hair and the round, angelic faces and china blue eyes of an Anglo-Saxon Madonna. They're both wearing pastel linen dungarees over tiny matching T-shirts, bucket hats and bug-eyed sunglasses, and look as fresh as if they just stepped out of the shower instead of having just endured a punishing long-haul flight.

'Girls!' Their mother takes a deep breath. 'Italy! Can you believe it? I was right: even the air smells good here.'

They all raise their faces, flowers to the sun, and Vivi takes a moment to appreciate how much the twins have grown. She wants to stop time, to freeze them like this, to keep them at an age where nothing catastrophic has happened to them, when they haven't experienced the loss of someone they love. Although if she were able to stop time, she should probably have done so months ago.

'Mia? Isla? Darlings?' she calls. 'My God! I almost didn't recognise you.' She hurries to greet her sister, nearly tripping on the steps in her haste. 'Such a cliché, I know, but has it really been three years?' She pictures them with dimpled elbows and cheeks, in toddler pyjamas, smelling of bubble bath, snuggling in for bedtime stories. As newborns, two impossibly tiny, perfectly round, bald heads peeking out of pink blankets. The back of her throat begins to sting and she blinks rapidly: those days are long gone, and she was only there for a handful of them, too busy with her own baby, the business she tended to with as much constancy and ferocity as any mother.

How did they get here so fast, the girls practically grown, their childhood already a memory that she was barely a part of? It feels like five minutes has passed, not fifteen – or is it sixteen? – years.

'Weeds, aren't they? They've left me a long way behind. They're even a head taller than Jeff,' Alice says, releasing a hair elastic to shake out her messy ponytail, her fair skin free of make-up. No matter how much free product Vivi sends her, she never wears any of it, caring little about such things. Alice turns to hug Vivi fiercely, mashing her face against her shoulder. It's even more of a comfort than Vivi expected, and she returns the hug with equal fervour.

'Not exactly an achievement.' Alice's ex-husband liked to pretend he was five foot nine, but he fooled no one.

'Fair comment.' Alice releases her, reaching into her bag and pulling out a pack of nicotine gum. She thrusts it at Vivi, but Vivi shakes her head. She has never had a habit and is surprised her sister doesn't remember that, but then Alice has always been oblivious to things that don't directly concern her. 'You look good.' She tilts her head to one side. 'All things considered.'

'Liar.' Vivi can't hide the plum-coloured shadows under her eyes, the wan skin. No amount of serums or expensive creams can conceal the indelible marks of grief.

Isla is looking around with interest, reaching out to touch the rough stone of the palazzo walls, while Mia is stabbing at her phone, frowning.

'How are my favourite nieces?'

'Good, thanks, Auntie Vee,' they chant in unison, smiles briefly lighting up their faces. They have Australian accents now. Five years down under will do that.

The two girls return Vivi's effusive hugs, Isla more enthusiastically than her twin. Nothing's changed: Mia always was the less approachable of the pair. Even as a toddler she'd shy away from any display of affection. She was the daring one, running laps around Vivi's back garden or trying to climb the fence into the next-door neighbour's place. Always wanting to live dangerously. Isla was the obedient one, the kind one, and although Vivi loves them both dearly and equally, she has an extra layer of admiration for Mia, a risk-taker after her own heart, stubborn in the pursuit of her desires.

'Sorry about everything,' Isla whispers, and Vivi squeezes her tighter.

'Precious girl.'

'I can't believe we made it here in one piece. I fear my life has been considerably shortened by that autostrada out of Turin.' Alice widens her eyes and mimes hands gripping a steering wheel, her clenched knuckles demonstrating her terror. 'Driving on the wrong side of the road with jetlag. I deserve a medal.'

'You didn't kill us, Mum,' Isla says.

'Not quite,' Mia chimes in.

Alice ignores her daughters, puts the packet of gum back in her bag and takes in her surroundings. 'It's bloody gorgeous,' she says, turning in a slow circle, her eyes widening as she sees the sheer face of the mountains, purple in the heat haze, sharp as cut-outs against the sky. 'We won't want to leave, will we, girls?'

The twins are inspecting the pockmarked stone walls, the broken shutters (painted a nevertheless charming shade of duck-egg blue) and the unruly gardens. Mia, snapping away with the camera on her phone, mumbles something unintelligible that Vivi chooses to interpret as positive.

'*Bellissima!*' says Isla shyly.

'She's been learning Italian on Duolingo ever since she found out we were coming,' Alice says proudly.

'Mum! You're oversharing. Again,' Mia grumbles.

'It's fine, really,' Isla says.

'What can I smell?' Alice ignores Mia, sniffing the air again. 'Garlic? Rosemary? It's going to be heaven to be catered to for a week!'

'Well done, Isla; I hope it comes in useful. This place isn't too shabby, huh?' Vivi isn't about to draw attention to the scuffed furniture or temperamental plumbing. As she looks back towards the palazzo, her gaze falls on a window on the top floor. A movement catches her eye. She squints, and for a moment thinks she sees someone there, a gaunt face peering down at them. She turns back to her sister, ignoring the unnerving feeling of being watched. 'I can't claim any responsibility, I'm afraid. Jade found it,' she admits.

The pictures on Instagram make the nineteenth-century palazzo seem more glamorous than it is, but since when is that a surprise. 'I'm sorry it's only Piedmont and not the Cinque Terre, or Sicily, or Puglia. That's where everyone is going these days, isn't it?' They both skirt the fact that not only is Vivi footing the bill for the entire group but she also had her travel agent arrange the flights for Alice and the girls. 'She'll get the best deal,' Vivi had said on the phone when she issued the invitation, batting away Alice's half-hearted protests.

Six months ago, Jade, her blessedly efficient EA, had been planning an extravagant fortieth birthday celebration with two hundred of Vivi's friends, colleagues and business acquaintances in the ballroom at Claridge's. A gilt-embossed invitation on heavy card had been approved and was waiting to be printed. But after Will's diagnosis, Vivi decided not to go ahead with it, insisting the party be cancelled, even if it meant forfeiting the deposit. 'But see if they'll waive the fee,' she instructed Jade. The alternative, a quick getaway with only the closest of friends and family, was all she could possibly cope with.

When Jade sent her the details of the Palazzo Stellina, a private estate staffed by a former Michelin-starred chef and accommodating up to a dozen guests, it seemed the answer to her prayers. More importantly, it was vacant on the date required. When Jade booked it, Vivi was still optimistic that Will would be well enough to make it.

Honestly, she could kill him for not being here.

It isn't the first time she's wished him dead, but if killing your spouse doesn't occur to you at least once during a marriage, who even are you? Her lips curve at the irony. Black humour and sheer bloody-mindedness are the only things getting her out of bed these days. You didn't get to where she was without people waiting on the sidelines for you to fall apart, and she was damned if she was going to give them the satisfaction.

'Don't worry. Half of the girls' class is in either Positano or Puglia.' Alice laughs expansively. 'At least we won't run into anyone we know here, right, Mia?'

'What?' Her daughter doesn't look up from her phone, and a faint frown briefly crosses Alice's face.

'Although I was hoping we'd be in Lake Como, inviting George Clooney over for an *aperitivo*. We could have gone for a hotel – the Passalacqua, maybe?' Alice grins wickedly and wraps an arm about Vivi's waist.

'The what?'

'The Passalacqua. I read about it in the in-flight magazine. It was just named number one in the top fifty hotels in the world. And it's on the shores of Lake Como.'

She's teasing, but it rankles – the assumption that Vivi has elbow-deep pockets.

'This will more than do, sis.' Alice leans in. 'I'm still so sorry about Will.'

'Me too.' And Vivi's brave face finally crumples as she allows herself to rest her head on her sister's shoulder, blinking away sudden, hot tears. It hadn't been a perfect marriage – does such a thing exist? – and in the weeks before his diagnosis they'd had one of the worst fights of their entire relationship – about the business, naturally – but it had still been a successful partnership, all things considered.

'I always did have my doubts about his commitment.'

Vivi lets out a strangled yelp of laughter. 'As it turns out, Will was extremely committed to dying.' She tamps down a spark of guilt. She won't tell Alice the truth, not yet. Maybe not ever.

'Fuck, I need a drink. I'm jetlagged to the eyeballs and drier than a witch's tit.' Her sister squints at her watch. 'I think it's maybe three in the morning our time?'

'Four, actually, Mum,' Isla corrects her and holds out a hand. 'And that's twenty euros for the swear jar.'

'All bets are off this week. I vote we let the bad language loose!' Alice cries, throwing up her arms with abandon and twirling in a circle while both girls ignore her, accustomed to her antics.

'Come on, let's get you on the outside of a negroni.' Vivi pulls her towards the huge, studded front doors of the palazzo. 'Thanks for coming all this way.'

'Sorry I couldn't stay for long … last time.' Alice pops a second stick of gum in her mouth.

Vivi brushes off her apology. 'You were there. I got through it. That's about the best you can say about these things. And you're here now.'

'The timing was good; the girls are on their winter break, though they *are* supposed to do some studying while they're here. Isn't that right, girls?'

Mia rolls her eyes as Alice leans into Vivi again. 'They run rings around me,' she whispers. 'Terrifyingly bright,' she adds, with none of the self-congratulatory boastfulness that would accompany such words from any other parent. 'I never know what they might be up to, so I try not to think about it too much.' Alice had her babies so young, becoming a mother at only twenty-two. Vivi has always admired her sister for it, not that she's ever told her that.

'There's a pool, yeah?' Mia asks, ignoring her.

'Sure is.' Vivi gestures behind them. 'Just wait till you see it – it's probably the best thing about the place.'

'Hey, Auntie Vee?' Mia shakes her phone. 'What's the wi-fi password?'

'I'll have to check with Jade. Or Marco will know. I'm surprised he hasn't come out to greet you.'

'Marco?' Alice arches one eyebrow suggestively at Vivi. 'Hot chef Marco?'

'Ew, Mum,' Mia protests.

'Too soon?' Alice says when Vivi doesn't respond. 'Are the others here yet?' she asks, trying a different tack.

'You three are the first. Pete and Nick's flight gets in tonight.' Vivi takes a breath. 'I also invited Caroline. I know, I know.' She holds her hands up in surrender. 'It was a moment of weakness. She knew Will as long as I did – in fact, she introduced us, don't forget.' She makes puppy eyes at her sister, fluttering her lashes. 'Don't be too mad at me. Besides, she's only a few miles away, so how could I not? If she heard I'd been here and not said anything to her … Can you bear it? She should have arrived by now, but then punctuality was never her strong point.'

Alice's expression flips from delighted to sulky, just as it used to when she was a girl. She pulls away from Vivi. 'You're kidding, right? Caro's like the *albatross* of friendship.' She sighs heavily. 'Just because you were once close doesn't mean you have to stay that way for the rest of your life.'

'Do you think you could be kind, just this once, for me? She hasn't had it easy, you know.'

'Do I have a choice? At least Pete's coming. I haven't seen him in forever.' Alice's face lights up again.

'You always were fond of him, probably because he indulged you,' Vivi teases, relieved to have got over the Caroline hurdle.

'I'd hardly call taking me and the girls out to lunch occasionally when my sister was too busy working an indulgence,' Alice huffs.

'Let's not fight, please?' Vivi takes her sister's hand again. 'Not yet, anyway,' she mutters under her breath.

'Well, now I've heard about Caroline, I definitely need a drink.' Alice looks about hopefully. 'Where's the bar?'

'Girls!' Vivi calls, seeing that Mia and Isla are heading for the pool. 'I have gifts. You too, Alice,' she says, taking her sister's hand and pulling her up the steps to the terrace. 'Your skin looks like it could do with some hydration. All that recycled plane air.' She shudders.

'Are you telling me I look like a wrinkled old hag? I'm still two years younger than you, remember.' Alice's voice has an edge; it'll take her a while to forgive Vivi for springing Caroline on her.

Vivi laughs again, and the doom-laden cloud lightens a fraction. 'Come on. We're all going to have a fabulous time. Promise.' She banishes the text messages to the far reaches of her mind. Nothing is going to spoil this week. Not if she can help it.

thetimes.co.uk
12 April 2023
Annelise Jones, business reporter

Beauty company Vivid Formulations announces death of CEO

Vivid Formulations, the cosmetics company founded by Vivienne Savidge, announced the death of William J Savidge late on Friday. A statement issued this morning said that 'the company is profoundly saddened by the sudden demise of its much-loved and highly valued CEO'. Calling it a 'shocking loss', CFO Robert Hutchings confirmed that he will assume the responsibilities of Mr Savidge's role until a replacement is appointed, adding, 'The company has every confidence in its senior management team moving forward, and is in full support of founder and creative director Vivienne Savidge, who is expected to take a short leave of absence.' Vivid Formulations posted net revenues of £25 million in the year 2021–22 on profits after tax of £5.2 million, a year-on-year increase of 32 per cent, and was one of the pandemic's surprise success stories.

NOTE: Comments on this news item have been suspended. Readers are reminded to refrain from making defamatory statements.

CHAPTER THREE

The easiest lies are the ones delivered over the phone. The person to whom you are speaking can't look you in the eye; plus, there's less chance of there being a record of the deception. Marco Bianchi dials his meat supplier and orders enough to feed seven guests for a week: legs of lamb for slow roasting over charcoal; veal that he will slice paper-thin, pan-fry in butter and serve with lemon and sage; and *bistecca* (the finest cut, but he's never been one to compromise). A haunch of prosciutto and logs of *salsiccia* and *soppresata*, made in the traditional way, are already strung from beams in the cellars beneath the palazzo, and he's just finished skinning a brace of wild rabbits.

Milk has been heated to precisely 85 degrees Celsius and the curds are now draining over muslin for ricotta. Figs are softening in the heat and must be eaten before they become jammy and spoil. Artichokes tumble on the counter next to tomatoes ripened on the vine and a bowl of eggs collected earlier that morning. He will use the yolks to make a light, silky pasta for the traditional *agnolotti del plin*.

It's a far cry from the sweatshop pressure of Cibo, the Greenwich Village restaurant with its brigade of twenty where he rose to the heights of sous chef, but this is honest food, honest work, even if he is sometimes forced to lie to get what he needs. The palazzo has been almost fully booked since opening only a couple of months ago, and it takes every ounce of his energy and many, many hours of hard work to maintain the standards he insists on. He is exhausted and will need a holiday himself after the summer is over.

He frowns at the basil already beginning to wilt and finishes the call with an assurance that the outstanding bill will be paid on the day of delivery. The falsehood slips across his tongue as smoothly as the bottle of Amarone he downed the night before.

Understated luxury and obsessive attention to detail is the guiding principle in everything he does, but compromises have had to be made. It took him nearly a year to make the former convent habitable (although the rooms are still tiny, at least they are less cell-like now), doing a lot of the work himself. The walls have been replastered, the floors refinished, there's a mix of locally made and antique furniture – just enough that the place looks welcoming rather than austere – and the mattresses and linen are the finest he could source. As with food, it's all about the best-quality ingredients, treated with care and respect.

The security gates were an inconvenient expense, but the calibre of guests he seeks to attract have an overwhelming requirement for privacy. The plumbing alone almost bankrupted him, the pool cost double what he was originally quoted, and the roof still needs repairing. Though bookings are steady, sluggish cashflow means he can't pay his meat supplier at the moment, let alone spring for a new roof.

Whenever the weight of the bank loan threatening to crush him becomes too much, he reminds himself to breathe, that these things take time, that he wants too much, too soon. Good things come to those who are prepared to put in the sweat, those who are willing to reap the rewards of patience.

'*Nonna*!' The old woman is sitting, hunched over, in the shadowy part of the kitchen next to the fireplace, almost invisible. 'Can I get you something?'

Stella tilts her head, her eyes like two shiny rosary beads, and stares at him without blinking. She's tiny and seemingly frail, but appearances are deceptive: despite being well into her nineties, she manages the two flights of stairs to the guestrooms without any assistance. She insists on helping where she can, checking tables are correctly set and that the rooms are perfect.

Her pasta is still the best he's ever tasted.

'Water?' he asks, going to the tap and filling a glass. It's already warm in the kitchen, despite the thick stone walls. The whole of Europe has been blanketed with a deadly heat that shows no sign of abating, and even up here in the mountains, the middle of the day is hotter than he remembers it ever being. She nods once and he places it beside her. After a moment, she extends a shaky hand towards it, and he watches anxiously, knowing he'll earn a slap if he tries to help.

'The rest of the new guests are arriving today.' Stella rarely replies to his comments, but he talks to her regardless, missing the banter of his former brigade. 'I'm running behind.'

Perhaps they'll be less demanding than the last lot, a group of investment bankers and their wives who thought that someone should be available to unpack and steam their clothes before dinner every night. He's met a couple of the new group already – Signora Savidge and her assistant, who arranged the booking. He can only hope that they'll leave a good tip, although Americans are much better at that than the British. As if on cue, the distant note of an engine pierces the silence. 'I've got to get on. Are the rooms ready?'

His grandmother blinks once, her sign that they are. He need not worry; she's as fastidious as he is when it comes to hospitality and keeps a close eye on Delfina, the young woman he has employed to waitress and help clean this summer. He hasn't told Delfina that he may not be able to keep her on over winter. The palazzo is still finding its feet, and bookings so far have come via word of mouth or a guest's diligent internet research. This summer has been busy, but the winter will surely be much quieter.

'*Grazie mille.*' He's about to step out onto the terrace when the dull glint of a pistol concealed among the folds of Stella's skirt catches his eye. '*Nonna!*' he hisses. 'What have I told you? *Please* don't carry that around!' He takes a step forward and she recoils, tightening her grip on the pistol. He holds out a hand. 'Please, give it to me. You don't need this. We're perfectly safe here. No one is going to harm us.'

She hesitates for a beat and then passes it to him, rolling her eyes as she does so, annoyed at being caught out. He checks, as he always does, that the safety catch is on and there are no bullets in the chamber. There are none kept in the entire palazzo, he's made sure of that, but he looks anyway. You can never be too careful.

He places the weapon on a shelf in the scullery, up high, where she can't reach it. He should get her some help, someone professional to talk to, but the last time he intervened it didn't go well. If one of the guests comes across her with a gun in her hand, it'll kill his business stone dead, or at the very least cost him dearly. Last month one of the children staying as part of a family group claimed that Stella had shouted at him, and it had taken all of Marco's charm and a hefty discount on the group's booze bill to calm the parents.

Putting the thought out of his mind for the time being, he sees the bowl containing the discarded rabbit entrails on the counter and picks it up. He's kept the heart, liver and kidneys, but the rest will go to the chickens.

Returning from the chicken coop, he reaches the terrace just in time to see a car pull up and a woman and two teenage girls emerge. He hangs back for a few moments, watching as the other woman greets them, eavesdropping on their conversation. You can learn a lot from watching people, especially without their knowledge.

CHAPTER FOUR

Caroline is all too aware that hers was a last-minute invitation, but now she'll be lucky to make it at all. Her twenty-year-old, third-hand car, bought off a fellow teacher several years ago, begins to steam gently from the bonnet not long after leaving the city. She isn't even halfway to her destination. Hoping that ignoring the situation will make it go away, it isn't until the temperature gauge is firmly in the red that she pulls over on the side of the autostrada to wait for the engine to calm down. She ponders the conundrum – a favourite word of hers – for a while. Should she even have favourite words? Or is that problematic, just as having favourite students has caused nothing but trouble. The thing is, words might be just about all she has these days.

As she left, she checked her rear-view mirror constantly, convinced she was being followed. Only after the narrow streets clotted with scooters and distracted pedestrians had disappeared behind her did she manage to relax, telling herself that the shadowy figure that had lurked outside her apartment building wouldn't dare pursue her beyond the city walls.

Now cars whip within a hair's breadth of her. Any closer and they'll scrape the paintwork of her ancient Fiat. She sits there, resting her head on the steering wheel, eyes closed, as she asks herself for the umpteenth time why she said yes to the invitation in the first place.

The email Vivi sent a fortnight ago contained a heartfelt offer to come and stay. She was going to be little more than an hour's drive away, she said. 'In fact, come for the week if you can. That is, if you don't have any other plans,' she signed off, adding a link to the website. A palazzo.

Caroline looked it up and discovered a building of soft grey stonework, a frankly amazing swimming pool with a jaw-dropping backdrop of snow-capped mountains, an outdoor terrace, a rustic kitchen, the table laden with baskets of local produce, *melanzane* and *carciofi*, plates of artfully arranged food, and a darkly handsome chef – 'brooding' is how she would describe him if she were writing about him.

Caroline lifts her head and brings her thoughts back to reality. *Buck up*, she tells herself. Feeling helpless never got a woman anywhere. Wiping her damp hands on her skirt, she risks turning over the engine, holding her breath until it miraculously grumbles into life again, then pumping the accelerator to merge into the traffic. She flips a middle finger at the driver who comes up too fast behind her and her mood lifts a fraction.

Everything goes smoothly until she turns off the autostrada onto the road that meanders along the Val Pellice and up towards the Italian Alps. She calculates she is about ten kilometres from the palazzo when the Fiat begins to steam again. This time it hisses and splutters and she coasts to a halt beside a collection of ancient farm buildings. 'Fuck!' She gets out, pops the bonnet and even more steam billows out.

Reaching into her handbag, she pulls out her phone. It's new, and she's still getting used to its ridiculous multitude of functions. She's angrily punching numbers when a man, eighty if he's a day, emerges from the nearest shed. She ends the call before it connects and begins to ask in rapid Italian if he wouldn't mind dropping her at the nearest village. She tells him she's staying with friends at the Palazzo Stellina, perhaps he knows it?

He pauses for so long after she finishes speaking that she wonders for a moment if he's deaf, or merely simple. Then he turns without a word and disappears again.

'Fucking great. Yeah, thanks for that.' She kicks her front tyre in frustration, forgetting that she's wearing open sandals, and succeeds only in stubbing her toe.

Moments later, there's the stuttering sound of an engine and a tiny three-wheeler truck that looks as decrepit as the shed from which it emerged pulls up next to her. This souped-up sewing machine – a Piaggo Ape, ubiquitous in small towns all over Italy – has a top speed of about forty kilometres an hour. They won't be going anywhere in a hurry.

'*Bagaglio?*' He gives her a wink of such lasciviousness that she second-guesses her decision to ask him for help, but she retrieves her weekender from the boot of her car and drops it onto a filthy potato sack that's spread out on the tray of the truck.

There's no room for her in the cab, so she hoists her skirts past her knees and climbs in next to her bag, doing her best not to reward him with an eyeful, and trying to avoid being covered in mud in the process. She repeats the details of the palazzo, speaking loudly so he can hear. He tells her that he knows it, that he will drop her there. Another wink and her stomach twists in revulsion. Thank Christ it's only a short trip.

As they set off, she reaches for her phone, fumbling with the unfamiliar settings as she types a brief message. She pauses only for a moment before pressing send, then shoves it back into her handbag and pulls out a worn compact. Grimacing as the wind blows her hair into a tangle, she begins to futilely dab powder on her shiny face.

She wishes it were as easy to disguise her other flaws.

After a while, she abandons her make-up and slumps back against the rear of the cab, already regretting her decision to see Vivi, just as she does any number of other questionable life choices that have led her to precisely this moment.

The truck lurches to one side, taking a hairpin bend too fast as they begin to climb, the road changing abruptly from tarmac to rough gravel. She checks their progress on her phone and sees that the farmer appears to have taken a wrong turn. They're not heading towards the pin dropped on her map. Fighting a rising sense of annoyance, she bangs her fist on the cab to get his attention, but although surely he must hear her hammering, he fails to turn around.

CHAPTER FIVE

'*Buongiorno!*' Marco approaches the women, so obviously related, though one is dishevelled and the other exudes glamour of the kind he was well-used to seeing in New York. 'We are so happy to have you stay with us.' He offers a broad smile, aware of the effect his even, white teeth and dark eyes have on both men and women. He's not afraid to use them to his advantage, especially if it leads to a more generous tip or a better review, or both.

Thanks to his earlier eavesdropping, he knows that Signora Savidge – Vivi – is recently widowed, and that her sister is mother to the two lanky teenage girls. He knows from the assistant's briefing notes that they have had a long journey to get here.

'Alice, this is Marco,' Vivi introduces her. 'Marco, this is my sister.'

'It is a pleasure to meet you,' he says, extending his hand for her to shake. Alice recoils. *That's odd*, he thinks. He's used to being met with a more positive reaction.

'Your hand,' she says, sounding horrified.

He looks down and sees blood and a stringy bit of entrail smeared across his palm. He immediately wipes it on his apron, kicking himself. This is not how he likes to greet new guests. 'Apologies. You caught me in the middle of preparing the rabbits.'

'We're not eating bunnies, are we, Mum?' One of the teenagers looks horrified.

'Isla is mostly pescetarian,' Alice says, smiling now.

'Pesce-pollotarian,' she corrects. 'I eat fish and chicken.'

'I'm sure Jade would have put that on the booking form,' Vivi says.

'It won't be a problem,' Marco assures them smoothly. There's always one. 'There will be plenty of choice, don't worry,' he adds.

The girl looks relieved. 'It's okay. I love vegetables, too,' she assures him.

'Yeah, she's weird like that,' the other girl chimes in. 'I'm Mia, and the fussy one is Isla.'

Her sister glares in response, but Marco can already tell which of them is likely to cause the most trouble.

'*Molto bene*. Welcome to you all.' He turns, pleased to see that Delfina, with perfect timing, has appeared at the entrance. She's carrying a large tray with glasses of iced water and a stack of cold rolled face towels, and once again he is grateful for her foresight. He has only to explain something once and she takes care of it.

She offers the tray to the women, who each help themselves to a towel and wipe their faces. Alice rubs hers across the back of her neck, closing her eyes in appreciation. 'Do you think we might get a massage, Vee?' she asks, her tone falling just short of pleading.

'We can certainly arrange that,' Marco replies quickly, nodding to Delfina.

'Brilliant.' Alice flashes him a smile that lights up her face. He has a weakness for blondes, especially ones who look like they've just stumbled out of bed.

'Perhaps you might show our guests to their rooms?' he suggests to Delfina, reining in his imagination. What is up with him today? Perhaps it is the sultry heat that is making him dream of lazy afternoon siestas between the sheets with a lover. Perhaps he has been on his own up here for too many months.

'*Allora.* Please, follow me. May I take the luggage?'

'Thank you,' Alice says, indicating the smallest of the three suitcases.

Delfina reaches for the largest one. 'I am stronger than I look.'

'*Grazie,*' the girl called Isla murmurs, lifting the handle of her own case.

'*Prego.*'

'We don't have to share a room, do we?' Mia pouts. 'Mum?'

'I'm not sure, darling. But even if you do, it's only for a week.'

'But Isla snores,' she complains.

'I do not!' Isla replies.

'I'll never get any sleep.'

'Okay, you've made your point.' Alice sighs, clearly exhausted at having to referee another argument between them.

'Don't worry,' Vivi says. 'Jade can track down some earplugs if necessary. In fact, I wouldn't be surprised if she brought several pairs with her — she seems to think of everything.'

'Don't worry,' Delfina repeats in accented English, frowning as she concentrates on the conversation. 'There are separate rooms. Two singles for the girls; they are next to each other.'

'Oh, perfect, thank you,' Alice says. 'See? Nothing to worry about, Mia. You'll have total peace.'

Marco feels Alice's eyes on him, and he turns to meet her gaze. 'Was there something else?' he asks.

'Oh, yes.' She shakes herself out of an apparent daydream. 'Mia wanted to know the wi-fi password.'

'Of course.' His eyes dance with amusement. There's an indefinable spark of electricity passing between them. 'It's on a note in your rooms, but I am afraid we have some issues at the moment.' He shrugs. 'Not of our making, but they are working on the towers this week.' He indicates the mountains behind them. 'It is supposed to only take a day or two, but …'

'Oh, okay, thanks. Sorry, girls, you'll just have to limit your screen time,' Alice says brightly. The statement is met with groans from them both.

As Alice and the girls follow Delfina up the wide stone stairs that lead to the terrace and the upper floors, Marco sees a movement out of the corner of his eye, a dark shadow moving along the path that leads to the swimming pool and the annex, a converted cowshed that he's cleared to use as overflow guestrooms when the main building is fully occupied.

Stella. The palazzo is her home, somewhere she has lived her entire life. She is the reason he has all this now – she welcomed his suggestion to turn her home into a small hotel when she could just as easily have chosen to live the remainder of her life here undisturbed, the palazzo gently crumbling around her. He will always be grateful to her for giving him a place in which to rebuild his life. He does what he can to keep her out of sight, although it's not always easy.

Arrival is stressful as he learns the guests' particular needs and they settle in. At the end of a week or a fortnight, he's in a rhythm and is even sometimes sad to see them go. That said, he can usually tell whether a group is going to be demanding within the first few minutes. In this case, the girls seem like they will be the hardest to please, although there are still three more guests to arrive, so he'll reserve judgement until then.

He met with Signora Savidge's assistant, Jade, when they arrived earlier in the day and spent some time clarifying the booking notes that she sent him. The *signora* is the first to bring an assistant, although several families this summer have been accompanied by their nannies.

The wealthier the guests, the more demanding they generally are, but it was the same at the restaurant, and he's had plenty of experience with difficult customers. Mostly they just want to feel important, to get what they want when they want it. They hate being made to wait, especially for a drink. It's come as no surprise that almost without exception, every guest over the age of eighteen (and some a year or two younger, to which he turns a blind eye) is immediately happier when they've got something alcoholic in their hand.

As he races to catch up with Stella and steer her somewhere safer, he runs through the remaining preparations but finds himself thinking about Alice instead, his imagination straying to wholly inappropriate scenarios.

CHAPTER SIX

An hour or so later, the metallic screech of the palazzo gates reaches the kitchen and Marco steps onto the terrace in time to see a silver car edge its way up the winding gravel road.

It pulls up at the front of the palazzo, where Marco stands waiting, and two men climb out of the low-slung vehicle. It is two of the remaining three expected arrivals, the men coming from the airport. Peter Hatchett and Nick Kinsella from Boston, Massachusetts, according to the information Jade supplied.

'Jesus.' The younger one lowers his aviator sunglasses. 'It's hot.'

'We are having a heatwave, but it is a little cooler in the mountains at least,' Marco appeases, choosing not to mention that someone in Lodi lost their life working in the noonday heat only yesterday. 'My name is Marco Bianchi, welcome to the Palazzo Stellina!' His smile is genuine: he never tires of saying that sentence.

'Thanks, buddy. I'm Nick, and this is my husband, Pete.' He offers a sweaty hand. He's a good twenty years younger and six inches taller than his partner, unsmiling, square-jawed and fair-haired.

'*Signori*. There are cold refreshments waiting on the terrace,' Marco says. 'May I take your luggage?'

Nick scowls, fussing with the collar of his shirt. 'It didn't make it.'

Ah. That explains his mood. Marco doesn't miss a beat. 'Not to worry, we have a small wardrobe of clothing for just such eventualities.' He sizes the man up, recalling what he has available. Nothing with as large a neck as this man has. 'I am sure we can find something to fit you.' He is used to guests arriving in a bad temper, especially when something has gone wrong on their journey, and his first job is to change that as soon as he can.

'Lucky one of us has carry-on, huh?' Pete says, grasping his leather weekender.

'Told you we should have got a couple of AirTags.' Nick purses his lips and slams the car door so hard that Marco jumps.

Pete sighs. 'You may have mentioned that several times already.'

'Last time this happened, my suitcase made it home ten days after I did.'

'I'm told the food here is outstanding, isn't that right, Marco?' Pete asks, ignoring Nick's furious expression.

'I shall let you be the judge,' Marco replies modestly. 'But that is the aim.'

'As long as it's healthy.' Nick pats a stomach that is flat as a board. There are almost certainly chiselled abs beneath the tight-fitting Ralph Lauren polo shirt.

'We're in Italy. Prepare for a carb assault. Pasta, pizza, ciabatta …' Pete warns. 'That high-protein regime you've had us on for months is about to hit the dust.'

'*La dolce vita*, huh?' Nick says in the kind of American accent that sounds to Marco like nails on a blackboard. He does his best not to wince.

'You bet.' Pete briefly rests his hand on Nick's muscled forearm as Marco ushers them into the cool dimness of the palazzo. 'Cheer up, we're here now. Look at this place.' Pete gives a slow whistle as they pause in front of the grand staircase. 'It's stunning.'

Lack of funds rather than aesthetics means Marco has left the painted walls untouched, and though the pattern is time-worn and faded, it has a distinctive charm.

'I bet we're the last to get here,' Nick says, still irritable.

'I believe there is still another to arrive. The *signora* and her sister are resting now.' Marco indicates the passage that leads to the terrace. 'That is where we often serve drinks, and dinner when the weather permits. But let me show you to your room first. You can freshen up.' He makes his tone as soothing as possible.

'Thank God. I need to get out of these ridiculous compression socks,' Pete says.

'Hey, I'm not about to let a blood clot ruin our vacation,' Nick snaps back.

'Don't mind him, the Zoloft must have worn off,' Pete jokes to Marco, who responds with a bland smile.

They climb the stairs, both men now slack-jawed with awe. Marco has become used to this, but the impression the palazzo makes on guests feels like a personal stamp of approval and never fails to make him swell with pride. 'You will find the swimming pool along the path from the terrace, and there is a tennis court beyond that. We have a selection of racquets and balls, and there are bicycles if you would like to cycle, perhaps into the village or beyond.'

'I'm not sure we'll get further than the pool in this heat,' Nick says, pulling a handkerchief from his pocket and mopping his broad, glistening forehead.

'The mornings are better,' Marco reassures him, though he is beginning to think this man would complain no matter what the weather. 'Or you can hike into the mountains where it will be most pleasant.'

'Here's hoping,' Pete says, panting slightly as they reach the top of the stairs.

Marco scans the corridor. He hasn't seen Stella for some time, and he'd rather they not encounter her until he's had a chance to explain her presence at the palazzo. He blinks as the shadows at the far end appear to morph and reshape themselves.

He comes to a stop at their room and opens the door with a flourish. This room faces the mountains and offers one of the best views.

'Thanks, Marco. This looks wonderful,' Pete says as he peers inside. The room is furnished with a king-size turned wood bedframe and sheets of the highest thread count money could buy. He gives a low whistle before adding, 'This must be costing Vivi a pretty penny. Must be nice to be able to afford this kind of thing on the regular.'

'There is a bathroom behind that door there,' Marco says, pretending not to hear, pointing towards a concealed doorway with a discreet handle. 'And a wardrobe for when your luggage arrives. If you let me have your paperwork from the airline, I will make sure it is chased up in the morning.'

Pete reaches into his pocket, bringing out a handful of notes. He examines them carefully before extracting a dollar bill and pressing it into Marco's hand. 'Much appreciated.'

'I will get someone to bring you clean clothes,' Marco says, not acknowledging the embarrassingly low tip but reasoning that it would cause offence to refuse it.

Further along the corridor, a door opens. 'I thought I heard voices. Pete!' Vivi rushes forward and greets the two men with effusive hugs. 'So glad you both could make it. How wonderful to finally meet you, Nick. How was your flight?'

'Fucking awful,' says Nick, banging his hand against the wall with such force that it infuriates Marco. Who the hell does he think he is? 'But I'm so sorry for your loss,' he says, and although it's a perfectly normal way to offer sympathy, it sounds to Marco as if the American thinks she mislaid her husband like he was a set of keys. The man's been here less than ten minutes and already he can't stand him.

'Thank you. It hasn't been the easiest of times. I only wish Will could have been here with us. He would have loved this place.'

As they catch up, Marco, forgetting his promise to bring clothing and curtailing his fondness for eavesdropping, hurries along the corridor towards the very last door. It is where the woman, Caroline, will be staying, but he could have sworn he saw his grandmother slip inside.

CHAPTER SEVEN

Vivi lifts her glass. A *bicicletta*, a cocktail of white wine, Campari and soda. She hasn't had a drink since they first found out Will was sick nearly eight months ago – it seemed selfish to enjoy anything in front of him – but now she thinks that it might do her some good. She takes a tentative sip, feeling the once-familiar kick of the alcohol as it slips down her throat. It's a relief that the heat of the day has subsided. The sun has dipped behind the mountains and it's the perfect temperature for outdoor dining. Fairy lights strung over the terrace and candles grouped along the centre of the table cast a flattering glow over the guests' faces. Tantalising smells of garlic and basil waft from the kitchen, and the occasional curse and clatter can be heard over the music coming from an outdoor speaker.

Jade passes around a plate of olives and prosciutto, even though Vivi has told her she is to think of herself as a guest here. She is wearing a simple linen shift not unlike Vivi's own, her wavy dark brown hair pulled into a loose ponytail and her skin touched with the barest amount of sheer foundation and mascara – all Vivid products, of course. 'Is that Nemesis?' Vivi asks, recognising one of Vivid's newest lip shines, in this instance a vibrant fuchsia pink.

Jade nods.

'It's the perfect colour for you.' Jade has been Vivi's rock these past few months, a calming presence in the maelstrom of admin involved in nursing a terminally ill person, the voice of reason when Vivi threatened to lose it. She never complained about schlepping halfway across London to the house instead of the office when Vivi found it necessary to work from home, even though it added hours to her journey. She brought coffee and delicious-looking pastries, salads and deli sandwiches, encouraging Vivi to eat when it became apparent that she had lost her appetite. Will adored Jade too, regularly threatening to poach her from Vivi for himself.

Jade had been right to persuade Vivi to keep the booking, even after it became apparent that Will wouldn't be well enough to join them, even after he went and died on her. Will should have been here, damn him. They should have had another thirty good years together at least. The last thing she wants right now is anyone's pity, but she tells herself that being with people who've known her forever will be the best kind of balm.

She sips her drink and studies the assembled group. Pete is wearing the years well. His hair is still thick and curly, the tiniest hint of grey at the temples only adding a distinguished look. He seems a little weary, his face drawn and the lines around his eyes deeper, but the time difference, though nowhere near as extreme as that from Australia, is still enough to mess with your body clock, so that might explain it. She watches Nick as he talks to Alice. He's not who she would have expected Pete to choose in a partner: a serious, very proper English accountant matched with a buff, brash, outspoken Irish-American half his age. Nick, she gathers, works in the fitness industry, and Vivi overhears him telling Alice about his gym, Kinsella's. He's been good for Pete in that regard: her old friend is in better shape than she's ever seen him. In the beginning of her marriage, Will was often away, travelling for business, and she and Pete spent hours together, working late into the evenings and coming into the office on weekends. He entertained her with stories of serial hook-ups, dodgy dates and occasional heartbreak with unsuitable men and, on rare occasions, women. Now, finally, it looks like he's found real love, and Vivi couldn't be happier for him.

'Still no sign of Caroline?' Pete asks, breaking into her thoughts.

'I haven't been able to reach her,' Vivi replies. 'But I expect she'll turn up eventually.'

'Typical,' Alice says, coming over to them. 'Considering she's the one who has the least distance to travel.'

'Be nice,' Vivi warns.

Alice sticks her tongue out at her sister then drains her drink and goes to the table to pour herself another one.

Mia and Isla, who apparently slept most of the afternoon, have thrown off their jetlag with the resilience of the young, snapping into the Italian time zone like new elastic. They are sipping chinotto through striped straws, and although Vivi could swear she saw Mia take a sip from her mother's glass when she thought no one was looking, she hasn't said anything to Alice.

Vivi is both proud and slightly envious as she watches them, taking in their denim cut-off shorts and midriff-baring tops, the casual, almost synchronised way they sweep their hair back over their shoulders as they chatter. They are so much more self-possessed than she was at that age. They seem utterly fearless.

'Did you manage a swim?' Vivi asks.

'Yes, thanks, Auntie Vee,' Isla replies.

'I can't believe there isn't a fence around it,' says Alice, looking faintly disapproving. 'Just as well we haven't got toddlers.'

'It's obviously not a requirement,' Vivi says.

'Well, it's unsafe. You wouldn't be allowed to do that in Australia – too many backyard drownings as it is.'

'Yes, but there are so many more pools there. Besides, fences are so ugly,' Vivi says.

'But they save lives,' Alice insists.

'Okay, you've made your point.' Surely they are not going to argue over something as banal as a pool fence?

Nick begins to recount the tale of their delayed luggage to Alice, who is listening sympathetically, if somewhat distractedly. 'Can you believe it?'

'He's stressed because his gym gear is in there,' Pete chimes in.

Vivi catches Nick's look of annoyance. 'I'm sure Marco can find you something.' She places an arm on his elbow.

'It's fine,' Nick says fussily, helping himself to an olive.

It doesn't sound like it's fine, but she lets the subject drop.

When she first started Vivid, she advertised for a part-time accountant, and Pete, who was juggling several sole-trader clients, got in touch. She told him later that he was the only applicant who appeared to take her seriously, who didn't sneer when she told him of her ambition to make Vivid the most successful cosmetics company in Britain when at the time it had only a dozen SKUs and a strangling cashflow issue. He did the company accounts for the first couple of years, by which time they had become the kind of friends who met for dinner at least once a fortnight and spoke to each other almost daily. They grew so close that by the time of her marriage, he (along with Caroline and Alice) was one of the bridal party.

The only hiccup in their friendship came when she brought Will in as CEO, a job that she later discovered Pete had his eye on. He left the company a few years later and moved to the States, but Vivi was determined to maintain the friendship, arranging to catch up whenever she was over and always remembering to send a birthday gift every year.

'You shall simply have to go into the city in the morning and shop,' Alice interrupts. 'You're in Italy, right? Fashion retail is fabulous here.'

'Exactly what Nick suggested.' Pete doesn't look happy about the prospect.

The twins' faces light up.

'Can we go too?' Mia asks.

'Yeah, there's a good Egyptian museum,' Isla adds. 'The oldest one in the world. And Ancient Egypt is our history study topic this semester, remember.'

'I'm sure it will be *fascinating*,' says Mia, clearly less enthusiastic about the prospect than her sister.

Their conversation is interrupted by the arrival of Delfina, her slim body wrapped in a long olive-green linen apron, bearing a basket of heavenly smelling bread that she sets on the table. Alice immediately helps herself to a chunk, tearing off a piece and dipping it into a grass-green bowl of oil. 'The food on the plane was awful,' she says by way of explanation.

Delfina returns moments later with another bottle of wine – a cold minerally white that Pete informs them is made somewhere near here – and fresh glasses as they take their seats. Alice chews another mouthful of bread while trying to talk and chokes as it sticks in her throat. Isla thumps her sharply between the shoulder blades.

'Are you okay?' Vivi asks.

'Want me to do the Heimlich?' Nick half-rises, ready to spring into action, but Alice holds up a hand and he sits back down.

They all fall silent as Marco emerges to explain the menu. '*Carciofi* – artichokes – *agnolotti*,' he mimes a pinching motion, '*scaloppini* …'

For months, food has held little interest for Vivi, and she's eaten more for necessity than pleasure, but hearing these melodious words, she feels her appetite stir. That said, he could be reciting the telephone directory for all she cares: the sound of his voice is soothing, like a bedtime story told by a famous actor. Her eyes momentarily flutter closed and she lets herself sink back against the chair.

'Pretty hot, huh?' Alice whispers.

'Hush!' Vivi hisses back, half-serious.

Alice bursts into delighted guffaws, causing Marco to cast a startled look in their direction.

Nick interrupts Marco's flow. 'I'll skip the pasta, thanks buddy. Unless you can do a low-carb version?'

Vivi opens her eyes in time to see a sneer of disdain flit across the chef's face. 'Perhaps a little extra salad for you instead, sir?' His cool tone goes right over Nick's head.

'It sounds divine, Marco,' Vivi says, smoothing over any awkwardness. 'All the more for the rest of us.'

'Yes, we're all about to die of hunger,' Pete adds. 'Sorry, Vivi,' he reddens. 'I didn't mean it like, well, you know … like that.'

She waves away his blunder. Will hadn't been able to eat anything very much by the end, and she'd seen the shock on Pete's face the last time he and Will shared a video call.

'Then I had better not delay,' Marco says, sweeping up the empty bread basket and returning to the kitchen.

Several minutes later, the first course, platters of artichokes prepared in three different ways, is served.

'What do you think?' Vivi turns to Nick, who has set the fried artichoke to one side and is stabbing at a piece of steamed vegetable with an awkwardly held fork. 'Have you been to Italy before?'

'It's … authentic,' he says, reaching for the word. 'And no, this is my first visit.'

'How wonderful.'

Soon everyone is talking at once, their words tumbling over each other in their excitement at being together. The first-night bonhomie is infectious, aided by several more bottles of wine. Alice and Pete are drinking like the tap might be turned off at any moment, taking full advantage of Vivi's generosity.

'How long has it been since we last caught up?' Alice asks Pete.

'Years. Five, in fact. Vivi's thirty-fifth.'

'Of course.' Alice puts down her glass. 'That was quite a night.'

Vivi leans back, allowing her glass to be topped up, and hears a vehicle in the distance. 'Caroline! At last.' She interrupts Nick, getting to her feet and going to the parapet that overlooks the front entrance.

'Finally,' says Alice. 'Classic Caro. Always the one to make an entrance.'

A tiny blue beaten-up truck comes to a halt at the palazzo gates and Vivi turns back to them, taking her seat again. 'It can't be her after all – probably a delivery.'

'Don't worry.' Alice pats Vivi's arm. 'She's like a bad penny, she'll turn up eventually. More's the pity.'

'Play nice now,' Vivi warns, sitting down again and scooting her chair in. Alice and Caro have never been friends. Alice thinks Caro is an intellectual snob who treats everyone around her like a fool (much like Alice's ex-husband, it occurs to Vivi), and Caro thinks Alice is a spoiled brat who cares only for herself. Vivi smiles to herself; they're more alike than they realise, both intolerant in their own way, but both capable of surprising kindness.

Marco and Delfina bring out the second course, tiny boat-shaped pasta glossed with butter and dusted with sage crumbs, and everyone except Nick (who looks both sanctimonious and aggrieved) falls on it as though they haven't eaten for days.

'What did you say Marco's surname was?' Pete asks, taking another bite of his pasta. Before moving to Boston, Pete lived in New York, and when Vivi visited, he whirled her around as many of the hottest new restaurants as there were meals in the days she was there.

'Bianchi,' Vivi replies. 'Why?'

Pete gives a faint shake of his head, as though trying to retrieve a memory. 'I swear I've had this dish before. He once cooked in New York, you said?'

'Uh-huh. We'll have to find out where. Maybe you ate there?' Vivi glances at everyone gathered around the table. 'Pete's superpower is his ability to remember almost every meal he's ever eaten,' she explains, though Nick is probably already aware of the fact. 'Where, when and with whom. It's quite impressive.'

'When it's as good as this, why wouldn't you?' Pete holds out a forkful to Nick, who hesitantly takes a bite.

After swallowing, Nick picks up his fork and spears another from Pete's bowl. 'Okay, you got me. The pasta is amazing.' They grin at each other.

Vivi has almost finished her food when a woman's voice rings out from the darkness below. 'It *is* Caro!' She drops her fork and rises from her seat, going to the kitchen and poking her head around the open door. 'I'm sorry, Marco, we will need to set another place. Is there any of that divine pasta left, perhaps?'

'No apologies necessary.' His voice is smooth, but Vivi detects an undercurrent nonetheless. 'And, yes, I can always feed our guests.'

Surely he can take such minor inconveniences in his stride – isn't that the point of paying a small fortune for the week? She'd thought she caught a whiff of stale alcohol on his breath earlier but told herself at the time that she must have imagined it. Now she sees the bloodshot eyes and wonders if perhaps she was right. Not that it's any of her business – if the food remains this good, she has no issues with what he does personally. She hurries down the steps to the front entrance of the palazzo. 'Caro! Darling!'

Caroline is scrabbling for her bags – a battered weekender that almost certainly dates from the last century and a creased leather handbag of a similar vintage – and fending off the help of the driver. She has hardly changed in the years since they first met. Her thick, wavy hair is drawn back in a messy ponytail, drawing attention to her strong jaw and sharp cheekbones. Silver hoops dangle from her earlobes, and she's wearing a loose, wildly patterned, crumpled dress with a pair of sturdy Velcro sandals on her feet. *She looks like a boho pilgrim on her way to walk the Camino*, Vivi thinks to herself, amused. Caroline always did dress like she threw on the first thing that came to hand, but somehow it always works for her.

'Sorry I'm so late. My car packed it in further down the valley.' Caroline tucks an errant strand of hair behind one ear and loops her handbag over her head and across her body. 'Managed to hitch a lift.' She says something in rapid Italian that Vivi can't follow, and the driver gets behind the wheel, giving her a wink. 'But the absolute bugger took a wrong turn and we ended up halfway to Pradeltorno before he realised his mistake. I wouldn't be surprised if he did it on purpose.'

'Well, I'm glad you finally made it.'

'So am I.' Caroline flashes an apologetic grin. 'It was so thoughtful of you to invite me.'

CHAPTER EIGHT

After dinner, Nick pleads exhaustion and Isla says she has some reading to do for school. 'She's lying,' Mia whispers to Vivi. 'She's probably snuck away to watch *Call Me by Your Name*; she's obsessed with Timothée Chalamet. She downloaded like a dozen Italian movies before we left home. Some of them don't even have subtitles.' She shakes her head as though this is the most deranged thing she's ever come across. 'Total nerd,' she adds more fondly.

The others drift inside to the living area, a lofty space with a soaring vaulted ceiling, where mismatched sofas and armchairs in muted colours of old rose, mustard and olive circle a vast stone fireplace. It's still too warm for a fire, though Alice can imagine it would be a necessity in winter. The chequerboard stone floors are partially covered with knotted rugs, bookshelves line two of the walls, and on another, tall square-paned windows are open to the night air. Several time-darkened oil paintings depict landscapes; a larger one shows the ubiquitous Madonna and her naked child. Alice straightens it as they enter the room, admiring the brushwork, though the light is dim and it might not stand up to her scrutiny in daylight.

The overall effect is one of a comfortable, albeit timeworn, European country house, though the overlarge crucifix with the bloodied figure of Christ hanging next to the door gives off a morosely gothic vibe and offers a clue to the palazzo's original purpose.

Mia challenges Pete to a game of backgammon and they sit at a small table underneath a window. Vivi and Caro settle themselves on one of the sofas, tucking their feet under them, while Alice makes a beeline for the sideboard, where a bottle of grappa and several glasses wait on a silver tray. 'Anyone?' she asks, pouring several generous measures.

'Just a splash,' Caro replies.

'Oh, okay, one for me as well,' Vivi adds.

'Is Jade not joining us?' Caro asks.

Vivi raises her head and looks around, surprised. 'I guess not.'

'I imagine she probably feels a little *de trop*,' Alice says, twirling her glass.

'But she's like family!' Vivi protests. 'She's been an absolute godsend this year.'

'But she's not, is she?' Alice reminds her. 'Family.'

'You have no idea,' Vivi says, her mouth a firm line, 'just how much I have come to rely on her.'

'Sorry!' Alice holds up her hands. 'I didn't mean to upset you.' Sometimes she forgets how sensitive Vivi can be.

'It's fine. And you haven't.'

'Doubles!' Mia indicates the dice and proceeds to move her remaining counters off the board with a triumphant flourish.

'I think that's what we call a thrashing.' Pete is gracious in defeat. 'Dammit, you're good, sweetheart. Too good for me anyway.'

'Another round?' Mia suggests, but Pete shakes his head, picking up his glass and draining it. 'Time for me to hit the hay, I think. Nick seems to think we're both going jogging in the morning.' He raises his eyes to the ceiling. 'My husband will be the death of me.'

The women continue to drink after Pete and Mia have left,

long after the sounds from the kitchen have ceased, and long after they probably should have stopped.

'How's the language school?' Alice asks Caroline. 'You've been teaching for, what, ten years?'

'I was there for thirteen years.'

'Was?' Vivi asks, her voice suddenly sharp. 'You mean you've left?'

Caroline shifts her position on the sofa. 'Something like that.'

'So what are you doing now?' Alice asks.

'Enjoying the summer. Working on my novel. I think I'm finally getting somewhere.' She lifts her chin like a boxer squaring off for a fight, daring them to doubt her.

'Your novel. Of course.' Alice takes another slug of her drink. 'Remind me, is this the one about the uni friends?' They've heard about this so-called 'novel' for decades now; in fact, Alice sometimes plays a kind of silent bingo with herself, taking bets on how long Caroline will wait before mentioning it. She consults her watch. Less than two hours: almost a record.

'Dark academia is making a comeback, as it happens,' Caro says stiffly. 'Remember how much we loved *The Secret History*, Vivi?'

'Kind of. It was a long time ago.'

'Well, anyway, I've put that in a drawer for now and I'm working on something fresh. This one is set in a language school.'

'Good for you.' Alice can't keep the patronising tone from her voice, and Vivi shoots her a stern look, though she chooses to ignore it. 'How enviable to be able to toss everything aside and follow your passion.' She conveniently forgets that she makes something only approaching a living from her art.

'Well, you certainly have the experience, setting it in a language school, I mean,' Vivi says. 'Don't they say to write what you know?'

'Were you sacked?' Alice blurts, putting two and two together.

'Alice!' Vivi scolds. 'If you're not careful, I'll get someone to put a gag on you!' She sounds as if she's only half-teasing.

'I'd like to see you try,' Alice snaps back. She enjoys making trouble, and alcohol only makes her more mischievous. Vivi cares about the good opinion of others, sometimes too much, but Alice has never been bothered by what other people think of her.

'You were, weren't you?' Alice asks Caroline.

'Not exactly,' she replies. 'We reached a mutual agreement that it would be best for all concerned if I did not return next year.' Her mouth pinches together as she finishes speaking, as if there is a whole lot more to say about the matter.

'Ooh, what was it? Did you steal the stationery? Have an inappropriate affair with a colleague?'

Colour rises in Caroline's freckled cheeks, reaching her hairline. 'Don't be ridiculous.'

'I knew it!' Alice says, delighted that she's hit the nail on the head. 'Go on, tell us all the juicy details. I won't judge, I promise,' she lies.

'You're wrong, as it happens,' Caroline says, but her voice catches, breaking on the word 'wrong' in a way that confirms Alice's hunch. 'And I'd rather not be the subject of your idle speculation if it's all the same to you.' She throws back the rest of her drink, places the glass down on the rickety side table next to her and gets to her feet, swaying slightly. She clutches the arm of the sofa to steady herself. 'I think I need some fresh air.' Not waiting for a response from either of them, she stumbles out of the room.

'Did you have to?' Vivi pleads.

'Have to what?' Alice asks, pretending wide-eyed innocence.

'You know she can't stand to be teased.'

'Who said I was teasing? Come on, she's such a supercilious cow. She thinks she's better than the rest of us, though I've no idea why.'

'Alice,' Vivi warns. 'It's just for a week, okay? Do you think you can manage that? Did you ever stop to think that she might be like that precisely *because* she feels inadequate around the rest of us? She's never had anyone – no partner to share things with, no children … and, it appears, no *job* now. Have a little compassion.'

'Oh, alright. Spoilsport.' Alice slurs the sibilants, hiccupping gently. 'I was only poking fun. I'll apologise to her in the morning. I'll be on my best behaviour from now on, Scout's honour.' Alice raises two fingers to her temple, not meaning a word of it.

'I've often thought we don't acknowledge enough the role luck plays in the course of a life, how everything can turn on a chance encounter, a tiny decision, meeting the right person at the right time … or the wrong person at the wrong time.' Vivi sighs. 'There but for the grace of God and all that.'

'Nonsense. You make your own luck – look at you. Preparation meets opportunity, that's what luck is,' Alice says stoutly, tipping her head back to drain the last of the grappa from her glass.

'Some people never get the privilege of opportunity,' Vivi counters. 'And you weren't a Scout, by the way. They chucked you out of Guides for stealing all the tent poles at camp, remember?'

Alice smirks as Vivi's phone buzzes with a notification. 'You promised you'd lock that thing away this week,' Alice reminds her sister, but Vivi ignores her, turning it over and squinting at the screen.

After a moment, Vivi gets to her feet. 'It's late, and you've been up for more hours than I can count. Why don't we call it a night?'

'I'm sorry, I didn't mean to push it. I'll apologise to Caro in the morning.'

Vivi doesn't answer.

Alice huffs and gets to her feet. 'I might go and see if Marco is still up. I want to get the lowdown about what there is to do around here.'

'Oh, I'm sure Marco will have plenty of suggestions for you,' Vivi says with a wink.

The morning after

The person is too still, and even in the dawn light it's clear their colour is not good, not the healthy pink or brown of a body through which blood rhythmically pumps but an unnatural greyish white, as if their skin was made of modelling clay.

'*Merda!*' The word bursts from Delfina's mouth, any concern about not waking the guests abandoned. She sprints the last few steps, throwing down her towel, kicking off her sandals and taking a flying leap, fully clothed, into the water.

Diving down and grabbing the person under their armpits, she scissor-kicks back to the surface and then drags the body, almost on top of her, towards the shallow end where she can stand. For the first time, she curses the length of the pool. The body is awkward and slippery, and she almost loses her grip. Summoning every bit of strength she's built up over the summer, every ounce of determination, she focuses on reaching the shallows, on getting the body out of the pool, out of the water.

Seconds slow until they feel like hours, and it is as though there is a wildfire roaring in her head. She must not panic, though her breath is coming in sharp, laboured gasps.

Finally, her feet gain purchase on the rough bottom of the pool and her shoulder bumps painfully against the coping.

She attempts to stand then strains to lift. As soon as the body leaves the water, it's a deadweight. There's no way she can do this on her own.

'*Incidente!*' she chokes, her breathing ragged as she wrestles with the body. She steals a closer look. It is unnatural, like a character in one of the zombie movies her little brother likes so much, the body as cold as a spring avalanche on the mountains behind her. '*Non respirare!*' She's no expert, but it looks like they haven't taken a breath for some time.

It's hopeless, but she won't give up.

'*Assistere!*' she half-cries, half-screams, the pitch of her voice an unfamiliar panicked shriek, her breath coming in heaving sobs now as the initial adrenaline wears off.

She stops for a moment, listening.

The palazzo is eerily quiet; even the birds have fallen silent.

Merda! Where *is* everyone? Surely someone must have heard her?

CHAPTER NINE

Four days earlier

When Vivi wakes the next morning, she eases out of bed, draws the curtains, and takes a full body stretch, feeling the ache in every joint. 'Bloody hell!' she says when she sees the heart-stopping view. Wisps of mist have gathered in the folds of the mountains overnight, and the sky glows pink and gold above them. The valley is marked by stands of slim cypress trees and acres of green vineyards, the ribbon of the track from the palazzo unspooling beneath her. She opens the window wide and inhales the fragrant scent of pine.

It is likely bleak and desolate here in winter, but for now, it's magical: lush and verdant. She stands there for a minute or so longer, listening to the birdsong as a breeze plays over her face, toying with her hair. She almost never takes the time to stop and just *absorb*, especially this year. Perhaps it takes coming somewhere new to give her a different perspective. She certainly hopes so, for she could do with a fresh outlook on life. And some more sleep.

Despite a bone-deep tiredness, every amplified creak and moan of the unfamiliar new accommodation made it impossible for her to drift off the night before. She could have distracted herself with a soothing podcast, or some sleep-inducing theta-wave music, or even checked her emails, but instead, like someone who can't help but pick at a scab, she went online, searching for bad reviews. Not the ones about her products but the ones about her. The ones she should really keep away from. The personal attacks. She never used to be like this, but since Will died it's become a compulsion, another way of punishing herself.

The wi-fi at the palazzo still wouldn't connect, but there was just enough phone signal to allow her to search. 'The Vivi you see on YouTube is nothing like the reality of working with her at Vivid Formulations. Beware …' Ouch. 'How dare she call herself a make-up artist? She looks like she'd suck the life out of you with those teef …' 'Girl has no idea how to apply foundayshun …' 'She's fat, old and sounds so fake. IDK how she ever got to be sucsessful.' She winced at the appalling spelling, but it didn't make the comments any less hurtful. It was hours before she finally turned off her phone and fell into a restless sleep.

Now she registers movement in the gardens below and looks down to see someone dressed head to toe in white overalls and a broad-brimmed veiled hat. Smoke emerges from what looks like a small bellows. There is the tall box of a beehive if she's not mistaken. If she strains, she can almost hear a gentle hum.

Then there's a splash from the swimming pool, and as she leans out, she can see someone swimming laps, a slim silhouette in a dark costume. She can't imagine who would be up this early. Movement beyond the pool catches her attention. Two figures on the road, tiny ants from her vantage point, heading towards the palazzo gates. Almost certainly Pete and Nick, out jogging.

She showers quickly before applying a layered cocktail of serums. Even during the worst of times, she still takes care of her skin: it comes as naturally to her as breathing. These days, however, she doesn't look as closely in the mirror. Grief ages you, guilt even more so, and no miracle cream can erase that.

Eight months ago, her main concern was staying relevant as the nearly forty-year-old head (and face) of a cosmetics company in a world that largely equates beauty with youth. As a young entrepreneur, she had based her brand on her status, but calling forty 'young' is too much of a stretch. These days, every other gorgeous actress or singer seems to be launching a beauty brand ('not to mention a tequila label,' Alice added when they discussed it). She takes some comfort in the knowledge that Charlotte Tilbury is in her fifties; Trinny Woodall just turned sixty. Bobbi Brown, too, is in her sixties (and has just founded her second beauty business), and they are all still killing it. And look at Estée Lauder, Elizabeth Arden and Helena Rubenstein – they went on for years. There is no reason she shouldn't.

Now she wishes that was all she ever had to worry about.

Will had gone to see his GP after Vivi noticed that his skin had a yellowish tinge. She still kicks herself for not insisting he went sooner instead of stocking up on antacids and accepting his assertion that the stomach pains were merely indigestion.

She is still astonished at how quick it all was.

She moves away from the window and walks to the carved wooden armoire, selecting a dress printed with a cheerful pattern of oranges and lemons, hoping it will improve her mood. Thrusting her feet into a pair of woven sandals, she heads down the sweeping staircase to see about breakfast. She is surprised to feel hungry again. Last night she ate more than she has in months, but now her mouth waters at the thought of what the next meal might bring.

She enters the kitchen where she finds Marco, wearing a frown and an olive-green apron, slicing an onion, the blade of his knife an alarming blur. You need total focus for something like that, not to mention years of practice. She likes to think she has steady hands when applying make-up, but if she ever tried to cut things that fast, she'd be a mess of blood and sticking plaster in no time.

On the counter, a glistening yellow-gold hunk of honeycomb drips into a bowl next to several loaves of bread. The smell of baking and the peppery scent of basil fill the air. She sniffs appreciatively. 'Good morning.'

'*Buongiorno.*' He stops slicing, wipes his hands on a cloth and looks up at her, his look of total concentration replaced by a smile. He seems less frazzled than the previous day. 'Coffee?'

'Tea, if that's possible. Milk, no sugar.'

'Certainly. Give me a minute and I'll bring it out to you on the terrace.'

'Thank you.' Vivi goes to leave the kitchen then stops, remembering. 'I'm having trouble connecting to your wi-fi, did Jade ask you about it?'

'It comes and goes,' he says. 'The tower …' He shrugs. 'The best place for a signal is in here, I'm afraid.' He sweeps his arm around the room and Vivi gives a start as a flurry of black fabric unfolds from a shadowed corner, assuming the form of an elderly woman. She peers more closely, seeing skin wrinkled as an old cheese, a body that seems as insubstantial as a wraith.

'Oh!' She takes a step backwards.

'This is Stella. My *nonna.*'

'Oh goodness, the same one as in the photograph? I didn't see you there.'

Marco nods, his attention focused on the knife again as he begins to slice tomatoes at breakneck speed.

Yesterday, when she and Jade arrived, Marco led them through the house, pausing at a framed black-and-white photo in the entryway. A young girl in a flowered dress was balanced on a bicycle, and by her side a taller woman was dressed in the style of a man, shirtsleeves rolled to her elbows, a thick belt around her waist, a bandolier slung across her body, a rifle strapped to her back. 'That one is my great-aunt, Gina, and there's my grandmother, Stella. She still lives here with me.' Marco pointed to the young girl. 'She was a *staffette*, only thirteen, a courier running messages across the countryside on her bicycle. The Germans didn't suspect pretty young women, let alone girls. They were practically invisible, which they used to their advantage. But if she was caught, she would have been tortured and killed just like anyone else. She ran that risk every day. My great-grandmother, their mother, sheltered partisans in the cellars below us, often for weeks at a time.'

'Incredible,' murmured Vivi, chilled by the story. 'I'd love to see that. The cellars, I mean.'

'There's nothing but wine and cobwebs down there these days,' he said, dismissing her request.

'Lovely to meet you, Stella,' Vivi says now.

The old woman nods at her and goes to the range to fetch a kettle.

'She doesn't speak much, I'm afraid. And her English is limited. But don't worry, she hears everything.' He goes back to his knife and chopping board. 'I'll bring your tea shortly.'

Vivi remembers the wi-fi issue. 'I need to answer some emails later,' she insists apologetically. 'You know how it is. No rest for the wicked.' She winces. Why did she say that?

'After breakfast?'

'That would be super.'

'I'll clear a place at the table for you. I'm sorry, it's the best I can do.'

'Thank you.' Vivi is gracious, reminding herself to release the things she has no control over, noticing the sunlight streaming through the leaded windows. So what if she has to work in this glorious kitchen, full of rickety antique dressers and charming ceramics, rich with character and history? It's more appealing than a sterile office.

She goes out to the terrace, where the table has been cleared of the previous night's detritus and laid for their next meal. Before long, Delfina brings out a tray with a pot of tea, a strainer, milk and a basket of pastries.

'*Grazie.*'

'*Prego.*' She unloads the tray and then slips away again, graceful as a ballerina.

Vivi reaches for a pastry, finding them still warm, not minding that the flaky crumbs stick to her lipstick. She takes a bite, savouring the buttery flavour. It's the best thing she's tasted in months.

Nick is the first to join her, exuding self-satisfaction and minty mouthwash, comb ridges furrowing his damp hair, biceps stretching the sleeves of his polo shirt. He carries a large plastic bottle, pouring in water from a jug on the table and adding the contents of a sachet before replacing the lid and giving it a thorough shake. 'Personalised blend of vegetable protein and minerals,' he says in response to Vivi's curious glance. 'Optimum nutrition.' He pushes the sachet towards her. 'Try some if you like.'

Vivi sips her tea, unsure how to respond. The liquid in Nick's bottle is a murky colour and looks disgusting. 'Mmm,' she says unenthusiastically.

Nick chuckles and takes a long draught from the bottle before leaning back, hands linked behind his head. He's wearing two watches, both complicated-looking digital sports models, which seems like overkill but somehow doesn't surprise her. She decides against commenting on it, afraid it might unleash a lengthy explanation.

'Is that all you're having?' she asks.

'Hell no. I'm on vacation,' he says. 'I'll allow myself some fruit, eggs. You only live once, right?'

'Tell me, Nick, how did you and Pete meet?' Vivi tears off a corner of another croissant, slathering butter onto it.

'You think it was on Grindr or at the gym?' he asks, and for a moment Vivi isn't sure if he's teasing. She hasn't been able to work out his sense of humour yet. God, she hopes he has one, for Pete's sake. She smiles to herself at the expression. Nick probably thinks she's amused by him. 'We walk our dogs at the same park, if you can believe that. It was about the only place to meet someone the last few years. Lockdown was brutal.'

'*Ciao*! How are we this morning?' Pete arrives, leaning over to kiss Vivi on the cheek and then Nick on the lips. 'Thank you for insisting we come,' he says, indicating the landscape with a sweep of his arm. 'It's even more stunning in the daytime.'

Vivi is about to ask him how he slept when Alice plonks herself down on the seat beside her, turns over a cup on a saucer and croaks for tea. 'Anyone got Advil?'

'Must be the jetlag,' Vivi says with a grin. 'Certainly nothing to do with the grappa last night, right?' She's already forgotten their terse exchange of the night before. She pours her sister a cup from the pot and pushes a milk jug towards her. 'How are the girls?'

'Spark out. Half their luck; I've been wide awake since four,' Alice complains, resting her elbows on the table.

'We thought we'd take them into the city this morning,' Pete says. 'There's still no sign of our luggage and I can't wear this T-shirt all week.'

'Thanks, honey,' Nick says as Delfina, damp hair escaping from a chignon, brings out platters of prosciutto, cheese and a bowl of tiny wild strawberries.

'You got any eggs? Three, poached?'

She nods and holds up three fingers. '*Tre*?'

'Yes, please. Hey, anyone know how you say "poached"?' Nick asks, draining the last of his disgusting-looking protein drink and smacking his lips in satisfaction. 'Coffee, too. *Per favore.*'

'*Si.*'

'Do you mind?' Alice asks, not waiting for a response as she reaches across Vivi to grab a croissant.

'Could you pass the prosciutto?' Pete indicates a plate at the other end of the table.

'After you.' Alice slides it towards him, sighing happily. 'I could eat my body weight in that. Doesn't food always taste better in the open air?'

'Amen, sister.'

Good food has always made Pete happy.

Jade arrives, all polished skin and jaunty ponytail. God, she makes Vivi feel like a total hag sometimes. Her perfume smells familiar, but it is a moment before Vivi places it. Portrait of a Lady. Beloved by Victoria Beckham, according to the internet anyway.

'Ah, Jade, hello. How did you sleep?' Vivi asks.

'Well, thank you.' Jade smiles warmly at them all, her voice carefully modulated, smooth and almost accentless. She takes a seat at the far end of the table, hooking her beach bag around the side of the chair. 'It must be the air here or something. It helps that it's so much quieter than London.'

'Where do you live?' Alice asks idly.

'Highbury. I just bought my first flat.' Jade blushes, and it occurs to Alice that she's embarrassed to be talking about herself. 'It's a shoebox, really.'

'You must pay her well, sis,' Alice jokes. 'Even shoeboxes in Highbury aren't exactly cheap. Neither are those sunglasses – very nice, by the way. Oliver Peoples, right? Almost the same as Vivi's,' she muses, shooting Jade an odd look.

Jade self-consciously adjusts the frames. 'Knock-offs,' she says.

Caroline appears wearing an ankle-length A-line skirt and a severe short-sleeved blouse buttoned to the neck. On anyone else it would look uptight, but on her the effect is art-school instead of frump. She slides in on the other side of Vivi, closely followed by Isla and Mia, looking even more impossibly fresh-faced than they did yesterday.

Mia whispers urgently to Alice, and Vivi overhears something about a 'creepy old lady', a bad dream she had. 'She was watching me, I swear!' She is insistent, but Alice rolls her eyes and asks her to pass the pastries.

Vivi is about to ask Mia about it when Delfina arrives with plates of fried eggs, sliced tomatoes, avocado and watermelon and jugs of orange juice, and the conversation shifts.

Vivi asks for more tea and some painkillers for Alice.

Jade immediately reaches into her bag and produces a strip of anti-inflammatories. She pours Alice a glass of water.

'She's always so well-prepared,' Vivi whispers to Alice, doing her best to cheer her sister up, for she really does look the worse for wear. 'I swear, whatever you asked for, she'd have it in that bag of hers.'

'Thanks, darling,' Alice says.

Jade flushes as Alice takes the tablets from her. 'I've got stronger ones if you need them.'

'These will be fine. Vivi's right: you are a gem.'

'Just doing my job.'

'Did you know that the word "pharmacy" originally referred to formulations used in witchcraft?' Isla says.

'That's enough now,' Alice warns.

'In fact, that's rather interesting,' Vivi says, smiling at her niece.

'Watch out, the wheels are turning.' Alice swallows the tablets with a mouthful of water. 'I've seen that look before. Don't forget, you're supposed to be switching off, Vee.'

'The perfect time for creative ideas,' Vivi reassures her calmly.

As they linger over more coffee and the last of the strawberries, they discuss their plans for the day. Vivi is swept along by the noise and energy and sheer boisterousness of her friends. Even Alice has perked up.

It makes a welcome change after the months of sickroom quiet.

Pete and Nick plan to go to Turin with the twins, dropping off Caroline (who will arrange a tow-truck for her car) on the way. Alice claims to need more sleep and then 'perhaps a swim', and Vivi says she will join her by the pool after checking her emails.

'Do you need me?' Jade asks, but Vivi waves her away.

'I know this is a working holiday, but let's put the emphasis on holiday,' she reassures her.

'You could do with taking your own advice there, sis,' Alice teases.

'Of course,' Jade says, her face serious, 'if you're sure. I'll be by the cabanas if you want anything.'

'Stay together, girls,' Alice says to the twins as they skip down the stone steps to the gravel driveway. 'And take your hats. That sun is just as fierce as at home, you know.'

They wave but otherwise pay little attention to their mother's words, carefree as only sixteen-year-olds on holiday can be.

CHAPTER TEN

By the time Vivi enters the kitchen, laptop under her arm, both Stella and Delfina have disappeared, and Marco has begun work on dinner preparations, aggressively pounding meat to paper thinness. A delicious smell of baking wafts towards her. When Jade booked the palazzo, she recommended the half-board option, featuring a three- or four-course dinner in the evenings. 'It's run by a Michelin-starred chef; it would be silly not to make the most of it,' she pointed out. Vivi remembers this now as she stands on the threshold, watching him at work. It was proving to be a sound recommendation, not only because the palazzo is so far from anything approaching a town or village but also because Marco is a true master.

She spies a clear area at the end of the large farmhouse table and settles herself, pulling out a chair quietly so as not to startle him. 'My assistant says you used to work at a restaurant in New York,' she says when he has finished bashing the meat.

He looks up, as if surprised to see her, then his expression shutters. 'That's right.'

'Last night, Pete said he thought he'd had that divine pasta dish before. Would I have heard of it?' she persists in the face of his reticence. 'The restaurant?'

'I don't know. Do you go to New York often?'

'Well, not recently, but before that, often enough.'

'It was a little place in Greenwich Village.'

'Called?' He's annoyingly vague, but Vivi is used to prodding until she gets the answers she needs.

'Cibo,' he says at last, his musical pronunciation pleasing to her ear. 'It means "food". I left because my grandmother needed me here.'

Somehow this statement doesn't ring entirely true, a false note in an otherwise seamless explanation, but Vivi's got more important things on her mind, and anyway, now that she knows the name of the restaurant, she can do her own sleuthing when she gets the chance. She types in the wi-fi password as he spells it out for her, relieved when her email begins to load.

'Is everything okay with your rooms?' he asks. 'With the palazzo?'

'Of course. It's wonderful. Such attention to detail.' Right down to the Aqua di Parma bath oils and Giomi vegan and paraben- and sulfate-free hair products in each bathroom – she, of course, notices such things. Little things, done well, with great care: it's always been her philosophy too, although lately she feels as though it is getting away from her. Vivid has too many product lines, too many distribution points, and not enough of her attention. Much as she hates to admit it, quality has suffered.

'*Bene.*' His mallet has stilled, suspended over the board.

'Was there something else?'

'This is our first season. I am interested in the feedback from our guests. But there is one other thing.' He hesitates. 'The payment. The balance owing for the week. I have not received it.'

'Really?' Vivi blinks, surprised. 'Jade should have taken care of that. It's not like her to forget. I'll ask her to check on it. I do apologise.'

'*Grazie.*' He goes back to pounding the meat, albeit with a little less force.

Vivi logs into her email and is soon absorbed in the most recent sales report, after which she moves on to updates from the various territory managers. The R&D department is working on refillable cosmetics jars and she scans a report on their progress, then there's an email relating to sustainable packaging options – the less plastic they use the better, as far as she is concerned, and the company stopped using microplastics years ago. The development of a new minimal beauty range, Pure V, has hit a few hiccups in formulation, and she fires back a series of questions to the head chemist. Next, she sees a message from Jade, sent much earlier this morning (Vivi remembers her saying she slept well, but this was sent at 4.30 am), forwarding a request from the *Vogue* features editor for an interview. Vivi used to be flattered by such profiles, but the novelty has long since worn off. She can't understand the seemingly insatiable appetite for stories about her, but if it's a publication or news outlet that will help drive sales, she almost always says yes. A profile in the coming months will give her a chance to shed light on the company's future direction after the sudden loss of Will and to emphasise that it is business as usual as far as she is concerned. She replies to Jade's email in the affirmative, but only if they'll guarantee a solo, lead feature. She won't share space with anyone else.

She almost misses the P.S. at the end of the email and reads it twice to make sure she's understood it correctly. The BBC – Desert Island Discs – requesting an interview. A small thrill shoots through her: you've really made it when Lauren Laverne wants to know your eight favourite songs. Would it be too on the nose to pick 'I Will Survive'? She and Alice have sung their hearts out to it more times than she can remember. Perhaps 'Dog Days are Over' might make the cut, even if it is wishful thinking.

It will be important to choose songs accompanied by anecdotes suitable for broadcast, ones that show her in the best possible light. Humble, self-deprecating, relatable. If there's anything she's learned after twenty years in the beauty business it's that image is everything. She's still thinking about what other songs have time-stamped her life when Marco places an espresso cup, a slice of biscotti resting on the saucer, next to her, saying nothing. He might be terse, but good service comes as naturally to him as breathing. She glances down, seeing his square, calloused palm, a tattooed forearm, the apron knotted taut around his hips ... even the kitchen clogs on his feet don't detract from his brooding aura. It's no surprise Alice has already taken notice of him.

'*Grazie*,' she murmurs, clearing her throat before clicking on the next email. Even the smallest acts of kindness undo her these days.

For some reason, sales in one of her best-performing outlets, an online beauty site, were down twenty per cent last month. The news doesn't send her into the panicked frenzy it once would have, but it's concerning nonetheless. Even in economically difficult times, the so-called 'lipstick effect' means that people are still inclined to treat themselves to little luxuries, cosmetics being among the most obvious ones. Post-pandemic lipstick sales (particularly smudge-proof formulations) have surged as people get out and about again. But Vivid is facing challenges that even she's not sure how to overcome: the construction costs of their new manufacturing plant have come in at more than double the forecast, the new make-up line she spent most of last year developing has been gazumped by a competitor launching something worryingly similar, and unless she and Robert, Vivid's CFO, can come up with a rescue plan, the company is in trouble. They've grown fast in the past five years, perhaps too fast. She's never had to make lay-offs, but the prospect is looking increasingly likely. She pushed her concerns to one side while Will was sick, but she doesn't know how much longer she can keep on ignoring them.

She massages her temples, attempting to ease her tension, then fires off an email to the category manager, asking for more detail on which products are affected, to see if there is a pattern. Fighting the small fires is all she can do right now.

Vivi always dreamed of success. Diminishing the size of those dreams is a lie she used to tell magazine writers to make them think she was less than she really was – less ambitious, less single-minded, less bloody-minded. It's a sad fact that readers generally like their female role models to be modest. You're not supposed to admit to the wanting, the all-encompassing drive to succeed. It's not entirely *feminine*. The plain truth is that she has spent the last twenty years fighting, scraping and clawing to get to where she is now, to build a brand, to get space in department stores and establish a strong presence online. Until this year, Vivid was the fastest growing cosmetics company in Britain five years in a row, but none of it has come easily. She sacrificed a family life, friendships, holidays, sleep … Perhaps she will use the *Vogue* interview to talk about the toll such ambition takes, all the parts that so few people ever hear about. Honesty: isn't that a radical concept?

'Everything okay?' Marco asks.

'Yes, fine. Thanks.' She hadn't realised that she'd sighed so loudly.

He dusts flour from his hands. 'We should discuss the dinner – on Saturday. Your assistant said it is your birthday. That this is the reason for your visit.'

'To be honest, after the year I've had, I'd rather not make a fuss, but somehow I don't think my sister, or my friends, will let me get away with that.'

'It is no trouble. Jade has given me a list of your favourite foods and preferred dishes.'

Vivi reminds herself to be gracious. 'Thank you, but please, a dinner like the one we had last night is more than enough. Your food is amazing.'

Marco gives her a genuine smile. '*Grazie*. I am humbled that you think so.'

'Oh, I know so,' she replies with absolute surety.

As she is about to finish up, she glances at Marco, who is now rolling pasta through a machine, draping the silky folds over the backs of his hands, humming to himself. She observes him for a moment: excellence is always mesmerising.

She shifts the laptop screen, angling it away from him, then does a quick Google search. *Marco Bianchi. Cibo, Greenwich Village.* Several pages of results appear. There's a mention of the restaurant being awarded a Michelin star in 2018, so that bit of information is correct, but there are also links to media reports from 2019 regarding the death of a customer. Her eyes widen and she is about to click on a result from the *New York Times* when Marco stops what he is doing and comes over to the fridge behind her.

She hastily closes the browser window.

Vivi's email pings with another message. She's about to ignore it when the subject line catches her eye: 'Ref. William Stanley Savidge'. It's from an email account she's never heard of: garybirdwhistle@richardsonandpartners.com. There have been numerous messages since Will's death, mostly from old friends she never even knew he had, offering condolences. She assumes it must be another of those. She's got a stock reply in a file somewhere, saving her the trouble of answering each one individually.

She clicks on it, drumming her fingers as the message loads. It is brief and to the point.

Dear Mrs Savidge,
We have recently been made aware of your actions in regard to the death of your spouse, William Stanley Savidge. Our client believes they are entitled to a discretionary fee, in the sum of £50,000.

> *We should be grateful if you could deposit the full amount in our bitcoin account no later than COB Friday 2 August.*

It's followed by a complicated string of letters and numbers, apparently the bitcoin wallet address, but it's the final sentence that kills the words of disbelief forming in her mind.

> *P.S. We have in our possession digital copies of the correspondence pertaining to the acquisition and supply of X on 21 March this year, together with voicemail messages relating to this matter.*

This is no phishing or spam email, no troll or crackpot. This is blackmail.

She closes her laptop with a snap, bile rising from her stomach. It is as though the air has suddenly left the room, leaving her breathless with shock.

Who could possibly know about this, and how the hell did they find out?

CHAPTER ELEVEN

Mia pauses in front of a larger-than-life sculpture of three figures, their arms linked behind their backs like an infinity symbol, and wonders what it would be like if their third sister had survived. Would being a triplet be even harder than being a twin? Sometimes Mia imagines she sees a girl, another who looks just like her and Isla, standing in the shadows at the end of the bed. Often, it's just as she's about to fall asleep, or if she wakes in the middle of the night. The girl's eyes bore right into her, as if trying to consume her. When she told Isla, her sister suggested she should stop watching so many horror movies.

She and Isla are in the Gallery of the Kings, a long, moodily lit room crammed with statues of pharaohs and gods and goddesses. She has been snapping photos from the moment Pete dropped them off outside the Museo Egizio, amusing herself by speeding through the galleries and pretending she's a contestant on one of those crazy travel adventure game shows while Isla dawdles her way around. If she continues at that pace, they'll never get out of here. Pete and Nick aren't due back for at least three hours, but Mia has other plans besides hanging out in this stuffy gallery.

Bored already, her hand strays to the back of her head, and despite the soreness there, she winds a hair around her index finger and begins to pull.

Finally, Isla appears next to her, rolling her eyes. Mia surreptitiously drops a strand of hair on the floor. 'Mia!' Isla's voice is a stage whisper, loud enough that several other visitors turn and fix them with dirty looks. 'You were zoning out again.'

'Sorry.' Mia is glad that, although Isla knows her so well, she can't read her mind, can't see the dark thoughts that threaten to overwhelm her. Sometimes, as a way of blocking them out, Mia pulls at each strand of hair, feeling relief as they come away in her fingers. Trichotillomania. She researched it, but even knowing its name hasn't stopped her. Straighty one-eighty Isla would be horrified. And then upset. There are things her twin doesn't need to know.

'Can we go now? I've got plenty of pictures, enough to impress Mr Baldwin for sure.' Mr Baldwin is their young, good-looking history teacher, and Mia is always searching for ways to be noticed, if only to watch him blush when she flutters her eyelashes at him, purely for her own amusement.

Isla checks the time. 'Pete and Nick won't be back for hours.'

'There's a really cool vintage store about five minutes from here.'

'But I've hardly seen anything yet.'

'Suit yourself. I'm going. I'll be back in plenty of time.'

'Mum said to stick together,' Isla hisses. But Mia is already walking away. 'Wait!' she calls out and, sighing, follows her twin.

Mia stops outside the museum to look up the address on her phone. 'It's this way,' she says, reaching for her sister's hand and dragging her along a side alley. She always has the power to call Isla's bluff. 'It's going to be so much better than anything we have at home,' she promises.

At first Mia thinks she's made a mistake. The shop, which they almost miss, is a sliver of a store with a cluttered, dusty display of acid-wash denim and nylon Adidas tracksuits from the eighties in the window.

'You think?' Isla says, wrinkling her nose.

'You never know,' says Mia, grabbing her hand and refusing to be daunted, 'what treasures might lie within.'

Inside is much better. Beyond the satin boxing shorts and Fred Perry polos there are black-and-white motocross jackets and stacks of old Levi's, a pile of pastel-coloured vintage sweaters, and a cache of gently worn leather handbags with labels like Furla and Fendi sewn into their lining or stamped on the outside.

'This is cool.' Isla holds out a fringed suede jacket.

'Yeah, if your name's Betsy-Lou,' Mia scoffs, flicking through a rack of tropical-patterned shirts.

Isla goes to the back of the cluttered shop and digs through a basket crammed with multi-coloured silk scarves. 'Do you think I could pull this off?' she asks, wrapping one around her throat. Mia has a keener eye for fashion than her sister and often has to tell her what to wear, or how to wear something. Sometimes Mia wonders if Isla defers to her on purpose to make her feel good. Occasionally they dress alike for the fun of confusing their friends, but Isla doesn't much care for it.

Isla strokes the sleeve of a ballet-pink cashmere sweater (only slightly moth-eaten), then drapes it against herself. 'Here.' Mia is beside her now, holding out a cotton pique blouse embroidered with tiny blue flowers. 'Try this.'

'Really?' Isla is doubtful.

Mia checks the handwritten price tag and quickly converts the price to Aussie dollars. 'It's a steal. Trust me, you'll look great in it.'

The young woman behind the counter comes forward and begins chattering in rapid Italian, but Mia looks blankly at her. '*Inglese?*' she asks. '*Australiani.*'

The woman's eyes light up. 'You want to try on?' She points to a corner where a sheet hangs limply from a circular rail.

'*Grazie.*'

'Knockout,' Mia says a few minutes later as Isla emerges. 'You look like a young Elle Fanning. No, you look *better* than Elle Fanning. You *have* to get it.' She reaches into her pocket and pulls out a lipstick. There's a flourish of a V on the lid: it's from the box of goodies that Auntie Vivi gave them yesterday. She sends them a huge gift of her latest products for their birthdays and Christmas every year. Mia's never told Isla, or her mum for that matter, that she sells the things she doesn't want to her friends. Isla usually doesn't wear anything but clear gloss, but she lets Mia apply a slick of raspberry pink to her lips now. She peers into the dusty mirror strung from the back of the changing cubicle. 'You're right. It's kind of cool.' She grins. 'I look okay.'

'Well, I wouldn't go that far, freak,' Mia teases.

'*Bella!*' The shop assistant appears behind her in the mirror, clapping her hands in delight. '*Bellissima!*'

'Are you sure you don't want it for yourself?' Isla says doubtfully.

'My shoulders are broader than yours. It wouldn't look half as good on me.'

'You sure?'

'Yes. You should get it.'

'Right, I will.' Isla goes up to the counter while Mia lingers in the back of the store, rummaging through a rail of dresses.

'Let's go,' Isla calls to her once she's paid. 'I'm thirsty. How about a *limonata* or a *gelato*?'

Mia drops the psychedelic-patterned dress she's holding and follows her sister out of the store, calling a cheery *arrivederci* to the assistant as she leaves.

They're halfway back to the main piazza when Mia pulls a satiny, sparkly handful of buttercup-yellow fabric from her backpack, holding it up to Isla, a mix of glee and defiance on her face.

'Oh no, you didn't!'

It's fun to shock her straitlaced sister. 'She was too lovely to leave in that dusty old shop,' says Mia. 'Look at her, she's a dress that's made to be worn.' She holds the fabric against herself, twirling around in the narrow alley. In fact, she thought she heard her sister's voice urging her to slip it into her bag, but Mia can't tell anyone that.

'How do you know it will even fit you?' says Isla. 'And why couldn't you have just paid for it, you know, like a normal person? If you needed money, I could have lent you some.'

'Where's the fun in that?' Mia calls, skipping ahead of her.

'But what will Mum say?' Isla asks when she catches up with her.

'She isn't going to know, is she?' Isla would never rat on her, not about anything. Their loyalty runs deep; it's a twin thing. 'Besides, she probably won't even notice, and if she does, I'll tell her Dad bought it for me.' She shrugs. 'Too easy.'

CHAPTER TWELVE

Vivi dumps her book – she is yet to open it – a towel and her suntan lotion onto the cushions of one of the loungers. Her hands haven't stopped shaking since she closed her laptop ten minutes earlier.

Alice bobs gently in the shallow end of the pool, eyes closed, chin raised above the water, legs stretched out in front of her, an expression of sheer bliss on her face. Jade is lying a short distance away, absorbed in a paperback. When Vivi arrives, she gets up and begins to fold her towel.

'Don't you dare leave on my account,' Vivi says, mock-scolding. 'I replied to your message about the *Vogue* interview, but tell me, what on earth were you doing on emails so early this morning?'

Jade is momentarily flustered, her careful vowels slipping from their usual neutral into something more rounded. 'I … er …' She lifts her shoulders. 'I've never been a very good sleeper. More so when it's a strange place.'

Vivi takes the excuse at face value. 'As long as you're not getting up at sparrows on my account.'

'No, no, of course not.' Jade picks up her beach bag, having hurriedly shoved her belongings inside it. 'I expect you and your sister will appreciate some time alone together. Besides, I'm rather hot,' she replies, making a show of wiping her face. 'I burn if I spend too long in the sun.'

'Well, only if you're sure. This is a break for you too, remember.' Vivi is standing closer to her now. 'I do have something for you today, but it shouldn't take more than half an hour or so.' She draws close now, speaking quietly. 'Can you look into a solicitors' firm called Richardson and Partners for me? Check that they're legit. Just a brief outline – location, size, key clients, the type of work they do, that sort of thing. Oh, and an employee of theirs, Gary Birdwhistle. Nothing exhaustive. You might have to log on in the kitchen, though, it's the only place with a decent signal.'

'Of course. Are they based in the UK?'

'No idea.'

'Not a problem. That's Gary with one r?'

'Yes. And Birdwhistle just like it sounds.'

'Is there anything else?'

'One other thing – Marco says he hasn't received the balance of the bill for the palazzo. Could you check on that?'

'I swear I actioned it last week.' A vertical line appears between Jade's eyebrows. 'But, of course, I'll make sure it's gone through.'

'Thank you.'

* * *

'Holiday mode has been activated. Come on in …' Alice calls when Vivi returns to the pool.

'The water's lovely,' Vivi finishes for her, forcing herself to smile.

'Sure is. Though I couldn't persuade Jade. Anyone would think she was afraid of getting wet, like she's the Wicked Witch of the West or something. You should have seen the look of horror she gave me when I suggested she might like to cool off.'

'What a waste of a very expensive swimsuit,' Vivi says.

'She's a little mini-me, isn't she?'

'What?'

'Come on. Don't say you haven't noticed – the same swimsuit, practically the same frock the other night ... she dresses like you, wears her make-up like you, even sounds like you.'

'I never really thought about it.' Vivi changes the subject. 'Are you feeling better?'

'Think so. A cheeky Aperol spritz would probably improve things. Dammit, I should have asked Jade to bring some back.'

'She might be my assistant but she's not our servant,' Vivi reminds her, using all her self-control not to snap at her sister.

Alice emerges from the water to sit on the side of the pool. 'Okay, okay,' she grumbles.

Vivi checks her watch, a delicate, jewelled bracelet that Will gave her more than a decade ago when the company reached the top five in UK cosmetics sales. Goddamn. Why does almost everything make her think of him? Is it ever going to get any easier? 'It's ten past eleven, don't you think you should pace yourself?'

'Lighten up, sis.' Alice squints up at her. 'God knows I don't often get a break – and I am so, so grateful for this. We all are.'

'I'm thankful you could be here.' Vivi sighs and shrugs off her wrap. She walks to the edge of the pool to join her sister, lowering herself onto the tiles and dangling her feet in the water. She hands Alice a tube of Vivid zinc sunscreen.

'Is it any good?'

'What do you think?' Vivi raises her eyebrows.

'I was teasing, jeez, chill out, Vee.' She reads the label then turns back to her sister. 'Are you okay? You seem a little on edge.'

'I'm fine, really.' It won't solve anything to share this with Alice.

'Can I keep it?' She holds up the sunscreen.

'Just as well I brought plenty.' Vivi slides into the pool beside her sister. It's already sweltering and the sun has a bite to it, but the water is deliciously cool. She pushes away from the edge, fanning her hands to stay afloat, and the lump of sorrow that's been sitting in her chest for months begins to loosen, replaced now by fury that someone thinks they can blackmail her, that they might know things she was certain were secret.

'Love ya.' Alice flicks water at Vivi, getting her fully in the face.

'Will you ever grow up?' she splutters in mock annoyance, dabbing at her eyes.

'Not if I can help it.' Alice shakes with helpless laughter. 'Honestly, I sometimes think Isla is more mature at sixteen than I am at thirty-eight.'

Vivi silently agrees.

'Don't look at me like that,' Alice warns, wagging a mocking finger. 'Anyway, how are you doing?' she asks. 'I mean really?'

Vivi shrugs, moving further away from her sister and contemplating swimming a few lazy laps. It's been months since she had the will to exercise. 'Being here is helping.' Or at least it was, until that email pinged into her inbox. She has no idea how to deal with it, if Gary Birdwhistle's client, whoever the hell they are, even has any real evidence. She's been racking her brain trying to think who could be behind the threat. Only a very few have that information. The purchase was supposed to have been untraceable.

However, she's all too aware of the consequences of her secret being made public. She could lose her company, face a trial, quite possibly a prison sentence. She will not allow that to happen. She's always been in complete control of her life, right up until Will got sick. But then, there's very little anyone can control when it comes to terminal cancer.

'Well, that's understandable. It's the first time something truly awful has happened to you.'

Vivi strokes back towards her sister and hauls herself poolside. 'I think I've had my fair share—'

'Not like this,' Alice interrupts her.

'Yeah, maybe you're right,' she concedes, letting her legs dangle in the water again. She looks across the pool towards the palazzo and sees Jade carrying a tray of drinks.

'Marco thought you might like some refreshments,' she says when she reaches them, putting the tray on a nearby table. It's laden with three glasses and a jug filled with a fluoro orange liquid. 'Naked and Famous, he said it's called. I think there's mescal, yellow chartreuse, aperol and fresh lime juice. It sounds lethal if you ask me.'

'Marvellous!' Alice calls. 'What a gem he is.'

Vivi catches her sister's eye. 'Be careful,' she warns.

'You're just jealous, Vee,' Alice teases.

'That is the last thing I am, and you know it.'

'Well, stop policing me then.' Alice leaps up and heads for the drinks.

Vivi sighs and slips into the water once more, apprehension and the sudden change in temperature tightening her scalp. She emerges to find Jade hovering a few feet away from the pool edge, as though she dare not get any closer, holding out a frosty glass adorned with a striped paper straw. 'Vivi?' She is speaking quietly, so Alice doesn't overhear them.

'Yes?'

'I've got that information you requested. Would you like me to email it to you?'

Vivi accepts the drink and thinks for a moment. 'Yes, but to my personal account, if you could. And use your Gmail address. It's not strictly a work-related thing.' She never has to ask Jade more than once to use her discretion, nor does she have to offer an explanation.

'Of course.'

'What was all that about?' Alice asks when Jade has disappeared again.

'Nothing, just boring work stuff.'

Alice sighs. 'You need to switch off this week, yeah? What with looking after Will and the business, you're going to burn out if you're not careful.' She wraps her lips around her straw, sucking hard. 'Vivi …?'

'What?' Vivi sighs, knowing from her sister's wheedling tone that it will almost certainly be a sob story about money, or rather the lack thereof. She has been bailing Alice out – a few thousand dollars here, a car loan, uniforms for the girls, contributing to school fees – ever since Alice's marriage break-up. When it comes to her nieces, she can't refuse. Most of the time it doesn't bother her – she's got plenty to share and no one else to spend it on, and family is family after all – but recently her patience with people wanting things from her has worn thinner than the embossed tissue paper her products come wrapped in.

A stranger looking on would see a golden life. A thriving business, awards and accolades, a big house on the edge of the heath, country home in the shires, appearances at any number of blue-ribbon events, her name in the society and business pages. But it hasn't always been the case. In the early days of the company, she channelled everything back into R&D, marketing, advertising … What no one sees are the years of hard work, the belief that there would always be time for children, the eight unsuccessful rounds of IVF, and now no husband: her sounding board, her cheerleader, her lover, her partner in life and business … the other half of her.

'Nothing,' Alice says, affronted as she sees Vivi's expression. 'What? I've sold a couple of pieces this month.' Alice is a talented but often distracted artist, creating life-size sculptures that are popular as installations in the foyers of insurance companies and private banks. There's even one in the Art Gallery of New South Wales. She's recently moved on to painting portraits of pissed-off women, who wear expressions that range from the mildly irritated to the downright livid, and has gained something of a following since Isla helped her set up an Instagram page to promote them. She's never short of models (mostly her female friends, who think it's hilarious and revel in not having to smile), but despite a recent solo show – Face Value – she admitted to Vivi last month that sales haven't been what they should be. 'Though my dealer is begging me to go back to sculpture. He just doesn't get it.' It's Alice's turn to appear pissed off now.

'I see,' Vivi says, noncommittal.

'Well, it is expensive having teenagers, and the mortgage on the house has gone through the roof,' Alice admits. 'Did you know we've had *fourteen* consecutive interest rate rises in the past two years? Bloody inflation.'

'How much?' Vivi asks, fed up with Alice's dancing around the subject.

Alice glances at her sideways. 'Twenty grand?'

Vivi nearly chokes. That's more than her sister has ever asked her for. 'Pounds?' She can't keep the incredulity out of her voice.

'Well, I meant Aussie dollars, but, yeah, twenty thousand pounds would be amazing.'

For the first time, Vivi sees red, her stress and tension and grief spilling over. Her sister is the closest, easiest target. 'I'm not the fucking bank of big sister,' she says, gritting her teeth. 'Despite what you might think, there's not an unending money tap I can just turn on.'

Alice's eyes are huge and round, and she looks at Vivi with a mix of fear and horror. 'Jesus, okay, I get the picture. You're the one who brought it up.'

'Only because I got there first!' Vivi snaps. 'I'll bet anything you planned to ask me for a loan at some point this week. Except it's never a loan, is it? Because it never gets paid back.'

Alice lets out a muffled sob and scrambles to her feet. She slams her glass down on the table and flees in the direction of the palazzo.

CHAPTER THIRTEEN

'Pants, three shirts, four T-shirts, two pairs of shorts, boxers, socks ...' Nick piles everything on the counter and Pete tries not to wince as the total is rung up. They should get most of it back on their insurance, right? He picks up the socks, disguising his horror as he converts the price into US dollars. 'Do we really need these? It's summer. A pair of flipflops will do.'

'I don't want my ankles bitten.' Nick pouts. 'Besides, I only have one pair of gym socks, and I plan on running most mornings.'

'Okay.' Pete reluctantly puts them back on the pile.

'C'mon, Grinch, have a little fun here.' It's a source of amused banter between the two of them that Nick loves nothing more than spending money on nice things, while Pete is reluctant to open his wallet for anything but essentials. Pete's managed to keep the precarious state of his finances a secret from Nick so far, and although they're married, they haven't committed to joint bank accounts, thank God. No one needs that level of intimacy in their life.

'Just think, every time you wear this –' Nick holds up a paisley-patterned shirt '– you can say, "Oh, thank you. Yes, I bought it in Italy. That fabulous trip my husband and I took together ..."' He grins winningly.

Pete holds up his hands. He knows when he's beaten. 'Okay, okay.'

'Really?' Nick looks surprised that he gave in without a fight.

'Sure, why not. You only live once, huh?'

'I'll drink to that.'

There's a moment's awkwardness when Pete's credit card is declined, but he pulls another from his wallet and it's accepted without incident.

'Lucky you've got more than one, huh?'

'Indeed.' Pete doesn't want to think about the unpaid balances on all four of his credit cards, something Nick also knows nothing about.

They pick up the carrier bags containing their tissue-wrapped purchases. 'I saw a great little bar across the square over there.' Nick points to where a waiter is setting out a series of wicker cafe tables and chairs under an awning. 'Coffee?'

'Or Campari?' Pete suggests. 'When in Rome.' He follows his husband out the door, which closes behind them with a pleasing chime. 'Or at least Turin.' It is so long since he was last in Europe that he's almost forgotten the delight of whiling away an hour or so with a strong coffee or a drink in a beautiful town square, watching the world go by.

They find a table under a shady colonnade and a waiter takes their order, depositing drinks and a small plate of fritto misto after a short interval. 'Ouch!' Nick drops a courgette strip back on the plate and blows ineffectually at his fingers.

'Hot?'

Nick nods and takes a sip of his drink instead, pressing his burnt thumb to the glass to cool it. 'Are you sure it's okay for us to be here? At the palazzo, I mean,' he asks, staring out across the bustling Piazza San Carlo, where throngs of well-dressed Italians criss-cross the square, all seemingly in little hurry to be anywhere else.

Pete lifts his hat and smooths back his hair. 'I could hardly say we couldn't make it, not after Will …' He hasn't told Nick yet the purpose of his meeting next week in Milan. When, or rather if, he does, his new husband might think it an even worse idea that they've accepted Vivi's hospitality. He selects a grissini stick from a glass on the table and waves it in the air, an imaginary conductor. 'And she's ridiculously sentimental about old friendships.'

'Hey, isn't that the twins?' Nick asks, distracted by the sight of two long-legged blondes crossing the corner of the piazza, about to duck down a side street. 'I thought we were meeting them at the museum?'

'We are.' Pete checks his watch. 'But not for another hour. They're teen girls.' He shrugs. 'Just the age to get up to no good when they think no one's watching.' He is about to wave to get their attention when a scuffle breaks out on the other side of the square. Shouts echo around them, angry voices in a stream of a language he barely understands bouncing off the tall stone buildings. Nick has already risen from his seat, hands clenched.

Pete's immediate reaction is to clamp a restraining arm around him. 'We're not getting involved,' he hisses.

There's the smack of someone throwing a punch, and then another, and a crowd gathers. A scooter zips past, inches from where they are sitting, coming to a skidding halt in front of the tight knot of people. The rider shouts something unintelligible and wades in, not bothering to remove his helmet.

Nick shakes Pete off and runs towards the scene, their waiter fast on his heels. 'Nick!' Memories of what happened the last time Nick got involved in a fight slam through Pete, much like the right hook the guy in the piazza has just thrown, but it's as though Nick hasn't heard him at all.

The wail of a siren cuts through the sultry air, and Pete at least has the foresight to grab their shopping bags, all other thoughts forgotten in his haste to hurry after Nick, to try to prevent him from getting involved in something he shouldn't.

Seconds later, Pete comes to an abrupt stop on the edge of the crowd, his heart thudding at the sight of blood smearing the cobblestones. Two men, their fists raised, pace in a circle, snarling what sound like insults at each other. Another – the scooter rider – is in the middle, arms outstretched, attempting to keep them apart.

Pete scans the crowd, but Nick is nowhere to be seen.

One of the men lands a punch to the other's head, knocking him off his feet. He rains blows on the man on the ground, his fists a blur as the crowd gasps, some cheering, others crying out and waving their hands in distress. The man in the motorcycle helmet weighs in. Then another man, stocky and muscular in khaki shorts and a white T-shirt, pushes his way into the circle and lunges at one of the fighters.

There he is.

There's a look in Nick's eyes that sends a thread of fear through Pete. Before he can call out, tell his husband to get the fuck out of there, two black-uniformed men appear, the word *Polizia* in white letters across their backs, batons raised, shouting what sound like orders. Pete shuts his eyes, feeling nauseous, and when he opens them again, there is a shiny crimson blaze on Nick's cheekbone.

Nick spits out a bloodied gob of saliva and Pete's stomach lurches.

The two fighters have scattered, melting into the crowd, leaving only Nick and the scooter rider facing each other, both looking dazed, as if they can't quite believe what just happened.

At first the police seem to think they are somehow involved and pin both men to the ground, holding their arms behind their backs. Pete winces as he watches Nick's already injured cheek slam against the cobblestones. The crowd surges around them, and he struggles against it, trying to get to Nick. The scooter rider is speaking in rapid Italian, as is another bystander who also seems to be giving the police an account of the events.

'He's with me,' Pete says, finally reaching Nick. '*Turistica*,' he insists, using one of the few words of Italian that he can recall. '*Turistica*. Innocent. He's innocent.'

It only takes a couple of minutes, though to Pete it feels far longer, for several more people from the crowd to convince the police that the men responsible for the fight have vanished, and that the two they have restrained were trying to break it up. The police have a brief conversation, and then, after a few dramatic hand gestures, the one holding Nick hauls him to his feet, muttering what sounds like an apology.

Nick dusts himself off – there's a smear of blood on his shorts – and catches Pete's eye, offering him a helpless shrug, looking faintly sheepish.

Pete's concern turns to anger. The idiot could have got himself in all kinds of trouble, locked up, killed even. He's waited so long for love, for companionship, for his person (and boy, there were times, years even, when he thought there would never be one, let alone someone he cares for as much as he does Nick). He wants them to be together when they're grey-haired and doddery, not for things to be cut short by a stupidly impulsive mistake. He swallows, taking a moment before he can trust himself to speak. 'We left without paying the bill,' he says, deliberately ignoring the bruise blooming around Nick's right eye. 'We don't want to get arrested for that, do we?' He tries to make light of the situation, but there's an underlying judgement in his voice that he can't shake.

'So we did,' Nick replies, resting a reassuring hand on Pete's shoulder. 'Come on, let's go back, shall we?' The crowd has dispersed now, sensing that the spectacle is over. Pete and Nick walk across the piazza to their table, where their glasses still sit, beaded with condensation.

As they take their seats, Pete signals to one of the waiters for more drinks and manages to ask for an ice pack, indicating

Nick's bruised face. 'Wh ..., wha ... what the hell was that about?' he asks. Thousands spent on speech therapy and he still stutters when he's upset.

'No idea. Quite a show, though.'

Pete forces himself to take a breath. 'I get that you thought you were doing the right thing, but let's try to stay out of trouble for the rest of the trip, okay?'

'Don't patronise me, Pete.'

Dammit. They have yet to argue, not in any serious way. He bites back a further reply, as much an attempt to keep the peace as to not draw any further attention to his stutter.

Fresh drinks arrive and a glass full of ice, and Pete sees to Nick's cheek, fishing out a cube and handing it to him. 'For the swelling,' he says, kinder now. While Nick presses the dripping ice to his face, Pete takes a sip of his Campari and looks across the piazza again, remembering the girls. Did they see what happened? He didn't think they got caught up in the fight, thank God, but where are they now?

'You want anything else?' Nick drops the ice onto the table and studies the menu in front of him, though Pete knows that he probably won't understand much of it.

'There should be a few more things coming. If you're nice, I'll share.'

'Hey!' Nick abruptly stands up, waving madly and attracting a few irritated stares from the other customers who are there in hopes of enjoying a quiet espresso, especially after the earlier kerfuffle.

'Mia! Isla! Over here!' His voice is loud enough to get their attention and they wave back, changing direction and heading towards the table.

'Jesus, what happened?' Mia asks, her eyes wide.

'Are you okay?' Isla looks at him with concern.

'You should see the other guy,' Nick jokes. 'Just a scuffle.'

'It looks like more than a scuffle,' says Mia.

'I'm surprised you didn't see it,' Pete says. 'We thought you two were just across the piazza when it happened. I could have sworn I saw you both.'

The girls exchange glances. Mia gives her sister an infinitesimal shake of her head, so quick that unless you were paying close attention, you wouldn't notice it.

Pete notices it.

'Nope. We've just come from the museum. Looks like we missed all the fun,' says Mia lightly.

'At least you've had a better morning than we have,' Pete replies, ignoring the lie. That girl has the best poker face he's ever encountered.

'Didn't we see you earlier?' Nick asks, puzzled.

'Don't think so,' Mia replies, flopping down on a chair next to Nick with an exaggerated sigh. 'Anyway, it was pretty boring.'

'It *was not*,' says Isla, pulling up another chair as a waiter delivers a dish containing a bright green mush studded with tiny white fish fillets. 'It was an awesome museum. So relevant to what we're studying.'

'Yum,' says Mia, looking at the dish, her voice dark with sarcasm.

'Did you order that?' Nick asks.

'Uh-huh.' Pete scoops some up with a hunk of bread. 'It's a local specialty: garlic and parsley sauce with anchovies. It tastes better than it looks, I promise,' he says, finishing a mouthful. 'Tell me, girls, how did you know where to find us?'

'You saw us,' Mia says. 'Across the square.'

'*Piazza*,' Isla says under her breath.

'But you were supposed to be at the museum.'

'Like I said, I was bored out of my mind, so we thought we might try to locate you. It was a safe bet that you wouldn't be too far from the shops.' Mia grabs a grissini stick and uses it to point to the Armani boutique a few hundred yards away before breaking it into pieces and feeding them into her mouth in rapid succession. 'Can I have one of those?' she asks through a mouthful of crumbs.

'You're under eighteen, remember? How about a soda instead?'

She mock-sulks and breaks up another grissini. 'Hey, Pete?' she asks.

'Yeah?' He's still trying to work out why she lied to him. Is it normal teenage behaviour, or is there something else going on? He takes a gulp of Campari, feeling it soften the edges of the stressful morning. This is supposed to be a chilled-out week. Plus, they're not his responsibility, he reminds himself. Keeping Nick out of trouble is more than enough for him to handle right now.

'Can we have another game of backgammon this afternoon?' she asks.

'You think I'm a sucker for punishment?'

'I hope so.' She grins.

CHAPTER FOURTEEN

After sulking in her room for half an hour, Alice decides to go back to the pool to smooth things over with Vivi, but when she gets there, there is no sign of her sister. Welcoming the peace, she lays her towel on a lounger and stretches out. Being able to laze around in the middle of the day like this is a rare treat: generally she is covered in paint-splattered overalls, her hair messy, up to her elbows in modelling clay or gouache, sipping on tea that went cold hours before.

She is still in shock at Vivi's response to her request for money. Of course, Alice hates asking, but Vivi's got more than she knows what to do with and has always told her how happy she is to help. Perhaps her timing was off; perhaps Vivi overreacted because of all the stress over Will's death. Whatever the issue, she hopes her sister doesn't stay mad at her for long or it could make for an awkward few days.

'*Torta?*'

Alice opens her eyes, shading them from the sun, and sees Marco standing before her. 'One of my favourite Italian words.'

Marco hands Alice a plate bearing a slice of cake dusted with icing sugar, then hovers while she picks up her fork and takes a bite, waiting for her verdict.

'Wow. That's delicious. It's so light,' she says, grinning at him. 'Hazelnut?' The others, wherever they are, are missing out.

'Correct.' He winks at her, and she feels a tiny flutter in her belly. She tells herself that the only reason he has such an effect on her is because of the complete and utter scarcity of men in her life. Unbelievably, she hasn't slept with anyone since splitting up with Jeff, the girls' father, five years earlier. Well, apart from one disastrous Tinder date that she's determined to wipe from her memory.

Her ex is one of those self-involved, inherently insecure types who never miss an opportunity to remind you of their superior intellect. He drops university names and qualifications like litter whenever he gets the chance, pointing out that all Alice has is a diploma from a second-tier art school. He wore her down with his insistence that she should never aspire to anything more than motherhood, and then insinuated that pregnancy had left her flabby and unattractive. Like a fool, she believed him. For her birthdays, while they were together, he always gave her gym memberships or beauty treatments, a not-so-subtle dig that she needed to lift her game. He had been impressed by Vivi, often comparing the two sisters, until one day Alice lost her temper and told him that if he liked Vivi so much, maybe he should fuck her instead.

Thank God she no longer cares what he thinks of her, or what anyone else thinks, for that matter.

Though Jeff never stopped singing Vivi's praises, Vivi wasn't a fan of her brother-in-law. She had completely failed to hide her delight when Alice told her their marriage had broken down. She said Alice got married too young, that she rushed into things because she was pregnant, both of which were true. More helpfully, she also sent a cheque that allowed Alice to put a deposit on a place for her and the girls to live, saying she couldn't bear to think of her nieces ending up on the street. She also offered plenty of advice along with outrage at Jeff's serial infidelity, which was what triggered the separation. Alice shudders now thinking of it, for she has never got over the humiliation of finding him in bed with one of their mutual friends.

Alice is in her late thirties, in her goddamn *prime,* she reminds herself, and look at her, chaste as a nun. It's a goddamn crying shame.

Marco *is* bloody attractive. And at least ten years younger than her, not that it overly bothers her. It is a sad indictment of her life that she's even thinking about pursuing him, a man she'll never see again after the week is over. But it's been a long time since anyone looked at her the way he is doing right now.

'It's *outstanding*. Really.' She surreptitiously sucks in her stomach. At least her swimsuit hides the stretch marks on her hips, a legacy from carrying multiple babies. She'd defy anyone to bounce back unscathed from that.

Alice tries not to show her dismay at her body in front of the girls. It's important to her that they grow up with a healthy self-image – not that they've got anything to worry about, but she's heard enough about body dysmorphia to know that it has little to do with the reality of the situation. She reminds herself not to be so shallow. She should be concerned about homelessness, world hunger, the war in Ukraine, the growing number of people living below the poverty line, end-stage capitalism, whether her latest triptych of paintings will sell … anything more compelling and important than whether she can afford a boob lift, which she knows for a fact she can't.

Alice read somewhere that grief is supposed to age you at least ten years, sometimes turning your hair white overnight. But her older sister doesn't look anything close to her age – a decade younger at least – unlike Alice, who has the sunspots and freckles to show for years living in a climate where the sun is akin to a weapon of mass destruction. Forty, in Vivi's case, is most definitely the new thirty. Good skincare and plenty of money will do that, she supposes. She tries but fails to quell a surge of envy. Now is hardly the time to be jealous of her sister, no matter how infuriating she might be. Even Alice can appreciate that Vivi has been through hell in the last couple of months.

To some people it might seem that, until recently at least, Vivi won life's lottery. Love, money, success, fame ... a life that oozes glamour, not that she has ever rubbed Alice's nose in it. Of course, Vivi also endured any number of gruelling, heartbreaking and ultimately unsuccessful IVF cycles, something that only those close to her know anything about.

Alice really doesn't have much to complain about: she lives in a peaceful country, has a (very nice) roof over her head, food on the table, good health, an artistic career (okay, so it doesn't exactly pay the bills, but at least she's doing something she loves – how many people can say that?), two strong, healthy, happy daughters, people to love and who love her. Look at her now, for example: eating cake by a shimmering pool in the beautiful Italian countryside. Attended to by an attractive Italian chef. In a fucking *palazzo*. She is on holiday – her first proper one for years – and other than a cold glass of rosé, cake is her favourite thing.

Life is good, she would do well to remember that. Savour every moment, for you never know when it could be your last.

She hadn't managed to find Marco the night before, but that was probably for the best. She'd been jetlagged and not entirely sober, a dangerous combination. Now, however, she is delighted to find herself alone with him and only wishes she could persuade him to linger. Damn the fact that she's suddenly tongue-tied.

'*Grazie mille*. I'm glad you like it,' he says, grinning even wider.

Alice is about to reply with something inane about the weather, but when she looks up from her plate he's already halfway back to the palazzo.

* * *

Later, she presses her thumb into the few remaining crumbs on the plate, then slips on her sundress, gets to her feet and takes the plate inside, telling herself that she does not need a second piece.

The kitchen is deserted, and she dithers for a moment, feeling a plunge of disappointment that Marco isn't there; she'd been rehearsing her best lines on the walk over.

'Can I help you?' It's Delfina.

'Just returning this,' Alice replies, indicating the plate.

'*Grazie.*' Delfina holds out her hand.

'Oh yes, right.' Alice passes the plate to her and then leaves, turning down the passage that leads back to the terrace. Hearing the creak of a door up ahead, she pauses, surprised to see a tiny, bent-over old woman emerge. She has a dusty bottle of wine in one hand, cobwebs trailing from its base. Before Alice can even say *buongiorno*, the woman disappears into another room further along the passage. *That's odd.* Alice blinks, unsure whether to trust her own eyes: the woman was as silent and stealthy as a ghost.

On impulse, she goes to the door the woman emerged from and pulls it open, revealing a set of narrow stone stairs that descend to a shadowy space below. The hairs on her arms prickle as cold air gusts towards her. Aside from the unrestored top floor, Marco hasn't explicitly said that any parts of the palazzo are off limits, but she's aware that she's about to go somewhere she probably shouldn't.

Since when has that ever stopped her?

With visions of discovering a priceless painting hidden away in a dusty alcove, she enters, blinking as her vision adjusts to the dim light. The door closes behind her, and she wishes she thought to bring her phone: its torch would be handy right about now. She descends the stairs, feeling along the wall with her hands until she reaches the bottom. Stepping forward, she nearly brains herself on a haunch of meat hanging from a hook fixed to the ceiling, a sixth sense making her duck at the last minute.

Before her is a long, dim, cavernous space with rough stone walls that curve towards the ceiling. A narrow beam of light comes from a chink in the wall at the far end. She wrinkles her nose at the musty smell, pinching it to stifle a threatening sneeze. To her left, cardboard cartons stamped with swirling logos are haphazardly stacked – this must be where Marco stores the wine – and she steps past them further into a space that seems as though it might stretch under the entire palazzo.

She squeezes between two upended barrels and a couple of broken chairs, their rattan seats sagging from overuse. Dirty gilt-edged picture frames lean against a mottled stone column, but they're disappointingly empty of canvases. Moving further into the space, she sees what appears to be a haphazard pile of sticks – walking sticks? – resting against a wall. Vivi mentioned that the palazzo was once a convent. Who knew: maybe the nuns were so old they needed help getting up and down the palazzo stairs? She giggles to herself at the image of dozens of old women clad in long black habits leaning on the sticks for support.

Wine aside, there's a lot of ancient, dusty shit in here, and probably not the Old Master she was hoping for (it was always a long shot, she has to admit), but she keeps going, wriggling past an armchair with half the stuffing missing, ignoring the voice in her head that's telling her to leave now.

'Holy shit!'

Those aren't walking sticks against the wall.

She edges closer.

'Fucking rifles! Are you kidding?' Involuntarily, she reaches out to touch one.

It's a rifle alright.

Next to them, on a shelf, is a lumpy piece of upholstery fabric. Still curious, she tugs on a corner, then gasps. Under the fabric are five – she counts them again to be sure – five pistols. They're covered in a fine layer of dust, the metal tarnished, and don't appear to have been touched for years. But still, guns? She picks one up, feeling its weight in her palm and finding it unnerving but also kind of thrilling. This is the first time she's ever handled a gun of any kind.

She thinks back to dusty fifth-form history, when they'd covered the entire Second World War in a term's worth of lessons. Didn't the Italian partisans put up a huge fight against the Nazis in northern Italy? She wishes now she had paid more attention. But Italy's role in the war doesn't explain why there would be antique firearms here, in a former convent. Somehow, she has trouble picturing a brigade of pistol-packing nuns.

A door slams distantly overhead, and Alice drops the gun back on the shelf as though it's suddenly searing hot. She turns and hurries back to the steps, tripping in her rush to get to the door. She grabs the handle, but it's stuck fast.

She bangs on the door, calling for someone to please let her out, but there's no response.

She rattles the handle, then throws her body against the wood, but it still doesn't move. She yells as loudly as she can then remembers that Vivi is probably in her room two floors above, that there's no telling where Marco is, or Jade, and that everyone else has gone to the city. Only the old woman and Delfina are likely to be nearby, but the door is solid timber. She's stuck in a thick-walled, dimly lit dungeon.

A cold sweat beads on her forehead, breaks out in her armpits, and the cake in her stomach threatens to make a reappearance.

Telling herself there's no need to panic, to take a breath and think for a minute, she tries the door again, twisting the handle as far as it will go, the rough wood of the door catching her bare shoulder, her sandals slipping on the steps. She twists harder, throws herself into it, desperate now, her heart racing like she's just sprinted a mile, but the door remains stubbornly shut.

Losing the battle with her fear, she resumes banging on the door and shouts as loudly as she can until her throat is sore with the effort, her breath ragged with scarcely contained panic.

No one hears her.

No one comes.

CHAPTER FIFTEEN

Caroline waits in the ever-diminishing sliver of shade cast by her car for the mechanic from the city to arrive, feeling her sandals pinch her toes and thinking about all the things people hide from each other. The things they don't say, not to mention the lies they tell to smooth things over, to make people think the best of them.

The average person lies at least three times a day, or so she once read online somewhere, surfing the net for inspiration when she should have been writing.

Of course, there are all kinds of lies: lies of omission, lies of self-preservation or to protect someone you care about, tiny white lies that ultimately harm no one, that smooth the minute, the hour, the day. There are lies of misdirection, of deception, bare-faced lies, and lies designed to inflict the maximum amount of damage. And then there are the lies you tell yourself.

She's probably told all of these at some point or another. She has, most recently, lied by not admitting to Vivi or the others that she was sacked from her teaching job, a job she now realises she loved, though she hadn't valued it much at the time.

However, she hadn't been lying when she told Gabriele that she wasn't in love with him, that it was over, that she couldn't see him again.

Has it only been five weeks? At first he called dozens of times a day, begging to see her, crying, *snivelling*, for God's sake, and she was forced to turn her phone off. And then, when she stopped answering, he began texting: long, desperate missives, telling her his life wasn't worth living, begging to see her, insisting they were destined to be together. That she was Juliet to his Romeo, for Christ's sake. And then the messages took a different tone, threatening, sinister ...

After that she blocked his number, but then he turned up outside her apartment building, waiting for her to appear, day after day, refusing to leave. The last time she saw him, he grappled with her handbag, nearly dislocating her shoulder, his face inches from hers, threats and declarations of love combining to form a garbled, terrifying message.

After that incident, she stopped going out, a prisoner in her tiny apartment, calling in sick to work and surviving on black coffee and pasta with bottled sugo she had made during happier times the summer before. There was no one she could call. She got so desperate she even googled 'how to get rid of a stalker', but all she learned was that one in five adult women would be stalked at some point in their life, a horrifying statistic.

There was no way she would go to the *polizia*.

She had brought it all on herself.

Eventually, the principal called her in. Escaping her apartment via a back exit not long after the sun came up, she checked behind her almost the entire walk to the school, convinced that Gabriele was following her.

At the school, things only got worse. It turned out that a relationship she thought was secret had become common knowledge, and her years of service counted for nothing. The principal terminated her employment immediately. Covered in shame, she couldn't bring herself to fight back. She had no doubt he would make the most of the opportunity and hire a younger, cheaper teacher to replace her.

What a total, sodding mess her life was.

Vivi's invitation, arriving by email two days after the ignominious sacking, had come at exactly the right time.

Of course, Caroline had emailed as soon as she heard about Will (after sobbing her heart out at the news), penning a long message of condolence, recollecting the early years, the good times, apologising for not being able to come to the funeral (not revealing that she simply couldn't bear to, that she was too much of a coward). She spent hours composing it, editing obsessively until she was satisfied that she had got the words exactly right.

Vivi, by contrast, sent a short, bald message of thanks in return.

The thing is, Caroline met Will first, though that snippet of information had long since been forgotten by everyone except her. A group of them went to the cinema to see something arty with subtitles, she can't remember what. Will was friends with someone she vaguely knew and had invited them both along. Afterwards, they sat in the beer garden of a hidden-away pub. She could still remember the smell of the roses that grew over the back door. The air cooled on her skin, but all she felt was an inner warmth, a glow as she basked in the attention of the lanky boy a year above her, a boy who offered his jacket as the night wore on, who listened to what she had to say as though she was the most fascinating person he'd ever met. Eventually, they were the only two remaining, barely noticing as the others slipped away. After last orders, he walked her back to her rooms and kissed her goodbye, pleading an early tutorial the next morning, his lips feather-light but leaving her giddy all the same.

She whispered his name to herself before going to sleep, remembering how she'd made him laugh, the way one of his teeth was slightly out of alignment with the others, the moment his hand reached out to briefly cover hers. With absolute certainty, she knew she'd met someone important.

And then she was stupid enough to introduce him to Vivi.

Though only a first-year, Vivi was one of those people everyone seemed to know, or know of. There was something about her: it wasn't that she was classically beautiful (Caroline was wary of such girls, they existed on a different plane to everyone else), but her wide-set eyes, which gave her a permanently astonished look, olive skin, thick eyelashes, effortlessly good hair, and her habit of always wearing red lipstick meant she was impossible to overlook. She also had an enviable knack of making you want to be around her, a magnetic energy that drew you in and kept you close. She always had a recommendation for a great book that no one was talking about yet, she knew where all the great cheap eats were and could show you the best way to get red wine stains out of your favourite top … She and Caroline were staircase neighbours, often running into each other on the way to lectures, juggling notes, textbooks and mugs of tea. Caroline was reading English, and although Vivi was a classics student, she spent a lot of her time with the drama crowd, which Caroline hung on the fringes of. Somewhat to Caroline's surprise, they were friends by the end of the first term.

A week after meeting Will, Caroline asked Vivi to come with her to the college bar, not wanting to look too obvious by turning up on her own. 'Just for an hour,' she insisted, literally dragging Vivi away from her seat in the library. Of course, Caroline was too shy to mention that there was a tall, brown-eyed, third-year business studies student who pulled pints there on a Thursday night and who she was pretty sure she had already fallen half in love with.

Three words. That was all it took. 'Two beers, please,' Vivi said, and Caroline knew any chance she might have had was shot. There was a sizzle of electricity between them that even she could feel. A romantic would call it fate; Caroline labelled it grossly unfair. She silently cursed her ability to self-sabotage; really, she should have known better.

She resigned herself to wearing an ugly bridesmaid's dress, catching the bouquet at their inevitable wedding, and managed to console herself with the idea that heartbreak was fuel for a writer. She never breathed a word of her own feelings, not to Will or Vivi.

Student Caroline was going to be the next Brilliant Young British Novelist. Will, they discovered when he joined them for a drink as the bar was winding down for the night, dreamt of being a CEO at a major listed company one day (and even managed to make such a dull ambition sound exciting). Vivi confessed she still had no idea what use her classics degree was ever going to be but insisted that she was going to Be Somebody. They all had such big dreams, were going to lead such big lives, but that's not how it turned out – at least not for Caroline.

Although she was brilliant at starting a novel, she wasn't any good at finishing one. Once she turned thirty, she mentally edited out the word 'young' from her imaginary biography.

Caroline left uni without graduating, faffing around at a series of part-time, casual, unstable, mostly awful jobs, usually involving waitressing, before signing up for a course to teach English to foreign students in an effort to secure a steadier income. She told herself teaching in the mornings would still give her time to write in the afternoons. She applied for membership of The London Library and, for a while at least, took herself Very Seriously. Now, she can no longer imagine being that young woman, the one who had such unassailable self-belief, the audacity to dream.

Will was snapped up for a trainee scheme with a management consultancy, and Vivi joined the Royal Shakespeare Company as a junior wardrobe and make-up artist. 'Honestly, it's only because my uncle knows the director that they even interviewed me,' she explained to Caroline before changing the subject and asking about her writing. That was part of Vivi's allure – she always made you feel like you were the most interesting person in the room, downplaying her own achievements and dreams and cheering for yours.

Two years later, and with Will's encouragement but Caro's misgivings, Vivi quit her job (despite the fact that she had just been promoted to head of make-up), borrowed ten thousand pounds from her parents, and created a range of five lipsticks named after characters from Greek mythology – Aphrodite, Athena, Artemis, Pandora and Medusa. 'See!' Vivi said gleefully as she showed Caroline the packaging. 'I knew my degree would come in useful someday.' Caroline didn't mention that the Greek naming thing had, in fact, been her suggestion, as had the introduction to a chemist who helped Vivi with the formulation. The trouble was, even when Vivi trod on your toes, she did it with such charm and enthusiasm that you couldn't hate her for it. Vivi also spent some of her limited seed money on packaging design, choosing the timeless, understated typeface that was now synonymous with the brand.

When Nicola Durham, leading lady at the RSC, wore Medusa, a dark, almost-black-red lipstick, on the red carpet, a stylist for *Vogue* happened to be there and spotted it, and the range sold out within a month. *Tatler* gave it the top gong in its annual beauty awards, lauding the lipstick not only for its saturated colours and staying power but also for its cruelty-free, vegan, sustainable ingredients and eco-friendly packaging. The words 'cult status' were thrown around like confetti and soon Vivi couldn't keep up with demand.

Three years after that, as predicted, Caroline followed a radiant Vivi down the aisle wearing a ballet-pink flounced dress that suited Alice and the five-year-old flower girl far better than it did her.

In her twenties and early thirties, while everyone else she knew got on with their lives, acquiring serious jobs, partners, mortgages and children, Caroline was still going on disastrous dates, sharing a dingy flat in Peckham with an out-of-work actor and a dude who fancied himself a musician, constantly arguing over whose turn it was to buy milk. In a fit of wanting to do something – anything – to change things up, she applied for a job at an English-language school in Turin, despite not understanding more than a smattering – *infarinatura*, she later learned – of Italian.

She was supposed to be there for a year, but somehow it had ended up being more than a decade. It paid peanuts, but the holidays, at least, were great, and with help from a small inheritance after her mother died, she bought herself a tiny apartment near the produce market in the Piazza della Repubblica a few years before the property situation went bananas. It was probably the only time in her life that she managed to find herself ahead of the curve.

She grew accustomed to the 3 am grind of the delivery vans and the musical shouts of the stallholders, told herself she was living the dream, and every January resolved that this was the year she would finally finish her novel, that it would be published to great acclaim and everyone would regard her with new respect.

Sometimes she even believed it.

Caroline also did a pretty good job of convincing herself that she had long abandoned her feelings for Will, but at Vivi's thirty-fifth birthday, the cocktails were heavy on tequila, which didn't mix well with the antidepressants she was taking, weakening her defences. His confession that he and Vivi were 'going through a rough patch', that their marriage was on the rocks, took her completely by surprise. She told herself it was her last shot, her final opportunity to tell him how she really felt, that she had been in love with him since uni, that she still, all these years later, got ridiculous butterflies around him, had never stopped thinking about him.

She was pretty sure it was Will who had made the first move.

Fragments of what happened next have come back to her over the years, but what she most clearly recalls is Pete's shocked face looming over Will's shoulder as she scrambled to yank her dress down. She remembers Pete leading – half carrying, if she's honest – her to the front entrance, hailing a taxi. Then waking, mortified, the next morning in the cheap hotel she'd booked.

The way Caroline sees it, shagging her friend's husband in a bathroom stall pales in comparison to what Vivi did all those years before, let alone what she's done since.

But God help her if Vivi ever found out.

In any other circumstances she would have declined the invitation to spend an entire week with Vivi, but the chance to escape her apartment, which had become a prison, was too good to pass up. Being away, even for a week, would hopefully give Gabriele time to come to his senses, to move on with his life, as she must with hers. Besides, she and Vivi have some unfinished business to resolve.

She's still pondering all this, wishing she brought a hat to shade herself from the sun, when the vigneron from the day before makes an appearance. He pops up among the vines and gives her a leer that makes her shudder, smiling widely enough to confirm that he's missing all his back teeth. She feels faint from the heat, which shimmers before her, and her feet have swollen, pinching at her Birkenstocks. She really doesn't want to exchange more than a brief *buongiorno* but feels guilty. After all, he *did* give her a lift the night before.

She is saved by a cloud of dust rising in the air down the road.

Please let this be the mechanic.

Her phone begins to chirrup and she scrabbles in her handbag, trying to retrieve it. Damn! She gets to it too late, stares at the screen. Whoever it was doesn't bother to leave a message, and she pushes down the thought that it was Gabriele calling from a different number, telling herself instead that it was probably someone trying to sell her double-glazing or solar panels or scam her with the threat of a fictional unpaid bill, or something equally annoying but mundane.

She's very good at lying to herself.

CHAPTER SIXTEEN

Mia holds out her phone as far as her arm will allow, tilts her head and smiles at the camera. Click. Adjust. Click. Widen smile. Toss head. Meaningful stare. Click-click. She examines the results with forensic attention, flicks her hair off her shoulders and poses again, widening her eyes and sucking in her cheeks, lowering her chin. *That's better.* Ignoring the voice in her head that tells her she looks gross, she applies a filter, adjusts the contrast, checks the background and then posts. #bellaitalia #turin #palazzostellina.

Mum doesn't know about this account; she thinks Mia has only @miahardy06, set to private. Mum doesn't use social media that much, so the chances of her stumbling across this one are close to zero. Even Isla doesn't know about it, not that she'd ever rat on her.

Pete and Isla are yammering on about the museum – yawn – and aren't paying the slightest bit of attention to her. Nick ordered them Cokes and a plate of fries, and Mia smirks as she sees him checking out his reflection in the glass of the cafe window. He's even more obsessed with his appearance than she is.

She inhales a handful of shoestring fries and looks out across the piazza. It's really chill here. Old buildings, great shopping, decent food … Perhaps she could come here for a gap year? Or a uni semester? The boys are cute, too. An Italian boyfriend ... that would be something. Despite being nearly seventeen, Mia has never had a boyfriend. Sure, she's kissed a few boys at parties, but that hardly counts. It would be nice to have someone who would bring her thoughtful small gifts and take her to fancy restaurants, out to cool clubs, do more than just snog, or pash, as her friends in Sydney call it. Her lack of experience weighs heavily, and she is determined to do something to change it.

Pete's phone beeps and he pauses his conversation to check it briefly. 'What's the name of this piazza again?' he asks.

'San Carlo.'

Isla knows. Of course she does. Her brain that retains everything. She barely pauses for breath in her conversation; now she's busy telling Nick about the museum's papyrus collection.

Mia smirks again. He doesn't look as interested as he thinks he does, his eyes sliding past Isla to the people strolling in the square beyond.

Pete texts a brief message, but she can't see who he sends it to.

When Mia has eaten enough fries (she did offer them to Isla as well, she's not a total greedy mare), she licks the salt from her fingers, gets up from her seat and positions herself behind the others. 'Selfie time!' she says, manoeuvring them all into position.

'Say cheese!' says Pete.

'*Formaggio!*' Isla chimes in, grinning.

On second thoughts, it's her sister who's more likely to come and study here. Mia might end up going to the local TAFE to learn basket-weaving (not that there's anything wrong with that, she's quite fond of baskets as it happens), for all the clue she has about her future. Who is she kidding? Neither she nor Isla have ever got anything less than an A since year seven. Great things are expected of them both, not that

Mum puts much pressure on them, but Dad does, and so does school. Isla never seems to stress when it comes to assignments or exams, though she studies her arse off. Mia pretends she doesn't do much revision but usually stays up the entire night before a big exam, hyped up on No-Doz Plus and fear of failure. She gets high marks by the skin of her teeth.

'Hello! Hi!' They all look up as a bony woman with straggly hair and Iris Apfel statement sunglasses trots towards them. It's Caroline, that tragic friend of Auntie Vivi's. She's got loser written all over her, a pathetic 'pick-me' energy that oozes from her like a bad smell. She tried to talk to Mia and Isla at dinner last night, showering them with questions about school and what they want to do with their lives. Did they have any hobbies? Had they been to Italy before? Did they like it here so far? What was their favourite pasta dish? Ugh. Cringe. Such a try-hard.

Pete and Nick are polite – of course they are – fetching her a chair and ordering another round of Campari and sodas. Caroline's mouth twitches at Nick's attempt to thank their waitress in Italian, and she can't help but correct him, a lesson he takes with little grace.

'Ooh, lovely, fries!' Caroline leans forward, like a seagull stealing a chip, and her handbag slides off her arm and whacks Mia across her shoulder. 'Oops!' She sits down next to Mia, clutching her bag on her lap like an old lady and flapping her hand in front of her face at the heat.

'Did you get your car fixed?' Mia asks, pretending sweetness.

'It's going to be a couple of days. There's a part that needs to be ordered or something. Though there are supply chain issues here. Like everywhere now, right?' Caroline gives a flighty laugh, looking around nervously as though she's expecting to be accosted at any moment. 'What I know about cars could be written on a postcard. Here's hoping it isn't too expensive.' She gives an exaggerated sigh, flopping back in her chair. 'I suppose it could be worse. At least the driver was able to drop me near here.'

'Not to worry,' Pete says. 'You can ride with us if we go anywhere, there's plenty of room. And I'm sure someone can bring you back into town when it's ready.'

'Thanks, you are kind.' More drinks arrive and Mia tries not to shudder at the sight of Caroline's crimson lips sucking on the paper straw, her long beaky nose as it dips towards the glass reminding her of an ibis (bin chickens, they call them in Australia). She recognises the lipstick colour: Auntie Vivi must have given them all the same package of cosmetics.

Bored now that the food is all gone, Mia gets up and takes more photos, noticing a detail of the carved stonework, gazing upwards and snapping a roofline jutting against the cloudless blue sky, the statue of a soldier, arm aloft, riding into battle on a horse. She takes a surreptitious one of a good-looking waiter delivering drinks to a nearby table, a candid shot of Pete, Nick and Caroline.

'Oh no, please, no!' Caroline covers her face with her hands and tries to turn it into a joke, but Mia can hear the edge of irritation in her voice. Wondering why she's so sensitive – she's not *that* ugly, just weird-looking – Mia pretends not to hear, going to the other side of the table and bending to take a selfie of all of them.

'I said no!' Caroline's jaw is clenched, her lips a red gash against her pale, freckled skin.

'These are for Auntie Vivi,' Mia lies. 'I was planning on making a digital album of this trip. Memories, you know? It's going to be a birthday present to her.' It isn't a bad idea, she realises, and will give her something to do other than lie by the pool and listen to her sister crap on about archaeology. She clicks the button again, angling the viewfinder so that Caroline is in the centre of the shot.

'As long as that's all it's for,' Caroline relents, still sounding annoyed. 'I hate having my photo taken.'

'I don't know why. For an older woman, you look great.' Mia smiles guilelessly, but the bite is there in her words.

'Mia!' Pete glares at her. 'That's hardly polite.'

'It's okay,' Caroline replies. 'The ignorance of youth, hey? Death by a thousand paper cuts.' She smiles just as saccharinely back at Mia.

Ooh, return of serve. Caroline might not be such a loser after all. Mia feels a grudging respect for people who stand up for themselves. 'I meant it as a compliment, honestly.' A wicked thought occurs to her. She goes to Instagram and searches for Caroline Fenning, remembering someone mentioning her surname the night before. There she is – friends with Auntie Vivi and Pete, who also both have accounts.

Mia flicks through her recent photos, selects a handful, making sure to include several of her mum, Auntie Vivi, Pete and then one of Caroline. She uploads them, tagging her sister, Pete, Auntie Vivi and, importantly, Caroline, captioning it: 'Chilling out at the #palazzostellina #italianholiday'. *That'll teach the silly cow to complain about having her photo taken.* She presses her lips together to keep her smile from spreading across her entire face. Luckily, Caroline is listening to Isla rave on about the museum, seemingly far more interested than Nick was, though her eyes flick across the square, almost as though she is looking out for someone.

'About time we got back, don't you think?' Pete gathers the shopping bags by his feet and signals for the bill.

'Thanks, Pete – for the fries,' Isla says. 'And the drinks.'

'Yes, thanks, Pete.' Never let it be said that Mia does not have perfect manners. No one ever sees the dark mess inside her. They only register the exterior, tell her she is pretty, that she would be even prettier if she smiled more … as if that's what counts.

They find the car, which is parked on a side street not far from the piazza, and pile in, Mia squashed against Caroline and trying not to inhale her musky perfume. She smells like one of those hippy stores her mum likes so much. Patchouli. It's foul. She'll probably end up reeking of it herself now.

Nick negotiates the snarl of traffic that clots the city centre. 'Dammit!' he says, slamming on the brakes as a tiny Fiat zips into half a space in front of them. 'These midget cars: you don't see 'em coming.'

Pete responds by clapping a hand on his husband's shoulder and laughing uproariously. 'Just don't get us killed, okay?'

Nick doesn't find it nearly as funny as the others.

CHAPTER SEVENTEEN

Vivi leaves the pool not long after the tiff with Alice, going upstairs to change, needing some time alone to think. She feels bad for snapping at her sister. After all, Alice has no idea what's really going on.

Several things helped set Vivid on its successful path, but Vivi's decision to formulate its signature Close-up Foundation in a staggering thirty-five shades, at a time when most beauty companies offered less than a dozen, was key. Now, of course, everyone's doing it. She followed this up with lipstick shades and blush formulated for darker skins, and Vivid began to use an increasing diversity of models in their campaigns. Then, fifteen years ago, Will suggested she spend her slim advertising budget online, bypassing the expensive glossy magazines, which were already experiencing a slump in sales. Timing, it turned out, was everything.

Recently, Vivi insisted on casting women over fifty (grey hair was suddenly fashionable – just as well she wasn't in the box-dye business), and the company also introduced men and transgender models into the mix. Customers, it turned out, like seeing make-up on people like themselves instead of on unattainably perfect models.

A bottle of Skin Science Face sold every thirty seconds. They had been about to launch a new bespoke foundation, created using a top-secret method of scanning the skin, when one of Vivid's closest competitors came out with practically the same concept. They'd been forced to put the launch on hold indefinitely.

Vivi's been telling herself that all she needs is a break, just a few days, and that after this holiday she will be ready to step back into her old life, albeit without her husband and business partner by her side. Trouble is, Will was there for so long, she isn't sure she can do it without him.

She flops down on the bed, not caring that she's still damp from the pool. She has worked her arse off for nearly twenty years now with barely a break. Will had too, and look what good it did him. How many more years does she want to keep slogging away, working twelve-plus hours a day, six days a week? The thought of losing everything she's built, however, is terrifying.

Like almost anyone who hasn't been closely touched by death, until recently Vivi never gave her own mortality much thought. She vaguely hoped she'd be like the Queen at the end, hale and hearty with all her marbles accounted for until well into her nineties. Popping off to the next life after a lunch of several G&Ts and a roast beef and horseradish sandwich. Vivi doesn't *actually* know what the Queen's last meal was, but she likes to imagine it was something equally delicious and sustaining. A long life well lived, that was Vivi's aim, not that she looked too far ahead.

Barring unforeseen accidents or sudden, catastrophic illness, her demise is likely decades away, but it isn't entirely surprising that with the sudden death of her husband, and with another birthday looming (forty candles, enough to burn down a house!), she too has become preoccupied by the final full stop, as Will used to refer to it.

Still, she realises as the fog of recent months begins to clear, she's not ready to do *nothing*, certainly not for another forty or fifty years. But what if she hasn't got fifty more years? What if she's only got ten, or five, or one? What then? Does she want to have spent it all working, drowning in a sea of emails and meetings?

Among the many emails this morning that nag at her was one from Vivid's COO.

There have always been whispers that one or other of the big beauty behemoths – Lancôme, L'Oréal or Elizabeth Arden et al. – is sniffing around, but since the company's solid results of 2020–21 and 2021–22, thanks to customers leaning into self-care during the pandemic, those whispers have been getting louder. And now even Vivi, in her grief, is unable to ignore them. It was the first item on the agenda at the most recent board meeting, but although Vivi is no longer the major shareholder, she nevertheless managed to persuade the other members that the company would not be best served by a sale. For now.

The COO's email concerned J&K Pharmaceuticals, a Milan-based chemical conglomerate. The company is looking to acquire a cosmetics brand and has Vivid in its sights. They've been making discreet enquiries for a couple of years; several months ago, Will had even tried to persuade Vivi that it would be in their best interest to engage with them, a suggestion that led to an enormous row and ended in days of frosty silence. At the time, Vivi had felt completely blindsided, furious that Will would even entertain such a thing. 'There is no way on earth Vivid will ever be associated with such a disgusting company,' she stormed at him. 'I swear on my life.'

Now J&K's CEO wants a one-on-one meeting with Vivi next week and won't be fobbed off on anyone else.

While they have extensive scientific and technological resources, J&K shares none of the brand values and principles Vivi has worked so hard to establish at Vivid – sustainable, environmentally responsible, using only ethically sourced ingredients, a philanthropic arm. She would be devastated if

Vivid was to end up as part of an organisation like J&K, which puts profit over people, tests its products on animals and was responsible for a large petrochemical disaster in Mexico in 2012. Three people died, three hundred workers were injured, and a cloud of toxic fumes spewed into the atmosphere for days. Vivi has never forgotten it.

Her thoughts chase each other around and around in her head, giving her no relief until a movement outside the window catches her attention. She goes over, resting her palms on the sill, and sees a girl on a bicycle speeding down the road, her long hair streaming behind her. Vivi wishes she were the one freewheeling down that road.

But before she gets much further with that fantasy, her phone beeps with another message notification and she reluctantly turns away.

CHAPTER EIGHTEEN

On the way back to the palazzo, Nick and the girls insist on having the top down – 'What's the point of a convertible otherwise?' – and by the time they arrive, Caroline feels the beginnings of a migraine pinch her temples.

'Lunch will be served on the terrace shortly,' Marco says, wiping his hands on a towel as he comes out to meet them. He's smiling, though it doesn't reach his eyes.

'Oh, we ate in town,' Nick says, and Marco's face falls.

'Only a snack,' Pete adds hastily. 'And thank you, that sounds delightful.'

'Let's swim!' Mia says, racing up the staircase. 'Come on, Is.'

Caroline is desperate to cool down, but the hasty shaving job she managed before leaving home is not something she wishes to reveal, especially not when Mia and Isla will be flaunting their lissom young bodies in doubtless tiny triangles of fabric. Not that she's judging them – God no, she'd do the same if she looked even half as amazing as they do. She surreptitiously wipes the film of sweat from her upper lip and asks Marco for a drink instead.

'I can bring it to the terrace,' he replies.

'I might go and change first, but *grazie mille*, that would be most welcome.' Her skirt is clinging to her damp thighs, and she thinks that even if she dares not swim, she can at least wear her swimsuit under a cover-up and cool her legs in the water.

She changes as quickly as she can, throwing on a lemon-yellow silk duster over her swimsuit, remembering Gabriele tugging on the delicate fabric, unwrapping her like a present the first time they were together. She chases the thought away and knots the belt firmly.

The girls are already splashing in the pool when she gets there; she's missed her chance to slip into the water unobserved. It's a gorgeous oasis, set far enough away from the palazzo to be quite private, the mountains providing a dramatic backdrop, like something from a movie set. She stops and watches as one of the twins – she can't tell who – does a faultless swan dive into the deep end. She emerges from the water, shoulders back, head held high, shaking out her hair.

Caroline stands at the shallow end and dips her toes in the water.

'Are you coming in?' Isla asks, wiping water from her eyes as she reaches her.

'Maybe later,' she replies. 'I'm working up to it.'

'Suit yourself,' Isla says, ducking under the water before emerging with a streamlined freestyle and stroking effortlessly towards her sister.

When Caroline backtracks to the terrace, she sees Vivi at the table. Her face is angled away and she's staring up at the mountains. There's something about her complete stillness that makes Caroline hesitate for a second. The Vivi she knows is nearly always in perpetual motion, a ball of kinetic energy bouncing from one idea to the next.

'Hey.'

Vivi's head flicks away from the view. 'Ooh, nice dressing gown. How was your morning?' she asks, looking a little startled, as if she had been somewhere else entirely.

'Sorry if I disturbed you,' Caroline apologises, reaching for a water jug and pouring them both a glass. 'It's a duster coat. Vintage,' she says, peeved that Vivi described it as a dressing gown. 'Are you okay? Would you like me to give you some space? I can go back to the pool.'

'No, no, not at all. I'm fine, really. A little tired perhaps. Anyway, I'm glad it's just us here. How are you doing? It seems like forever since we last got together. I was so delighted when you said you could come this week.'

'Oh, you know how it is. Never anything that exciting to report in my world.' Caroline tries to sound bright.

Vivi lowers her sunglasses. 'But you have a rich inner life,' she teases.

'Something like that.' *Not really.*

'Come on, darling. You don't have to pretend with me.' Vivi smiles, an open, kind expression, and the walls Caroline has been trying to shore up around herself threaten to crumble.

She takes a deep breath. 'Actually, things aren't great right now.' To her horror, a rogue tear begins to slide down her cheek.

'Everything's a bit shit, isn't it? We're all sad about Will.' Vivi pats her hand, and while to someone else it might feel patronising, Caroline finds it comforting.

'Of course, I'm desperately sad about Will,' Caroline sniffs. She remembers the last time she spoke to him and her resolve steadies. In case Vivi should think that the only reason for her tears, she begins to recount recent events, giving her the *précis* version of her entanglement with Gabriele. She is too ashamed to tell Vivi how young he is. 'It was stupid,' she concludes.

'We've all been fools for love at some point or other,' Vivi says, not seeming to mind that Caroline is preoccupied with something far more trivial than the death of Vivi's husband. 'Surely there are other language schools?'

'I shan't get a reference, and they're going to want to know why I left so suddenly.'

'What about setting up on your own? Private lessons? That would give you even more flexibility to write.'

Caroline can't bring herself to tell Vivi that she's practically given up on writing, that she's concluded she doesn't have an original thought in her head. 'I guess. I'd rather not think about it this week, though. I've spent far too many nights worrying about what to do next. I think I need to give myself a break from trying to work out my next move.'

'Of course, sorry.' Vivi squeezes her hand. 'And I do know how that feels. Hopefully this is a week for us all to switch off, cast our cares to the wind.'

'Besides, it's nothing compared to losing Will, is it? Again, I am so sorry.'

'You loved him too.'

Caroline nearly chokes on a mouthful of water, but Vivi's expression is guileless. She means in a platonic sense, of course she does. 'It was a total shock; I wish I had known he was so ill.' That's a lie, but Vivi doesn't register it. 'And he was such a good man. So many will feel his loss.'

'Yes, he was a very good man,' Vivi echoes, staring into the distance again. A silver thread in her hair glints in the sunlight, but her skin is still youthful. God, she's even ageing more gracefully than anyone else, whereas Caroline has begun dyeing her roots, a badger stripe of white appearing at the crown of her head with depressing regularity.

Vivi has had everything Caro ever wanted: a hugely successful career and the man Caro saw first, loved first, never stopped loving. What's even worse is that she has always made it look so effortless, as if she was born to it.

'And don't feel bad about not knowing; he asked me not to tell anyone. He didn't want anyone to feel sorry for him, didn't want their pity. He hated people thinking he was weak.'

'But surely his friends would have wanted the chance to say goodbye? I know I would have liked to.' Caroline stifles the sob in her voice. She still can't believe she will never see him again.

'Believe me, I tried to convince him. But you know what Will was like once he made up his mind. He said it was about them and their egos, not what he needed.' Vivi blows air out of pursed lips then gets to her feet, grabbing her phone, which is sitting on top of an unopened book on the table.

'Oh, Vee, I'm sorry. I didn't mean to upset you. I shouldn't have brought it up.'

'No, it's fine, really. Please excuse me, I need to make a call.' She glares at her screen. 'One bar? Really? Couldn't Jade have at least found somewhere with decent mobile coverage? Is that too much to ask?' She looks fit to spontaneously combust, and Caroline has a surreal vision of flames extending from the tips of Vivi's scarlet nails.

'Where the hell is Jade, anyway?' She is fuming now. 'Has anyone seen her? Come to think of it, where's Alice? I haven't seen her for hours either. She wasn't at the pool when I went back there. Have you seen Jade, Caroline?'

'No, but she won't be far away.' The girl hangs on Vivi's every word. It's quite sickening and reminds Caro far too much of her younger self; there was once a time when she would have done anything for Vivi.

'Calm down, sweetheart.' Pete arrives and places two hands on Vivi's shoulders, which have risen somewhere close to her ears. 'You're supposed to be on vacation, remember?'

Vivi shakes off Pete's hands. 'Things are getting to me more than they usually would. I'm probably overreacting. Sorry, Caro.'

'Grief will do that to a person,' says Pete, 'but fortunately we have the antidote.' He grabs a bottle of prosecco from a sweating ice bucket on a stand in the shade and eases the cork out with his thumbs. 'Good friends, good food, and …' Pete holds up the bottle with a flourish, his palm slipping on its damp surface. 'Whoops … good wine!'

'At least there's that,' says Vivi, reluctantly putting her phone down and picking up her glass instead. 'Good friends,' she toasts.

'Good friends,' Pete and Caroline chant in unison, as Pete sloshes a generous amount into waiting glasses and Caroline chokes down a rare surge of guilt.

CHAPTER NINETEEN

Alice slumps against the door, wondering how long it will be before someone misses her. It's already past lunchtime. Will she be stuck here until mid-afternoon, when the girls return? Or until the evening, when her place at the dinner table is vacant? She thinks of how worried Mia and Isla will be when they realise she is missing. She's not worried herself, not yet, just pissed off at being in this position in the first place.

But she'll need to pee at some point. Oh Christ, it's going to be mortifying if she can't hold on. She starts calling out again, alternating between hammering on the door and yelling until her voice cracks.

She stops abruptly as there's a moan from the metal handle, a grinding noise from somewhere in the mechanism followed by a sharp click, and then the door swings open. 'Hello?' she calls out, bursting into the hallway and running slap bang into Marco.

'Oof! Alice?' He staggers with the force of her. For a few tantalising seconds, his arms surround her and she slumps against him, weak with relief. 'I don't understand. What were you doing in there?'

Alice reddens. She has no excuse. 'I, er, I got lost.' Part of her wants to shout at someone for having been trapped for so long, but she's embarrassed at having gone somewhere she shouldn't have. She only has herself to blame.

'Really?' He doesn't sound like he buys it even for a minute. 'You're lucky I came to get some more wine or who knows how long it would have been.'

'Yes, really,' she insists, though she can feel her cheeks flame.

'I am so sorry.' He has the good manners not to call her out on her lie. 'This should never have happened. I hope you weren't there for long?'

'No, not long,' she lies. 'And it's hardly your fault,' she adds, breathing more evenly now that she can see daylight and breathe air that's not musty and stale.

He is still holding her, perhaps fearful that she might collapse again, and the feel of his fingers as they curl around her back is sending pleasantly disturbing shivers up and down her spine. The last vestiges of her anger evaporate. Then his muscles tense against her. 'What?' she asks. 'What is it?'

Marco doesn't quite meet her eye. 'My grandmother …' He releases her, running a hand through his hair so delightfully that Alice feels a ridiculous desire to erase the lines of worry from his face. 'My grandmother is having a few problems.'

That must be the old woman she saw earlier. Is he telling her that *she* locked Alice in there? 'What kind of problems?'

'She is …' he circles a finger next to his ear, 'losing her touch on what is real. She has had a very hard life. The war …'

'But there are guns down there! Is that … is that entirely safe?' she asks, knowing that it entirely isn't.

He shrugs. 'If you had looked more carefully you would see that they are ancient – none of them have been fired in decades, they're all rusted over. And besides, there's no ammunition anywhere here, let me reassure you. There is *entirely* no danger. This is not America.'

'Oh good, well, that is a relief,' she says.

'Although Stella was a pretty good shot in her day.'

'She was?' A faint smile plays about her lips now.

'In the Resistance, she carried messages between the partisans, and more. She and her younger sister helped to eliminate dozens of Nazi soldiers. They were eventually caught and sentenced to death. She spent four months in a cell in Le Nuove, a prison in Turin used by the Nazis.' His eyes darken. 'It's a museum now. Gina died there a week before liberation, but Stella survived. By the skin of her teeth, as they say.'

Alice visibly shudders. 'Jesus, the poor woman.'

'She was *thirteen*. Younger than your own daughters.'

'I'm so sorry.'

He shrugs again. 'Maybe stick to the main areas of the palazzo from now on, hey?'

'Of course.' She pauses, considering. 'Do you think she'd let me sketch her? She's got such an interesting face. I'm an artist, a proper one,' she reassures him. 'I'm quite good, as it happens.'

He brightens. 'I'll ask her – she doesn't understand English very well, and I imagine your Italian …'

'Is pathetic. Thank you. I'd really appreciate it.'

'Sometimes she thinks our guests are, perhaps, the enemy. Sometimes it is as if she is thirteen again, that no time has passed. That there is still a threat. I found her a nice place in the city where she would be looked after, but do you know what?' He laughs as if he still can't believe it. 'She escaped. Caught a taxi all the way back here and stuck me with the fare!'

It's so absurd that Alice can't help laughing too, until tears of mirth and relief at no longer being trapped leak from her eyes.

Marco abruptly stops laughing and traces a finger along her jaw, wiping away a tear, and she's touched by the tenderness in his voice. 'I am not saying she did this, but please, if you are lost, just ask and I will get someone to show you where to go. I should hate to think of you being distressed by anything.'

Alice nods, feeling slightly ashamed.

'Are you okay now?'

She nods again, unable to speak, and for a moment she thinks he is about to kiss her. She almost forgets to breathe, not wanting to break the tension, willing his lips to find hers but too nervous to make the move herself.

'Marco?' It is Delfina, her eyes flashing disapproval as she takes them both in, the way they are standing only inches apart. 'Did you call for me?'

'Yes, I wanted to know if you had finished the rooms,' he replies. 'I must go.' He turns and walks away. Delfina follows him, ignoring Alice completely, and for a moment Alice wonders if in fact Delfina was the one to lock the door, if she perhaps did so deliberately.

CHAPTER TWENTY

Lunch is a long, languorous affair, a steady parade of delicious plates materialising from the kitchen: juicy tomatoes, oozing stracciatella, char-grilled lamb cutlets with rosemary, tender asparagus, fragrant peaches accompanied by thick cream studded with pistachios. They sit for hours, shaded by vines and lubricated by several bottles of bone-dry white wine.

Marco looks uncharacteristically cheerful as he collects each empty plate, and even Nick approves, licking his fingers after snaffling the last of the lamb. Alice grumbles at Mia, asking her to put her phone away. She rolls her eyes at her mother but otherwise takes the reprimand good-naturedly. Isla engages Nick in a conversation about his gym, and Vivi begins to feel as if life might yet have something to recommend it, especially if there are more days like this one in her future. She will apologise to Alice for snapping at her, blame it on grief, stress. And she'll lend her the money she wants, of course she will, though she won't tell her that until the end of the trip.

Only Caroline seems ill at ease, her face strangely blank and her eyes impenetrable behind her sunglasses, contributing little and responding with a tiny jolt anytime someone asks her a question. Vivi notices Jade make several attempts to engage her in conversation, but it appears to be mostly one-sided, her efforts going ignored. Caro is clearly finding it beneath her to talk to Jade. Such rudeness grates on Vivi.

After lunch, Caroline disappears upstairs. The twins and Alice decide to head to the pool, but Jade refuses all entreaties to join them, pleading a headache.

'Perhaps a nap might help,' Vivi suggests. 'And, Jade, don't take Caroline's behaviour personally – she can be a bit moody sometimes.'

'Oh no, really, it's fine. And please don't worry about me; I'm just happy to be here – it's so beautiful, and it's bliss to get out of London for a few days, even if it is scorchio. And lovely to get to know your family better as well.' Jade smiles. 'I'll check in with you by about four o'clock, unless there's anything else?'

Vivi waves her away, shaking her head.

'If you need me, I'll be in my room,' she promises.

Vivi and Pete linger over a glass of limoncello.

'Won't you join us?' Pete asks Marco as he delivers a plate of biscotti and tiny cups of espresso.

'*Grazie*, but I have work to do.' He says it lightly. 'It pleases me that you enjoy this.'

'It was wonderful,' Vivi assures him. 'We couldn't ask for better.'

'*Prego*.' He pushes the biscuits towards them and collects a handful of abandoned glassware.

'It's good to see you so happy,' Vivi begins when Marco has disappeared.

'I'm still rather astonished by it all, if you really want to know. I mean,' he pats his stomach, 'look at me, and then look at him.'

'He's the lucky one,' she says. 'I'm just so glad you could both make it.'

'Of course.' Pete leans forward and takes her hands in his. 'It's what old friends are for, right? Living it up in European palaces together.'

She smiles. 'I have something I'd like to ask you.' She plays with her glass. 'It's been good these last few days, hasn't it? The old partnership back together?'

'It has.'

'I was wondering if you might consider coming back. To work at Vivid.'

He drops her hand and sits back, stunned. His eyebrows raise, but only a fraction. Botox is probably responsible, not that she's judging. She's not above getting a little help herself. Her entire business is predicated on the transformational properties of skincare and make-up, but that doesn't stop her resenting the fact that society judges women so much more harshly than men, particularly when it comes to ageing. It also doesn't stop her doing what she can to stay looking as youthful as possible.

'Oh dear, that wasn't quite the reaction I was expecting.' She takes a slug of limoncello, choking slightly as it catches the back of her throat.

'No, it's not that. You took me completely by surprise.'

'We need someone to step into the CEO role. The past few months haven't been easy, as I'm sure you can imagine. I could really do with someone on my side, someone who knows what it's like to work with me ... especially now,' she says, willing Pete to meet her eyes. 'You were there at the beginning. And you could write your own ticket. Whatever it takes. Of course, it would mean relocating to London.'

'But there's Nick to consider ...' Pete begins.

'Of course!' Vivi rushes to reassure him. 'We'll help you find a nice little mews cottage. He'll love it. Don't all Americans find England delightfully quaint? I'm sure you'll be able to persuade him to move to London. They have personal trainers there too, last I checked. Hell, I could introduce him to any number of prospective clients.' She pauses, thinking. 'If he wants, he could even be an in-house PT. Corporate wellness is a high priority of ours. I'm sure we can find a budget for it.'

He spreads his hands wide. 'I can't deny, it's very appealing, but I'd have to think carefully about it, and speak to Nick, of course.'

Consulting work doesn't pay as well as most people think, and when you add in a global pandemic … well, she can imagine that he's been doing it tough the last few years. She's betting on him jumping at the offer, Nick notwithstanding.

'Since Will …' She swallows as her voice catches in her throat. 'Since Will died, I find myself without a sounding board, a right hand. I need someone who knows the business and who isn't afraid to disagree with me. I'd like you to be that person. You'll stand up to me, you always have. But most importantly, you know the industry almost as well as I do.'

'I'm flattered, obviously, and it would be an incredible opportunity, but …'

'But what?'

He looks as if he is wrestling with something, and Vivi goes for broke. 'It would be with a view to becoming CEO permanently, after a suitable period of transition, and with the board's approval, of course. But I'd be one hundred per cent behind you.' It's a job he once really wanted, and she is betting on that desire still being there, even all these years later. 'I think it would be an excellent opportunity for both of us,' she says firmly. 'There would be no surprises: we know each other's strengths and weaknesses. Have a talk to Nick, think it over, and get back to me with any questions, but sooner rather than later if you can. There's a lot going on, and to have your input would be invaluable. Just between you and me, J&K has been making enquiries.' She studies him, wanting to see his reaction. 'They're a pack of hyenas, but you already know that.'

Pete narrows his eyes. He looks as though he is about to say something more when Isla appears, a towel around her waist, her long hair dripping onto the table.

'Pete, can you come and swim with us now? Nick's never played Marco Polo before and he wants to learn. Please?'

Pete turns apologetically to Vivi.

'Go!' she says, waving towards the pool. 'We'll talk some more later.'

CHAPTER TWENTY-ONE

'So, what did you manage to find out?' It's late afternoon and Vivi and Jade have found a quiet spot at a bench on the other side of the tennis court, as far away from potential eavesdroppers as possible. 'My emails won't load right now.'

Jade doesn't need to be reminded what Vivi is referring to. 'It's a small family business, two partners – brothers, I think, or maybe cousins – based in Putney, dealing mainly with wills, property settlements, divorces, personal matters and so on.'

Vivi purses her lips, thinking.

'I confirmed that Gary Birdwhistle is an employee there. He went to a school called Cranleigh, in Surrey, and then to Southampton Uni, unless there's another Gary Birdwhistle, solicitor, out there. Not likely, though – it's a relatively uncommon name. His social media accounts are locked down tight. Not even a profile pic,' she says, sounding surprised. 'If I knew more about what it was for, I could keep investigating. My boyfriend's a solicitor, so there's a slim chance he might have come across him, or know where to find out more. I didn't call the company; I wasn't sure how deep you wanted me to dig.'

Vivi appreciates that Jade always goes the extra mile. She's the soul of discretion and empathy as well as being utterly reliable. Vivi doesn't know what she would do without her.

'No, no, it's fine.' She shakes her head. 'That's enough. Leave it with me for now.'

'Of course.'

They rise and begin to walk back towards the palazzo.

'Thanks, Jade. I know this is supposed to be a holiday for you.'

'A working holiday,' she replies with a smile. 'And nothing is too much trouble, you know that.'

'It's always appreciated. Now go and enjoy the pool – the water's lovely.'

Jade is about to reply when Vivi's phone chirrups with a stream of text messages. She thought it odd that her phone had been silent for the past hour. 'God, the coverage is shit,' Vivi complains, peering at her phone. The sun is so bright, it's almost impossible to see the screen. 'I can't read these here, I'll have to go inside.'

***

Vivi is almost at the stairs that lead to the second floor when Delfina calls out to her. 'Signora Savidge!'

'Yes?'

Delfina is carrying a long rectangular white box. It's so large, she has to hold it with both hands. 'I have something for you. It was delivered earlier. Some flowers, I think.'

'Oh, thank you.' There had been so many flowers after Will died that she ran out of vases, and now the perfume of lilies takes her right back there, haunting her as they slowly wilted. These must be for her birthday, perhaps from the office. She takes the box from Delfina and sees a small envelope taped to the front.

'If you would like them in your room, I can bring *una secchia*?'

'*Una secchia*?'

'*Vaso di fiori.*'

'A vase. Yes, please. But I'd prefer to have them down here where everyone can appreciate them.'

'Of course.' Delfina hurries towards the kitchen, and Vivi puts the box down on a side table, opening the envelope with her name on it and pulling out the card. It is edged in black and sends an immediate prick of warning through her. The message is printed in cramped letters: *Shame on you.*

'Delfina!' she calls, her voice sounding far stronger than she feels, the card quivering between her fingers.

The young woman comes hurrying back with a large glass vase in her hand. 'Sorry, I had trouble …'

'No, it's not that. Can you tell me who delivered this?'

'It came from the florist, Fiori della Mele. See – the name is on the box.' Sure enough, there is a small embossed sticker in the bottom corner.

'Right. Thanks.'

'Would you like me to arrange them for you?'

'No, that won't be necessary. I'll do it myself.'

'Okay. I brought a knife, to open it.' Delfina places it next to the box and, alarmed by the look in Vivi's eyes, backs away.

When she has gone, Vivi picks up the knife and slices through the twine and the tape, not sure what she might find inside. She takes a step back as she opens the box. The lid crashes to the floor.

Creamy trumpet lilies, each one open and perfect. The smell is almost overpowering, the aroma sickening. The flowers are identical to the ones Vivi ordered for Will's casket. His favourites.

dailymail.co.uk
Alison Archer
Published: 3.15 pm, 30 July 2023. Updated 7 pm, 1 August 2023

Death at Italian hideaway

Reports have emerged of a suspicious death at a luxury hideaway in the Italian Alps. Disgraced former New York star chef, Marco Bianchi, proprietor of the newly opened Palazzo Stellina, is no stranger to controversy, see our story HERE, but even he must be distressed by this latest development.

The group staying at the palazzo is rumoured to include society darling and beauty boss Vivienne Savidge, and the incident comes only weeks after the tragic death from cancer of her husband and Vivid CEO, William, 43.

According to sources, the as yet unidentified body was found floating in the resort's swimming pool by an employee in the early hours of yesterday morning.

Members of Ms Savidge's extended family, including her teenage nieces, are also believed to be staying there, as are several close friends. A male member of the group flew into a rage at *Daily Mail* photographers, uttering threats and obscenities.

It is unclear whether charges will be laid, and sources close to the family state that the investigation is ongoing. It is rumoured that drugs may be involved.

NOTE: Comments on this news item have been suspended.

CHAPTER TWENTY-TWO

Three days earlier

'Stretch out your hamstrings, placing one heel down at a time, lift your hips high ... higher ... and don't forget to breathe. *Bene. Molto bene ...*'

Alice, wearing yoga pants and a T-shirt knotted at the hip, is in downward dog and fighting off a wave of nausea as all the blood in her body rushes to her temples, making them throb painfully.

At dinner the night before, Delfina announced that they had arranged for a yoga teacher to visit, and for those who were interested, there would be a gentle stretch class at eight the following morning on the deck next to the pool. It seemed like a good idea at the time, especially after several glasses of wine and a second helping of zabaglione.

Now, however, Alice is not so sure. The teacher, who introduced himself as Riccardo, a tall, dark god with a Roman nose and a truly impressive physique, strolls between them, speaking softly and occasionally leaning in to adjust a pose.

Alice, Vivi, Jade (whose black tights and singlet are identical to Vivi's, and the subtle logo stamped on the waistband tells Alice all she needs to know about how eye-wateringly expensive they are) and Nick have joined in, and even Pete is there, doing his best to imitate the others.

Riccardo is wearing shorts and a singlet, and Nick's eyes haven't left him for a moment. Nick is also straining at every pose, taking it deeper, holding it longer. Alice strongly suspects that if competitive yoga were a thing, Nick would be at the front of the queue.

The twins are still fast asleep in their tiny bedrooms, single-person cells that used to house nuns. She looked in on them before coming downstairs, seeing them twisted around their sheets, silk masks shielding their eyes from the light. Just as when they were little, she sometimes feels like she loves them most when they are sleeping and can't come to her with their inexhaustible demands.

There's no sign of Caroline.

'And breathe in for six ... hold for six ... out for six.' Riccardo's voice is soothing and melodic with an accent that goes up at the end of each sentence, but Alice is far from relaxed.

Jade moves effortlessly through the poses, bendy as a strand of cooked spaghetti. 'How does your body even do that?' Alice mutters as she twists herself tighter than a pretzel.

Jade smiles serenely, her eyes focused somewhere in the middle distance. 'A shit-ton of practice.'

Alice snorts and collapses onto her mat.

Sounds of clattering pans and coffee grinding come faintly from the kitchen, and despite stuffing herself the night before, the smell of baking bread makes Alice's mouth water. Stifling a groan, she stands up, and as she lengthens her arms into warrior pose, a movement at the edge of the terrace snags her attention. She's a beat behind the others, who have moved into peaceful warrior, realising that Stella is watching them as she slowly skims fallen leaves from the pool. The old woman's thin, silver hair is pulled back into such a severe bun that it stretches the skin on her forehead. Who needs a security detail when you've got Nonna Stella, huh? A tremor of unease slides along her spine. She doesn't fancy being locked in the cellar again anytime soon.

Still, Alice is keen to sketch her, to discover what's hidden behind the wrinkles and the eyes that have doubtless seen so much. Hopefully Marco has mentioned it to her by now. She should have brought her paints on this trip, but Mia had more clothes than would fit in her suitcase, so Alice had let her have the remaining space in hers and as a result had only been able to squeeze in a small sketchpad and a couple of charcoal pencils.

She swallows, turning her head and refocusing her attention on Riccardo, who leads them through a flow series. Her body is beginning to feel slightly better as she eases out the final kinks of a long-haul flight. Maybe she can persuade everyone into a hike this afternoon? There's a trail leading from behind the palazzo up into the mountains that looks spectacular. Mia's not much of a walker, but Isla might join her. Then again, if she drinks as much at lunch as they all did yesterday, she might get no further than a nap on one of the sun loungers.

Finally, Riccardo invites them to take up corpse pose: *savasana*. Alice lies prone with relief, her spine pressing into the mat, and closes her eyes, trying not to think about the old woman staring at them. 'Remember,' he intones, 'yoga is not about self-improvement; it's about self-acceptance.'

'Amen, brother,' says Nick.

Alice tries not to cringe.

Riccardo is silent after that, and she almost falls asleep until the chiming of tiny cymbals rouses her and he invites them to roll to one side to complete their practice. When she opens her eyes, Delfina is there with a tray of juice and water.

'Thanks, man. That was awesome.' Nick is openly flirting with Riccardo, although Pete doesn't seem to have noticed. Or maybe he has but is deliberately turning a blind eye?

'*Grazie mille.* You are supple.' Riccardo flirts right back, self-consciously tucking a strand of hair back into his man-bun. 'You practise regularly?'

Nick shrugs, but a small smile crosses his lips and he is clearly flattered. 'I should do more,' he says. 'Yoga, I mean. Will you be coming again?'

'That depends ...' Riccardo looks to Vivi, who has helped stack the yoga mats and is now sipping on a glass of juice.

'Of course. If you're available, we'd love to do it again. Maybe tomorrow? Are you keen, Alice?'

'Sure.' She finds she means it. Before dinner the previous evening, Vivi apologised for losing her temper, and Alice graciously forgave her. After all, she's been through a lot recently. Still, Alice is more than a little miffed that Vivi didn't offer to lend her the money – even some of what she asked for. She might need to bring it up again before the trip is over. Her mortgage is three months in arrears, and she can't ignore the calls from the bank forever.

'Then I shall be here,' Riccardo says with a little nod, mainly directed at Nick.

'Oh, did I miss the class?' Caroline, dressed in a tragically baggy pair of shorts and a crocheted halter-top that Alice suspects she made herself, emerges from the house. 'Sorry, I overslept.' She runs a hand through her unbrushed hair and yawns, not sounding at all apologetic.

Doesn't it bother Caroline that she's such a freeloader? Of course, Alice and the girls are here because Vivi is paying for the accommodation, the food, the drink, and for their flights too. But that's different, they're family, and anyway, Vivi insisted the flights were an early birthday present. Alice is so wrapped up in her loathing of Caroline that it doesn't occur to her to mind that Nick and Pete are also benefitting from her sister's largesse.

Alice's irritation with Caroline is coloured by the fact that once Vivi went off to university, she hardly ever came home, and when she did, Caroline was almost always with her, leaving Alice feeling second-best and shut out. Alice didn't have the easiest of teenage years. She was bullied the year she turned sixteen – mean notes in her locker, raw eggs in her school bag, whispers behind her back, name-calling. The torment only stopped when she was finally able to go to sixth-form college in a different town. She tried to talk to Vivi about it, but there never seemed to be a good time.

It's ridiculous that she hasn't got over her resentment and illogical and unfair to blame Caroline, but there you go. Some things never leave you.

Now she thinks that Caroline could be a little more appreciative and bloody turn up when Vivi's organised something for them all. Admittedly, Mia and Isla haven't got themselves there in time either. Alice will insist the girls get their Lululemon-clad backsides to tomorrow's class.

'Those beds ...' Caroline rolls her eyes. 'I obviously needed the sleep.'

'Good,' says Vivi. 'And not to worry, Riccardo will be here again tomorrow, so you'll get another chance to *appreciate* him.' She gives Nick a teasing smile, but he pretends not to notice.

'Let me help you carry these to your vehicle,' Nick says, gathering an armful of mats and straps.

'*Grazie.*'

'Pete?' Alice asks, mainly to draw his attention to the fact that his hot young husband appears to have gone off with the hot young Italian yoga instructor, something that he might want to be aware of.

'Yeah?' He seems oblivious.

'You guys are so cute together,' she says. 'I always say that trust is the foundation of any relationship.' She looks pointedly in the direction of the path back to the palazzo, where Nick and Riccardo have stopped to chat, their bodies angled towards each other less than an arm's length apart.

Pete narrows his eyes, saying nothing, then deliberately turns his back, as though he doesn't want to watch, as if this isn't the first time he's observed such a scenario. 'What is that woman doing?' he asks in a stage-whisper. He's watching Stella almost, Alice thinks, as a distraction. 'She looks like she's dressed for a coven.'

'Shush. Don't *judge*. I think that's what all old Italian women wear. She's Marco's grandmother, Stella.' Alice is still too embarrassed to reveal that she wound up trapped in the cellar the previous day. 'Completely harmless, even if she does look like an extra from *The Godfather*,' Alice reassures him. 'She's lived here forever.' It only then occurs to her that this might be the woman Mia claimed to have dreamt about on their first night. She wonders if the situation is perhaps more sinister than it seems … Could the old woman be stalking the halls at night, slipping into the bedrooms of strangers? Surely not. She brushes off the ridiculous thought.

'So it's her place then?'

'I suppose.' Alice hasn't stopped to think about who might own the palazzo. 'I wonder if her family bought it off the nuns? Maybe it was going cheap.' She's half joking, but of course there just aren't as many girls and women with a vocation these days, so it stands to reason there would be abandoned nunneries, and monasteries for that matter, scattered throughout a country even as baked-in Catholic as Italy is. She's certainly never met anyone who ever wanted to be a nun, not after puberty anyway. That thought sends very un-nun-like thoughts of Marco floating into her head, her concerns about Stella entirely floating out of it. She grabs a glass of water, fanning her face with her other hand to cool herself down. 'I asked Marco if I might sketch her.'

'There's one way to find out,' Pete says, going over to the pool edge and dragging Alice with him.

'*Buongiorno!*' he says brightly. '*Come stai?*'

Alice watches as Stella simply blinks, angles her head and continues skimming leaves from the pool. She doesn't reply to Pete's question, though he tries again, this time in English.

Suddenly, the old woman reaches for Pete, gripping his forearm with her bony hand, her eyes bright and inquisitive as a bird's. Alice remembers the guns, which are, according to Marco, practically museum pieces. Nonetheless, she can picture this old woman wielding a rifle, the butt hard up against her shoulder, the same fierce look on her face as there is now. According to Marco, as one of the Italian Resistance, even so young, she had learned how to handle a gun.

Just as suddenly as she grabbed it, Stella drops Pete's arm, and he beats a swift retreat.

'What was that about?' Alice asks.

'Damned if I know. But I don't think she likes me very much.' He tries to brush it off but seems shaken. 'How about some breakfast, hey? I'm starving.'

They leave the pool and return to the terrace, where Vivi and Caro have already taken a seat. Alice spies Nick coming back up the steps, stuffing something in the pocket of his shorts. She nudges Pete, and his expression shutters. Perhaps things aren't as straightforward as they seem?

'Hey, Mum.' It's Mia, clear-skinned, bright-eyed and, for a change, smiling.

Isla was always the easy one, even as a baby, only crying when she was hungry or tired and easily soothed and settled. Mia, on the other hand, was impossible from the moment she emerged three minutes after her sister, full of outrage that she'd been made to wait. She's been like that ever since, and it's just as well that Isla's sweetness softens her twin's hard edges, though Alice doesn't love her any less.

'Hey, sweetie. Sleep well?'

Her daughter flips her hair over her shoulder and pulls out a chair. 'Pretty good. Do you think they have Vegemite?' she asks.

Alice shakes her head. 'You'll have more luck with Nutella, I'd say. Any sign of your sister?'

'Dead to the world.' She pours a glass of juice and smiles to herself. 'Snoring like a bull elephant with swollen adenoids.'

Alice can't help grinning at the mental image.

'So, what's on the agenda today?' Pete asks, helping himself to a basket of rolls. 'Pass the jam, would you, sweetheart? God, that's what I love about vacations – one day sliding into the next until they became a blur of swimming and sunshine, food and wine.' He sighs happily.

'Anyone feel like joining me on a hike later?' Nick asks, emerging from the kitchen with a blender full of a violently green smoothie.

'We were just thinking the same,' Alice replies, giving Pete a sly look. 'Burn off some of the insanely delicious food we're eating. Plus, it'll be a lot cooler up in the mountains.'

'According to Riccardo, there's a trail that leads to that pass there and a kind of hostel at the top.' He points towards the sharp-toothed mountains then raises the blender jug. 'Can I interest anyone in a green goddess?'

Alice coughs.

'I'm sure Marco has more ice and some straws,' he says, but no one responds.

'Do you think my sneakers will be up to it?' Pete asks, looking doubtfully at the sheer granite that soars skyward behind the palazzo. 'My boots are in my suitcase, the one that didn't make it to Turin.'

'Not to worry, sir.' Marco has emerged, carrying a bowl of berries in one hand and a plate of salami in the other. 'Your luggage has been recovered. It was delivered late last night. I will arrange for it to be taken up to your room.'

'Hallelujah. No excuses then.' Nick appears far more delighted than Pete about this turn of events. 'How about it, Mia? Care to join? Caroline? Vivi?'

'Absolutely,' Vivi replies.

'I'll come too.' Caroline says, reaching for another pastry, glossy with apricots.

It's her third, Alice can't help noting. *Freeloader.* Alice's annoyance has as much to do with the fact that not an ounce of fat clings to Caroline's body as it does with the way she is blithely taking advantage of Vivi's generosity.

She immediately regrets the thought. Jesus. She really can't stand herself sometimes: would it kill her to be a little less bitchy? 'I think this might just be my favourite meal of the day,' Alice says, spooning raspberries onto her plate.

'I know,' Caroline agrees, licking her fingers. 'Could you pass the fruit when you're done? I think those are local. Wouldn't it be nice to live like this all the time?'

Alice raises her eyebrows. 'I'd be the size of a small bungalow if I did. Not to mention my weakness for antipasti.' She says it quietly, conscious of commenting about her body in front of Mia.

'*Caffè?*' Delfina brings around a silver pot, filling their cups with one hand and offering steamed milk with the other.

'Perhaps we could take a ride into the nearest town one day, hey, Mia?' Alice asks. 'Didn't the website mention there were bicycles somewhere?'

Mia makes a noncommittal sound in the back of her throat and reaches for the juice. Her phone buzzes with a message and she flips it over, her expression brightening as she reads it.

'Who's that, darling?' Alice asks.

'Just a friend. They're staying nearby. In Turin.'

Alice raises her eyebrows. It's not that she doesn't trust her daughter, but, honestly, what are the chances? 'Really? Who?'

'Morning, everyone.' Isla appears, wearing cut-offs and a midriff-baring top, and slides into the remaining empty seat.

'Morning,' Vivi and Alice chorus back.

'I was just talking to Mia about taking the bicycles out,' Alice says. 'If you're interested. And maybe this afternoon, a hike if you're up for it?'

'Yeah, maybe,' Isla replies, sounding unenthusiastic.

'That was a girl from school,' Mia says, turning her phone over again. 'Eleni — you know her too, Isla.'

'I'm not sure — is she in the year above us?'

'Yeah. Her grandparents are Italian. She saw my Insta post yesterday and she's invited us — Isla and me,' she hastily clarifies 'to their place in the city for the afternoon. Can you drop us off, Mum?'

Alice hesitates. This is supposed to be a family holiday, and they're here to support Vivi. She glances at her sister.

'Don't be weird about it,' Mia says to Alice.

'Of course,' Vivi says. 'We don't all have to be joined at the hip here. Besides, it'll probably be much more fun for them than hanging out with us boring oldies all day. Anyway, you're coming on a hike with us, aren't you, Alice?'

'Sure. We can go for a bike ride another day,' Alice says. 'There's plenty of time.'

It's only after everyone has finished breakfast that Alice realises Mia never asked Isla whether she even wanted to go, whether she had any other plans.

Just sometimes, she wishes Isla would stand up to her sister.

CHAPTER TWENTY-THREE

Marco lets out an exasperated sigh as he checks his account. The balance owed by the Savidge group still hasn't been paid. It's an awkward situation, made more so by the fact that he's already asked her about it once. He'll have to speak to her again as soon as they've finished breakfast. He hates having to discuss money with guests: it makes him feel like a beggar.

'Oh good, you're here.'

It's the other woman he's been thinking about, and he blinks. If she knew how much she occupied his thoughts at present, she might be alarmed. 'I needed to see you as well, Alice.'

'Lucky me.' She grins at him, and he feels an answering curl of lust in his belly. It's been far, far too long. 'Oh, Vivi asked me to tell you that the bill is settled now. She says the money will be in your account by the end of the day, tomorrow at the latest.'

Has she read his mind? Regardless, he breathes a little easier. '*Grazie*.' His pride won't let him admit that unless they settle the account, he will struggle to feed them.

This group is one of the easier ones he's had so far this summer. They're not noisy (unlike the women on a girls' weekend, who shrieked around the pool area until after midnight) or drunk (unlike the stag party, who brought seven cases of beer and three bottles of whisky with them for a two-night stay *and* managed to break two of the new Riedel glasses) or messy (unlike the two families with toddlers, who left a trail of plastic toys, juice bottles and dummies in their wake and complained about the lack of a fence around the pool). A nice, normal group for once.

He has learned to his cost how tricky it is to get payment after a holiday is over, having had to chase one party for a month when he first opened. He usually insists on settlement in full at least a week before the arrival date, but this past fortnight has got away from him, and it wasn't until after they arrived that he realised Signora Savidge hadn't settled the bill. The amount in his account is barely at four figures. Sure, he's worked in restaurants that have been late paying their suppliers, but this time it's all on him — it's his business, his reputation. He is a week late with the money for Delfina and he hates not being able to pay his staff almost more than anything else.

'You said you needed to see me?'

'Yes.' Marco recovers himself. 'Your sister's birthday celebrations. A cake?' He flicks through several pages attached to a clipboard. 'Her assistant suggested chocolate, but I think we can do better than that.'

'Oh yes?'

'I will make a *torta* of mascarpone, grappa and lime, with amaretti and raspberry layers.'

Alice's eyes glaze over, and for a second he wonders if he's boring her. Sometimes he does go on about food too much, and not everyone is as passionate about it as he is.

She leans against the table towards him, eyelids lowered. 'That sounds amazing. You can talk *torta* to me all day, Marco.'

He laughs, relieved.

'Now, my sister, she will swear black and blue that she doesn't want all that candle nonsense, but I think we should go for it. Make a fuss of her. Although maybe not the exact number for her age.' Alice's eyes sparkle with mischief. 'If it's not too much trouble.'

'It is never too much trouble.' *Cristo*. He needs to stop flirting with her, but everything she says seems to have a double meaning and he can't help but respond in kind. 'She deserves a special night. To remind her that after sorrow, sweetness will come.'

'What a beautiful sentiment.'

'It is no trouble at all. It is the purpose of the Palazzo Stellina to ensure you all have the most memorable *vacanza* of your life.'

The future of the palazzo, everything he's invested – far too much money and his own sweat and even occasional tears – hangs on the reviews these first-season guests leave on social media as well as what they say to their friends and family. If Signora Savidge and her friends are as well-connected as Jade tells him they are, it's especially important that this week goes smoothly.

There's only the kitchen bench between them, but Marco can feel the air almost sizzle as Alice's eyes linger on his. He is impossibly drawn to this woman, who laughs easily and apparently refuses to take life too seriously. She takes a step around the bench towards him …

'Where are the extra wine glasses?' Delfina flies into the room. Her gaze flashes between the two of them.

'Thanks, Marco,' Alice says nonchalantly. 'You're a marvel.' She saunters out of the kitchen, hips swaying as she throws him a searing backwards glance.

'You are very popular this week,' Delfina says, and the comment brings him up short. He's an idiot. Getting involved with a guest is almost as bad as getting involved with a member of his staff.

'Keeping the guests happy,' is all he offers in reply.

'*Molto felice*,' she mutters under her breath.

CHAPTER TWENTY-FOUR

Mia sits in the shade while she waits for her mum and sister, squashing ants with the toe of her sandal and watching the survivors scoot around jerkily as if warning each other of the unbelievable, terrible ant massacre that just occurred. She wants to laugh, but no one will understand why she finds it so funny. Sometimes the bitterness inside her is frightening, but it's a familiar companion; she wouldn't feel like herself without it. She sighs and checks her watch. What is taking them so long?

She can't wait to get away from this boring place. There's no one her age to flirt with – well, possibly Marco at an absolute stretch, but he seems to only have eyes for her mum. Yuck. There is honestly nothing to do except swim in the pool, and even she can't spend all day in the water or on a lounger. Besides, she doesn't want her hair turning green: who knows what kind of chemicals they put in foreign pool water.

She wishes they were closer to Florence, Rome or even Venice, or somewhere much cooler like Positano or Puglia, but Turin will have to do. She wants to explore the city, just not the museums that Isla loves. She wants to be sitting in a bar or a cafe, flirting with cute Italian boys like the one she's arranged to meet later today.

'All set?' Her mum jangles the car keys in the air, and Mia forces herself to beam at her, all sweetness and light.

'We'll wait for you to get back,' Vivi calls from the terrace. 'It'll be better to hike later anyway.'

'Okay. I'll try not to be too long.' Alice squints up at her sister before returning her attention to the girls. 'I'm taking our lives in my hands again, I hope you realise.'

'I'll put Google Maps on; it'll be fine,' Isla reassures her calmly. 'What was the address again?'

'Near that square, the one we were at yesterday with Pete and Nick,' Mia says, heading towards their hire car.

'The Piazza San Carlo. Got it.' Isla taps away at her phone screen and they set off after stopping to open the security gates. They reach the centre of the city with the minimum of swearing on Alice's part, and Mia only grips the door handle once as Alice almost turns the wrong way down a one-way street.

'We're nearly there,' Isla says. 'What was the name of the road?'

'Anywhere here is fine.' Mia picks up the bag she brought with her. 'Just pull over there, Mum. We can walk the rest of the way.'

'But where exactly is she staying? I should come in and meet her family.' Alice startles as a car horn blasts them from behind, annoyed that they've slowed down. She pulls the car as close to the edge of the narrow road as it will go without scraping the stone buildings that butt directly onto it. Her phone rings, its tone incessant, demanding.

'Mu-um. God, do you have to be so embarrassing? Just drop us off here, it's fine. There's nowhere to park, anyway.' Mia has already unclipped her seatbelt and has the door half open. 'Answer your phone. We'll be fine.'

'We'll text you later,' Isla says as Alice reaches to answer the call.

'Damn, missed it.' Alice puts her phone down and glances in the rear-view mirror. A van is heading towards them, and there isn't room for it to pass. 'But what about picking you up? How will I know where to find you?'

'It's okay, Eleni said her cousin will bring us back later.' Mia is outside the car now, trying not to let her impatience show. Her mum can be oblivious to most things, but just occasionally she gets suspicious and insists on knowing inconvenient details. 'Thanks, Mum. Come on, Isla.'

They wave their mother off, watching as the car is swallowed up by the river of traffic.

'Do you think she'll make it back okay?' Isla asks.

'She'll be fine, stop worrying.'

'So where is this place?' Isla asks, looking dubiously at the façade of the building across the road.

'Just around the corner, I think. But, listen, we're meeting Eleni's cousin.' He's not really a cousin of anyone they know, but she's counting on her sister believing this. 'He commented on a photo I posted on Insta yesterday and offered to show me – us – around.'

Isla frowns. She opens her mouth to object, but Mia heads her off.

'Chill out, won't you? Don't you want to have a little fun? Something we can tell our friends about that's more exciting than going to our aunt's birthday party?'

Isla crosses her arms and looks properly annoyed now, though there's a hint of resignation in her expression too. She's used to going along with Mia's crazy plans.

Ignoring her, Mia reaches into her bag and pulls out a small mirror and one of the lipsticks Vivi gave her ('Always have a lipstick and an opinion,' her aunt says), circling her mouth in red. She smacks her lips together, checks her teeth and returns the lipstick to her bag. Mia gives Isla a sly glance and shrugs off her denim jacket. Underneath is a silky handkerchief-style top tied tightly across her breasts.

'Hey, did you steal that yesterday too?' Isla narrows her eyes.

Mia shrugs. 'It's a scarf. No big deal.'

'Did you *have* to? You know I would have paid for the scarf *and* the dress if you couldn't.'

'Chill the fuck *out*,' Mia repeats, tugging at a strand of hair and wincing as it comes away from her scalp.

'And stop doing that – do you want to end up *bald*?'

Mia sticks her middle finger up at her sister. 'Yeah, well, maybe you drive me to it. He said he'd show us around. Come on, do something spontaneous for once in your life. You never know, you might actually enjoy it.' She skips across the road in the direction of the piazza, narrowly missing an oncoming scooter. The driver beeps the horn at her. 'Hurry up, we're already late,' she calls back.

They reach the cafe they went to the day before, and Isla orders them both lemon sodas. Mia must admit, her sister's Italian isn't half bad. She experiences a rare moment of envy, conveniently forgetting that she, too, could have spent some time practising useful phrases like 'How much is that necklace?' and 'Where is the bathroom?'

'Well, where is he?' Isla asks when they've drawn out their sodas for nearly half an hour.

'*Ciao*, Mia?' A slim, dark-haired boy bounds up to them. He's carrying a backpack and wearing torn jeans and a T-shirt with 'Duke University' stretched in faded letters across his chest.

'Hey, Luca!' Mia gives him a shiny smile, pretending she already knows him.

He pulls a chair up to their table and beams at them. His eyes are the colour of hazelnuts and Mia fights a desire to pull on one of his silky corkscrew curls to see how far it will stretch. A delicious feeling of wellbeing spreads through her as she meets his gaze, and she can't look away. He's even hotter than his Insta photos suggested. And this is so much better than hanging out with her mum and aunt.

'*Buongiorno*,' she says, feeling self-conscious at her pronunciation. 'This is my sister, Isla. Isla, Luca.'

'Ah, *tu parli Italiano*?'

Mia has a feeling he is teasing her. '*Un poco*.' It's about all she can remember, and that's only because she heard Isla repeating it over and over on their way to school in the mornings. 'You said you wanted to practise your English?'

'Of course! Shall we go? I will show you the city if you like, and we can talk.'

Isla pays for the drinks and then they head off down one of the streets that leads from the piazza. 'Are you sure this is a good idea?' she whispers urgently.

'Oh shush,' Mia replies, skipping on ahead to catch up with Luca. There's not really room for the three of them to walk alongside each other, and Isla trails a few steps behind them as Mia chatters away, more comfortable now they are speaking in English.

'You are staying near here, right?'

'Not exactly. We're out in the middle of nowhere. The Palazzo Stellina – have you heard of it?'

He shakes his head. 'Where is it?' he asks, staring at her intently.

'About an hour away. North of the city, I think, towards the mountains. It's cool – there's an incredible swimming pool, and the chef is amazing.'

'I'd like to see it,' he says. 'And spend some more time with you, of course.'

Mia shivers pleasurably at his tone. 'I'm sure you can come over, my aunt's chill. We're there until the weekend. It's my aunt's birthday on Saturday.' Mia turns back to her sister. 'That's right, isn't it, Is? My aunt's husband – my uncle – well, he was …' She flushes, embarrassed. 'He died recently, so we're all here to cheer her up.'

'You're going drop us there later, right?' Isla asks.

'Drop you?'

'Take us home.'

'Oh, for certain.' He brightens. 'My friend has a car. He will lend it to me.'

'Cool.' Mia isn't worried, but she doesn't fancy having to call her mum to come and pick them up.

They wander some more, but all the streets begin to look the same after a while – at least, they do to Mia. Luca isn't that great a tour guide, she has to admit, but it's fun to pretend she's a cool girl hanging out with her Italian boyfriend … even if her sister is third-wheeling it.

'That's the museum,' Isla says, stopping abruptly. They turn back to look at her as she unleashes what sounds to Mia like a stream of flawless Italian, faint colour tingeing her cheeks. She turns to Mia. 'I told him we're studying Ancient History,' she explains. 'If you don't mind, I'd like to take another look. I didn't get time to see everything.' Isla hops from one foot to another, the way she does when she's excited or anxious. 'Can I meet you back here in a couple of hours?'

'But there's a bar near here that we can go to,' Mia pouts.

To Mia's surprise, Isla digs in her heels. 'Tell me where you will be and I'll come and find you later.'

'You're ditching us?' Mia jokes. Honestly, her sister is such a stiff sometimes, but hey, it's her loss, and this way Mia gets some one-on-one time with this hot Italian boy.

'I just need an hour.'

'Okay, your call.'

'Wait!' Luca holds up his phone. 'A selfie.' He slots himself between them and they dutifully smile. Then Mia holds up her phone and takes another, angling the camera so she and Luca are the only two in the shot.

'*Arrivederci*.'

'See you later.'

They leave Isla to her boring museum and find a fountain, taking a seat on a bench nearby. It's even hotter in the city than at the palazzo, and Mia leans into the spray coming off the bubbling water and closes her eyes. 'It's warm, hey?' she says, eyeing the fountain. She slips off her shoes and heads over, perching on the edge and swinging her feet into the water. 'Come on,' she says, wiggling her toes. 'It feels so good.'

'I don't think that is allowed,' he says.

'So? Who are you going to tell?' He's turning out to be less fun than she hoped. 'Can we get something to eat? I'm hungry,' Mia says when she's had enough of paddling in the fountain by herself. Luca seems oblivious to all her signals – accidentally brushing against him, flicking her hair, lowering her eyes whenever he turns in her direction … She's not giving up on her plan for an Italian fling just yet though. She looks at the photo she took earlier and reminds herself to get more photos of the two of them for her private Insta page. That will be something at least, evidence of her little adventure. 'Pizza?'

'Sure.' He laughs. 'You are in Italy, of course you should eat pizza. But no pineapple or they will do terrible things to you.'

She can't decide if he is taking the piss out of her or not.

'Let's go then.' She swings her legs out of the water, reaching for her shoes.

Luca leads them down a narrow laneway to a tiny shopfront at the end with a red awning. 'You wanted pizza,' he says, pointing at the window. 'Best in Turin.'

'Cool.' They take a seat at a tiny, rickety outdoor table, and she attempts to decipher the menu before giving up and getting out her phone. He orders for them both and she doesn't put her phone down until after the food arrives, having run out of things to say. With the pizza in front of her, she asks him to take a photo of her grinning cheerfully with a slice of pepperoni on its way to her mouth, and then one of them both, heads angled together, almost touching, the pizza in the foreground. That's one for the grid. #bellaitalia #pizzalovers

They drink bottles of a local *birra*, although it's bitter and makes her feel woozy after a few swigs. She wishes she'd asked for Coke instead.

The tacky music coming from the cafe is doing her head in, but he doesn't seem to mind it, tapping his foot in time and singing an occasional snatch of the lyrics. He orders more beers, not giving Mia a chance to say she doesn't want another. She sips the second beer slowly, finding it unpleasant now.

'If we don't leave soon, Isla will be wondering where we are,' she says. 'You are able to give us a ride home, yeah?' she reminds him. She doesn't want to admit that her mum will start to wonder where they are soon.

'*Si, si*,' Luca replies, then bursts out laughing at something he's watching on his phone.

They gather their things and head into the street. 'Hey!' she cries after him. 'Don't we have to pay or something?' He keeps walking, leaving her to scrabble in her purse for a fistful of euros as the waitress approaches. He could at least have offered to cover his drinks.

Isla is waiting outside the museum when they arrive. 'You're late,' she says, 'I've been waiting for ages. And my feet are killing me.'

'Sorry.' Mia raises her hands. 'We stopped for something to eat. And drink.' She stifles a burp and feels the sourness of the beer repeat on her, burning the back of her throat.

'What happened to your mouth?' Isla whispers as they follow Luca to where he says the borrowed car is parked.

'What?'

'Your lipgloss is all smeared. Have you been *pashing*?' Isla whispers, giggling, and Mia joins in, her good humour restored.

'No!' She giggles again. 'I wiped it off. Maybe it's pizza sauce.'

'I thought it looked good. The lipgloss, I mean.' Isla gets a tissue out of her bag. 'Here, let me sort you out, you look like roadkill.'

Luca stops in front of a tiny, two-door vehicle. 'Wow. Vintage,' says Mia, her sarcasm sailing right over his head.

'*Si.*' He opens the door with a flourish.

'How do you even get into the back?' Isla asks. Neither of them has been in a two-door car before; Mia didn't even know such things existed.

Luca reaches in and lifts a button and the seat pops forward.

'Oh, right. I'll sit in the back,' Isla says. 'Um. Seatbelts?' She casts around, grimacing as she runs her hand between the seats for fear of what she might encounter.

'Nup. Come on, chill, Is. It'll be fine.'

'I really think we should get Mum to come and pick us up.' Isla's hand is on the top of the seat in front of her and she looks ready to climb out of the car.

God, her sister can be a pain sometimes. 'They were all going hiking, remember? She probably won't even be there. And it would take her ages to get here, anyway. Besides, it's too late now.'

Luca guns the tiny car into the street, taking off in a cloud of rattling exhaust. 'Hold onto your tits!' he shrieks with manic laughter, both hands on his chest, only replacing them on the wheel when Isla complains.

CHAPTER TWENTY-FIVE

'Jesus!' Caroline gasps, resting her hands on her knees, bent over at the effort of dragging her creaky body up the steep incline. She is pretty sure her face is puce. Sweat is starting to drip into her eyes, making them sting like she's been cutting onions. She wipes the perspiration from her forehead with the back of her arm, screws up her eyes for a moment and pauses to catch her breath.

The path falls away to her right, and she's angled in towards the cliff for fear of falling. One leg may be permanently longer than the other if this keeps up. Nick and Pete are way ahead, dots in the distance, but Vivi and Alice are only a little in front of her, matching her snail's pace. Her thighs are *actually* trembling. She's so unfit! The short walk from her apartment to the language school is generally the only exercise she gets.

Her phone beeps with a notification and she reaches for it, glad of the excuse to stop for another minute or two. Is there phone service all the way up here? She glances around. A mobile tower. Of course. Funny how she almost never sees what's right in front of her.

It's a message from Gabriele, from a new number, not the one she blocked.

You can't hide from me. Not for long. Gx

Does he know she's left the city? Did he see her drive away?

Suddenly light-headed, her legs crumple beneath her, skidding on loose rocks as her backside hits the ground with a painful jolt. Her blood thuds in her skull, her heart racing now, pulsing faster and faster, the edges of her vision blurring until she thinks she might black out.

'Caro! Are you okay?' Vivi and Alice are coming towards her, concern on both their faces.

Caroline manages to wave a vague hand in their direction. 'The altitude ...' she says weakly, still breathless. 'Gimme a minute.'

The words 'poor Caro' float towards her. Normally she'd hate anyone pitying her, but right at this moment, she's got other things on her mind. She reaches for her phone, which has skittered away, and reads the message again.

How fucking dare he?

Not for the first time, Caroline regrets getting involved with Gabriele. Yes, he was charming, he was persistent, not to mention gorgeous, and the attention was flattering, but she should have known better. She is an intelligent woman, but the way she behaved was dumb. Although she won't admit it, she was lonely. Still, that is no excuse: she had no business encouraging him.

The final meeting with the principal was one of the most unpleasant of her life, though she knew she deserved every ounce of his disdain. She couldn't meet his eyes for a single second she was in his office. He would not tolerate such behaviour from a staff member, he said. She was the teacher, he reminded her, she owes her students a duty of care, the school owes its students a duty of care, and she is lucky he is not going to report her to the *polizia*. They both knew that was a bluff – Gabriele is over the legal age of consent – but she was shaken nonetheless.

When she told Gabriele it was wrong, that she had taken advantage of him in a way that was unforgiveable, that she was to blame, he cried. *He cried.* That was almost the worst thing. That sweet boy who cried is the same person who has sent her *this*? She can't reconcile the two.

He had shouted, in between noisy sobs, that he would be twenty in September, that then he will be a man, and they can be together. She insisted it was impossible, that they could not continue to see each other. That he had to stop hanging around her apartment building, stop calling her. She has spent the past few weeks hoping that he'll come to his senses, forget about her, find someone closer to his own age, but he has maintained his almost daily vigil.

God, how she wishes her life were different, that she had made many, many different choices. But right now, her biggest regret is sleeping with a student. She's a fucking idiot and probably deserves everything that has come to her. She has no idea how she's going to get another job, to keep paying her mortgage, support herself, *survive*. She has only the smallest buffer of savings. None of the rest of them have the slightest idea what it's like to worry about money, not in any real sense. She slips into despair.

'You sure you're okay?' Vivi and Alice have walked back down to where Caroline is sitting. 'Perhaps we should call it a day,' Vivi says, squinting at the lowering sun. 'Don't want to overdo it. Besides, I think I've just about hit my limit.'

Caroline swallows, her tongue thick and swollen, recognising that they're being kind, and struggles to get a grip on herself. She checks her watch. 'Fine, yeah. How long do you think it will take us to get back?'

'In time for cocktails, I hope,' says Alice. 'Why?'

'No reason.' She suddenly wants to be at the safety of the palazzo, behind those strong gates. It feels too exposed up here, as if anyone can see her.

'I'd kill for a bucketful of ice-cold rosé as soon as we get off this mountain. Jesus, I'll get vertigo if I keep looking down.'

Alice waves her hands towards the valley far below them. 'I had no idea we'd climbed so far.'

Caroline's breath is coming in short puffs and she's got pins and needles in her arms. She doesn't cope well with heights, but she can't have a panic attack here, not on the side of a mountain. She focuses on a clump of wildflowers on the side of the trail, their spiky pink petals shivering almost as much as she is. Slowly, the ringing in her ears recedes and her vision clears.

Vivi and Alice confer and then Vivi calls up to Nick and Pete, making a megaphone with her hands. 'We're ready to head back.'

Nick shakes his head, pointing up to the summit of the trail they've been following for the past couple of hours. 'We're going to head to the top,' he shouts down. 'It's not that much further.'

Vivi gives him the thumbs up and then a wave and points down the slope, back the way they've come. 'Okay, see you later.'

'We've had enough, isn't that right, Caro?' Alice asks, kind for once.

Caroline nods and gets shakily to her feet, gulping the last of the water from her bottle, not caring that it sloshes down her front and soaks her T-shirt.

She flicks to the notification on her phone again, angling the screen away from the two women. *Stop harassing me*, she types, pressing send on the message and breaking her zero-communication rule. The way Gabriele has been behaving this past month, messaging her dozens of times a day, at first begging and later threatening to hurt himself, to hurt her if she won't see him, she wouldn't put it past him to ... to do anything to get back at her. To hurt her as much as she has hurt him.

The trek down the mountain is, if anything, even harder, and Caroline's knees scream in protest at every step, but her fear and self-pity have turned to anger, the energy of it powering her towards the palazzo ahead of Vivi and Alice. She's too agitated to appreciate the beauty of their surroundings and goes from sweltering to shivering as the sun disappears behind the ridgeline, casting them in shadow.

When she is nearly upon the palazzo, she sees a car in the distance approaching the gates, and two tiny, slim figures emerge. 'There they are,' Alice calls out from above her. 'The girls – they made it back before us.' Alice and Vivi begin to holler and call, waving frantically, but they are too far away to be heard.

* * *

'Water?' Marco is out on the terrace with a tray of tumblers. Delfina stands next to him holding another on which several rolled snowy white facecloths have been stacked in a pyramid.

'*Grazie*.' Caroline takes a glass and a cloth.

'Did you have a good afternoon?' Alice asks the girls.

'It was okay,' Isla replies, taking a sip from her own glass.

'How was your friend?'

'She was … happy to see us.' Mia smiles at her mother. Butter wouldn't melt.

Isla looks as though she wants to say something, but Alice is paying little attention to either daughter, focused instead on asking Marco if they might open a bottle of wine. 'Rosé, if you've got it, would be lovely.' She flashes him a grateful look and sinks down onto one of the chairs. 'She didn't want to come in and say hi? Stay for a drink?' Alice asks, unlacing her sneakers. 'It would have been nice to meet her. Oh lord, my feet are so sore.' She wiggles her toes, an expression somewhere between ecstasy and agony on her face.

'She had to get back before it gets dark, you know?' Mia grins like a Cheshire cat.

CHAPTER TWENTY-SIX

Pete is already regretting the decision to keep climbing. His breath is coming in little gasps, and thanks to the thin air, he's struggling to inhale fully. Nick, meanwhile, looks as fresh as he did when he woke up that morning. He forgets that Pete is nowhere near as fit as he is, and Pete is determined not to show what it's costing him to keep up. Vivi, Alice and Caroline have turned back, and there's only the sound of his laboured breathing and the rushing of the stream that flows alongside the path. 'Are we there yet?' He stops at a red-and-white trail marker, resting his hand on one knee and squinting up at the forbidding saw-toothed mountain that looms in front of them.

'Not far now.' Nick reaches behind and offers his hand, but Pete brushes it away.

'Didn't someone say there was a hostel?'

'A *rifugio*, according to Riccardo. Rumour has it you can get a cold beer there. It's keeping me going.' Nick grins, and Pete's mood lifts. 'Should be around the next bend.'

'Yay to that.' Pete mops the sweat off his forehead with a bandana, wishing he'd remembered to bring his hat. His hair is thinner on top than it used to be but he's too vain to ask Nick for sun lotion. 'Oh, and by the way, don't think I didn't notice you noticing the hot yoga guy. *Riccardo*.' He says it lightly, but there's a sting in the words.

Nick chuckles good-naturedly. 'Were you jealous?'

Pete shrugs. 'Maybe.'

'Liar. Of course you were. I'm all yours now. Don't forget that.'

Pete wants to believe it. 'Wh ... what did he give you?' The stutter is back. 'I saw you stuffing that baggie in your pocket,' he adds when Nick looks at him, all wide-eyed innocence.

'Wait? What?' Nick erupts into laughter. 'Medicinal mushrooms, honest to God.'

Pete snorts, hoping it's true but still not convinced. He changes the subject. 'Jesus, this is steep.' Now would be the perfect time to bring up Vivi's London job offer, but he can't quite work out how to broach the subject, too afraid of what Nick's reaction will be.

'You okay?' Nick asks a little later, slowing down for Pete to catch up.

'Doing my best,' Pete puffs.

The wooden chalet appears like a mirage, and Pete collapses onto the seat of a vacant picnic table out the front. Several other hikers, including a couple they saw on the trail earlier, are also taking a break, their trekking poles resting against toned, suntanned thighs. He waves and then turns to Nick, groaning for maximum effect. '*Birra, per favore* ...' They're in the shade cast by the chalet and the sweat cools rapidly on his skin.

The valley spread below takes his breath away, a blanket of green pastures and striped vineyards dotted with squat wooden houses that must have weathered some bitter winters. From somewhere unseen comes the hollow chime of cowbells. If he squints, Pete thinks he can just make out the tiny figures of the three women on the trail far below him, Caroline in front, Vivi and Alice lagging behind.

Nick returns with a tray containing two large, frothy beers and a packet of nuts. 'Check out the moustache on that guy, seriously impressive. As are these.'

'Thanks for making me carry on,' Pete says, raising a frosted glass. 'I was ready to quit with the others, but this view makes it totally worth it.'

'I figured as much. See what happens when you listen to me, huh?' Nick takes Pete's hand and curls it in his own, and Pete feels some of his earlier doubt vanish.

They sit for a while, watching the shadows cross the valley.

'Say, what's up with Caroline? She talks to me like I'm a dumbass, completely uncultured American.'

Pete grins. 'And?'

'Hey, that's enough,' Nick says, swatting at him playfully.

'I feel a bit sorry for her. I know she can be a patronising cow, but she's got a good heart.'

'No one could ever feel sorry for Vivi.'

'She just lost her husband, don't forget. And she doesn't have a family – children – either, though I'm not sure she ever wanted them.'

'Some people keep that stuff private, you know.' Nick gives him a sideways glance. 'Do you? Want a family, children, soon?'

This isn't the first time they've talked about it, but in the past the conversation has been fleeting, and Pete's managed to dodge the hard questions. Nick talks about his nieces and nephew with such fondness, it's obvious he'd love children of his own.

'I did at one time,' he finally admits. 'But I'm not sure I'd be a good father; I'm far too selfish. Besides, I'm too old now. I'm forty-eight, for God's sake. People would think I was the grandpa, not the dad.'

'That's a crock; you can be a father at any age.' Nick is thoughtful. 'I want to take my kid to Little League games, have him sit on my shoulders and teach him how to ride a bike, tie a tie, cook a steak …'

'So you've always imagined having a boy?'

'I guess I could learn to tie hair ribbons and paint fingernails. Daddy-daughter dances would be fun.'

'How would we even do such a thing?' Pete wonders out loud, immediately thinking how much the whole process was likely to cost.

'Are you serious? Would you consider it?' Nick's eyes light up. 'There are ways …'

'It's a big decision,' he stalls. 'And not one taken on the spur of the moment.'

'You'd be an incredible father.'

Nick is beaming at him now, and Pete is suddenly exhausted. He hasn't ever really allowed himself to think in those terms. 'If we had a kid, it would be the end of vacations like this.' He sweeps his arm across the valley. 'And who would stay home? I can't see myself as the primary parent, I'm afraid. Plus, kids are *expensive*, in case you hadn't realised.'

'So?' Nick refuses to be dissuaded. 'We'd do some things differently, that's all. It would make us much less selfish. Better people. You'd think about it?'

'Maybe.' Put on the spot, it's the best Pete can come up with. Are they really discussing having a family? With Nick being so much younger, he supposes it was bound to come up. They've made vows to each other, promises, but none of that has been really tested yet. Can he truly trust Nick? He wishes he could be certain.

'I think my knees have seized up,' he says, hoping to steer the conversation into safer territory. He's about to suggest another beer when he realises they are the only ones left still sitting outside the *refugio*. The other hikers have disappeared, either inside or heading back down to the valley. As he speaks, a fine mist begins to gather around them. 'We should probably get going. I don't fancy stumbling around in the dark on the way back.'

'It's always the descent that kills you,' Nick replies, sounding disappointed that Pete has dropped the subject of children. He pulls a small fabric pouch from his pocket and proceeds to unfold a rain jacket.

'What?'

'That's what they say in mountaineering — you're at most risk of dying when you're tired. People stay too long at the top, celebrating the summit, thinking that's all there is to it, and forget they've got to get down the mountain again.'

'That's encouraging.' Pete heaves himself to his feet, doing his best not to groan like an old man. He's never told Nick this, but one of the reasons he's never allowed himself to picture a child in his life is because after what he did, he simply doesn't deserve it.

CHAPTER TWENTY-SEVEN

Vivi's legs ache, but she's more energised than she has been since they first learned of Will's diagnosis. Had it really only been a matter of months since the appointment with the specialist? The one where they learned that the stomachache Will had been complaining of was, in fact, late-stage pancreatic cancer. Further investigation revealed that it had spread to his liver, and after a first, unsuccessful round of chemo, the doctors had recommended palliative care. There was nothing to be gained from drug trials, no miracle cures, no time left for bucket-list adventures. 'Let me be at home,' he begged. 'Until the end. Can you do that for me?'

She couldn't refuse him that.

She steps out of the shower, towels herself dry, wraps her hair up and lies down on the bed for a moment, closing her eyes, consumed with thoughts about the threatening email and the goddamn flower delivery. She had told an astonished Delfina to dispose of them, claiming that she was allergic to lilies. She didn't want them anywhere near her.

Then there's the money. Getting her hands on fifty grand in a hurry is no small ask, even for someone in her position. Besides, it doesn't sit well with her to give in to blackmail, although the alternative is something she can hardly conceive of. No matter how she spins it, in a business that relies on perception as much as performance, she would be ruined, her reputation destroyed. The board would sack her, and she'd almost certainly be prosecuted. Everything she has worked for her whole life, gone, thanks to one leaked story. The haters would rub their hands with glee at such a fall from grace, not that she cares what they think. She doesn't doubt whoever this is has proof; the email gave that much away.

She's still lying there when Alice knocks softly on the door. 'Sorry, I didn't realise you were asleep,' Alice whispers, and Vivi opens her eyes. 'I'm worried about you.'

Vivi rolls over and pats the space next to her. 'I'm fine. Just can't help thinking of Will. He would have loved this.'

'You mean even the fifty shades of beige?' Alice asks, lying down beside her sister and rubbing the nubbly linen sheet between her fingers.

Vivi raises a fleeting smile. 'He was a man for whom the colour camel was invented,' she jokes, remembering the drawerful of light brown cashmere sweaters she had donated to charity after he died. 'Besides, don't knock it – all the cool kids are living beige lives these days. Boring routines involving plenty of self-care.'

'Whatever happened to going out all night and falling asleep with your make-up on?' Alice jokes.

'It's been an absolute boon to the beauty industry, I don't mind admitting.' Vivi sighs, her face growing serious again. 'We had so many plans ... We were going to take a "round-the-world gap year", as Will called it. South America, Japan, come and see you and the girls in Australia ... After the pandemic, we decided to bring the trip forward, but then ...' She pauses. 'More fool us to tempt fate like that. What's that saying? Tell God your plans and watch him laugh at you? Sorry, I don't mean to be a downer; it's your holiday as well.'

'You are not to even think of apologising,' Alice says firmly. 'You just lost your husband, I think you're allowed to be down about it. It's been, what, six weeks? That's no time at all.'

Vivi nods. 'It's only now and then, you know.' Her voice is thick as she struggles to get control of herself, tears threatening. 'Most of the time I can deal with it. It's not like it came as a huge surprise, you know? At least we had a little warning.'

'It's always a surprise, whether you're prepared for it or not.' Alice smooths back the hair from her sister's forehead, as if, for once, she is the older, wiser sibling.

'I keep looking for him, expecting him to appear in the doorway, or come around the corner, eyes gleaming with his latest plan, excited to tell me all about it, but he never does.' She sniffs. 'He's just not *there* anymore.'

'It's good that you remember him like that. I can't imagine how hard it was at the end. For you both.'

'It's absolute bollocks that drugs can manage the pain. He was hallucinating. Some days he hardly recognised me.'

'Jesus. Oh, you poor thing.' Alice wraps her arms around her sister, rocking her like a small child.

'It's not just that. There's something else, something even worse.'

'Worse than losing your husband?' Alice stops, looks stricken. 'Oh God, you're not sick too, are you? Please tell me you're not.'

'No, no, I'm perfectly healthy, touch wood.' Taking a deep breath, Vivi explains about the email, the threatening messages, the lilies. 'I tried calling the florist, although I could barely make myself understood well enough to find out who placed the order. As far as I could make out, it was done online and paid for by PayPal. And they – whoever they are – want fifty thousand pounds, in bitcoin, however you do that, or they'll go to the papers. I'll be ruined; I could lose my stake in the company. I'll end up in jail.'

Alice releases her, studying Vivi's face. 'What did you do?'

Vivi tells her, in as few words as possible, justifying nothing.

'Jesus Christ, do you have any idea who it could be? And they say they have proof?'

'They say they do. I have no idea how.'

'What are you going to do? You can't let them get away with this – you can't give in, you know that, don't you? Blackmailers always come back for more.'

'I know. But it's easier said than done. I've got until next week – the day after I get back – to get them the money. If I don't, it'll affect you, the girls … not just me and my business, my employees.'

'Don't even worry about that.'

'That's kind of you to say, but it will. You'll always be known as the sister of the woman who …' Her voice falters. 'I've seen accusations like this destroy entire families, not just the person involved.'

'We'll work it out, Vee. You're not on your own, okay?' Alice goes to the window, opens it, and stands there for so long that Vivi begins to wonder what she's doing. Finally, she turns to face Vivi. 'Right. Give me your laptop and show me that email. You said you haven't replied yet? We need to find out exactly what they think they've got on you. Demand that they show you proof before you do anything.'

'A lie is one thing; it'll soon fizzle out. But a scandal … a scandal will ruin me.'

'Stop talking like that. You're Vivienne Goddamn Savidge. These people, whoever they are, have no idea who they're fucking with.'

CHAPTER TWENTY-EIGHT

'I think we should start anyway.' Caroline drums her fingers on the table as Marco comes out from the kitchen for a third time to check on them.

Vivi, Alice, Mia, Isla and Caroline have been sitting outside for more than an hour, drinking prosecco and snacking on olives and crostini topped with white anchovies and red peppers. The women are showered and dressed in linen of various shades, thin-strapped sandals on their feet, skin lightly sun-kissed. Pete and Nick have yet to return from the hike.

'Do you think we should send out a search party?' Alice asks. She doesn't sound like she wants to volunteer for the job, and Vivi can't say she blames her. They're all tired, and although the aperitivo is delicious, she is ready for something more substantial.

Vivi glances at her watch. Gone nine o'clock. They should have been back at least an hour ago, depending, of course, on how long they lingered at the top. The sky has deepened from purple to nearly black, and the men will only have the torches on their phones to guide them. 'Do you think we should be worried?' she asks, torn between annoyance and concern.

'Wait, that might be them.' Isla points to the hillside behind the palazzo where a faint bobbing light can be seen amid the darkness.

Vivi gets to her feet and goes to the back of the terrace. She cups her hands to her mouth. 'Cooo-eee!' she shouts as loudly as she can. 'Pete! Nick!' After a moment, a call comes back. It's faint, but there's no doubt it's them.

She returns to the table and picks up her glass, downing the remainder. 'They're coming. I'd say we give them about twenty minutes, then let's eat,' she says to Marco, who has emerged at the sound of the shouting.

'*Sono d'accordo.*' He retreats to the kitchen with a scowl.

The missing hikers arrive just as bowls filled with a thick browny-yellow soupy mixture are ferried to the table accompanied by plates of tiny spears of radicchio, chicory and carrots. 'It looks incredible, thank you,' Vivi says to Delfina as she sets out bread and dishes of deep green olive oil.

'*Bagna cauda,*' says Marco, emerging from the kitchen. He's all smiles now.

'*Bagna* what?' asks Mia, wrinkling her nose.

'Shush,' Alice scolds her gently. 'I'll have yours if you don't like it. I could eat a horse.'

'They don't do that here, do they, Mum?' Isla asks, horrified. 'Eat *horses*?'

Alice doesn't get the chance to reassure her as Nick appears through an archway at the rear of the terrace. 'Evening, ladies. Sorry we're late, Vivi.' He grins. 'Totally lost track of time, and the descent always takes longer than you think.'

'We might have been slowed down by a couple of beers at the *rifugio*,' says Pete with a wink, reaching across the table to pop an olive into his mouth. 'I hope you're not all starving to death.'

'We're pretty close,' Mia says grumpily.

'As long as you're both okay, that's the main thing,' Vivi says, her irritation subsiding. 'I was starting to worry.' Now they're back safely, there are far more pressing concerns than simply having dinner an hour later than planned.

'We'll wash up and then be right down,' Pete reassures her. 'Two minutes at most. And don't wait for us, please.'

He keeps his promise and the men return to the table in record time.

'*Buon appetito*,' says Marco, reappearing to pour more wine and then leaving them to their first course.

Suddenly everyone is talking at once, passing bread and pouring wine. Nick fills Caroline in on the *rifugio* experience – 'such a shame you guys turned back' – and Mia whispers something to Alice while Isla begins to tell Pete about her second visit to the museum.

'I thought you went into the city to see a school friend?' Vivi asks, overhearing.

Isla reddens and hesitates before speaking. 'We did, but …'

Mia jumps in. 'Isla caught up with us later. Couldn't keep away from the museum, could you, Is?'

Isla nods, looking relieved, but Vivi is certain she caught her niece in a lie. Alice doesn't appear to have noticed, however, and for the sake of keeping the peace, Vivi says nothing more. Let them have their harmless secrets.

'Auntie Vivi …' Mia is clear-eyed and glowing from the sun, and once again Vivi is struck by the quality of her skin. It would make even Hailey Bieber jealous – plump, naturally dewy, luminous, the product of youth, good nutrition and an outdoor lifestyle, but mainly youth. She looks like she lives on sashimi and mangoes, which, come to think of it, she probably does. Vivi is sure neither she nor Alice ever looked that good when they were that age. Teenagers these days seem to take better care of themselves, eat better, have access to better skincare. Even pre-teens – eight-year-olds, Jesus! – are getting in on the act, clamouring for their older sisters' skincare, some of which is totally inappropriate. At least they're aware of sunscreen now. Small mercies.

If only she could bottle it, that radiant glow, she'd be worth squillions. She remembers the pot of Nivea that was the sum of her beauty regime as a girl.

Maybe it's time to launch a tween range. She already has a potential name for it: Clean Slate.

Mia's eyes slide sideways. 'I was wondering if we might invite Eleni over. She has plans tomorrow, but perhaps the day after, and maybe she can stay for dinner?'

'But that's Vivi's birthday, darling,' Alice interrupts.

Mia's face falls. 'I'm sorry, I lost track. Sorry, Auntie Vivi, that probably isn't a good time.'

Vivi thinks about it for a moment. 'Of course she can come. I'm happy for you to have a friend over, and I'm sure Marco can cope with one extra.' It'll hardly faze a former Michelin-starred chef.

'Oh, thank you, Auntie Vee. You're the best.' Mia grins, and Isla casts her a worried glance.

The morning after

Delfina presses her forefingers against the clammy skin of the person's neck. There should be the tick of a pulse, but there's nothing, no reassuring thrum, not even a weak one.

She leans over and tries to perform resuscitation, managing to keep their head out of the water, but no matter how much air she tries to force in, they will not begin breathing on their own.

Marco told her he had deliberately chosen to locate the pool at a distance from the palazzo, wanting it to be a secluded oasis among the trees, but now that seems like a mistake, not that he could have ever foreseen such a tragedy. She has shouted and shouted, but no one is coming, and she cannot do anything more; she simply does not have the strength to drag the body out of the water on her own, and anyway, there is nothing to be gained by doing so, no precious seconds that will be the difference between life and death. Those moments have long passed.

She must leave the body, find someone who will tell her what to do next.

She has no voice left, and as she pulls herself out of the water, her limbs feel oddly boneless. She bends down, leaning towards the body, but it is submerged again, inches below the surface, and her fingers can only grab at strands of gossamer hair. She stops, knowing it's futile, watching in a daze as the body begins to slowly drift to the bottom of the pool.

After a minute, she straightens, and though haste no longer matters, she hurries nonetheless.

She almost trips over the towels on the ground but doesn't look back.

CHAPTER TWENTY-NINE

Two days earlier

Despite drinking enough at dinner 'to sink a battleship', as her father would have said (try as she might, no amount of alcohol can quench her self-hatred right now), Caroline is determined to make it to yoga the next morning.

Gritty-eyed, and with her thigh and calf muscles screaming in protest after the hike, she pulls on leggings and an old T-shirt, dragging her hair into a messy ponytail. Even Vivi's gift of an enriched night crème (for mature skin, huh) and a jade roller can't do much for her puffy face.

She tries not to groan as Riccardo leads them through a gentle salutation facing the rising sun. It's a still, clear morning in a gorgeous location; she should be grateful for this day, but inner peace is frustratingly elusive.

It's just her and Nick. 'I feel like a third wheel,' she mutters grumpily as Riccardo and Nick swap increasingly searing glances. Riccardo seems unable to keep his hands off Nick, whether it be adjusting a pose or deepening a stretch.

Vivi and Alice said they'd be up in time, but Caroline wasn't the only one who got stuck into the wine, and then when Delfina brought out a bottle of grappa, they all had a glass or two. This isn't the sole reason her head feels so fuzzy, but it hasn't helped.

She does her best to concentrate on Riccardo's lilting intonation and his suggestion to be fully present in the moment.

As she struggles for focus, Vivi appears. 'So sorry I didn't make it, Riccardo. Forgot to set an alarm.'

Caro observes her more closely. Vivi doesn't look like she slept at all, and there are uncharacteristic shadows under her eyes and a brittle note to her voice that Caroline hasn't heard before. 'Anyone else desperate for coffee?' she asks, getting to her feet. Caffeine will do a better job than yoga when it comes to clearing her head, and she can't stand to watch Nick and Riccardo make goo-goo eyes at each other for a moment longer.

* * *

It's not until the others have nearly finished breakfast that Mia and Isla emerge, yawning, hair unbrushed and rubbing sleep from their eyes. The twins mumble their hellos before piling their plates with honeydew melon, tiny wild strawberries and paper-thin slices of prosciutto. 'Can we eat like this at home, Mum?' Mia asks, licking her fingers, but Alice doesn't appear to be listening.

'Sorry, what?' she asks eventually.

'Don't worry.' Mia rolls her eyes at her sister.

'Nick and I thought we might explore the valley today,' Pete says, running a possessive hand along his husband's spine. 'There's room for three more if anyone wants to join us. Marco says there are a couple of cafes as well as a local wine co-op. Delfina can arrange for them to open just for us, so we thought we might do some wine tasting this afternoon. There's also a church with frescos, apparently, as well as a small gallery …'

'I think we're going to chill by the pool today,' Mia replies, yawning again.

'Had enough of a culture fix this trip?' Pete asks.

'That's right.' Mia shoots him a defiant look, daring him to say otherwise.

'I really should spend a few hours studying,' Isla adds. 'I've got an assignment due.'

'How about you, Jade?' Pete asks.

'Uh, I'll be fine here, if that's okay?' She looks to Vivi for confirmation. 'Unless you need me to come?' She reaches into her bag and pulls out a folder, searches briefly through it and then hands Pete a stapled sheaf of paper. 'I did some research on the church. It's all here if you're interested.' She goes to her bag again, pulling out a tube of Vivid zinc sun cream. 'And you might want this.'

'Wow, thanks, Jade. You're certainly thorough.' Pete raises his eyebrows. 'Alice? Vivi?'

'Why not?' Vivi turns to her sister. 'You up for it, Alice?'

'Sure.'

It's as though they've all forgotten Caroline is even there.

CHAPTER THIRTY

Alice throws a bottle of water and some sunscreen into a straw tote, grabs a hat and sunglasses, and is ready to go at 3.30 on the dot. She stops by the pool to remind the girls to wear sunscreen. She'd prefer it if their cossies covered a little more flesh, but is there ever a better time to wear a skimpy bikini than when you're in the best shape of your life? Jade is there too, sitting in the shade a little way apart from the twins, apparently absorbed in a book. Alice sneaks a look at the title, smirking when she sees that it's something called *The 48 Laws of Power*. Christ, does that girl take her career seriously.

'Forty-eight?' That's borderline psychotic. Who can remember that many anyway? 'What's the first law of power, Jade?' she asks, coming closer for a better look.

'Sorry?'

'Just give me one. Law of power.'

Jade lowers her sunglasses and flicks to the front of the book. 'Never outshine the master.'

She says it without an ounce of irony, but Alice laughs out loud. 'No kidding. Tell me some of the others, I need cheering up.'

'Conceal your intentions. Always say less than necessary. Create an air of mystery,' Jade says hesitantly. 'Would you like me to go on?'

'Oh do, please.'

'Pose as a friend, work as a spy. Crush your enemy totally.'

Caroline, who has just arrived at the pool, bursts into peals of derisive laughter. 'Are you serious? That's idiotic. Honestly, honey, do yourself a favour and forget that kind of pseudo-tech-bro bullshit.'

'It's a *New York Times* bestseller.' Jade has gone scarlet. She flicks the book up to shield her face.

'Well, enjoy,' Alice says. 'And take no notice of what other people say – I'll tell you that for free.' She looks more carefully at Jade. 'Isn't that Isla's sunhat?'

'It's cool, Mum. I said she could borrow it,' Isla replies.

'Okay.' She turns to face her daughters. 'See you later, girls. We'll be back in time for dinner.'

'No worries. Have a nice afternoon.' Isla raises an idle hand in farewell. Mia appears to be asleep.

It's nearly four by the time everyone else arrives. Alice squeezes herself in the back of the convertible next to Caroline, with Vivi on the other side of her. Pete connects his phone and puts on some music. 'This'll wake you all up,' he says, grinning as the hypnotic beat of Beyoncé's 'Crazy in Love' echoes through the car.

Funny how a song can take you right back to where you were when you first heard it, how it brings an echo of that feeling, even decades later. Alice was a teenager when this was a hit, and hearing it now brings back a rush of complicated emotion.

'Just like old times,' Caro says as they pass through the gates and descend into the valley. She sounds fine, but her knuckles are white, hands pressed against her thighs. Is she a nervous passenger, or is something else bothering her?

'What?' Alice shouts over the sound of the music, the engine and the wind whipping past them. Pete and Nick can't hear them at all.

'Remember that weekend when you came to visit us?' Caroline says, seemingly out of nowhere. 'You were, what, sixteen, seventeen?'

So Caro remembers it too. Alice had been so excited to visit her sister at university. She'd imagined that she would have Vivi to herself, that they could do grown-up things, maybe even go to the pub or out for dinner. But Caroline had muscled in, insisting on joining them on an open-top sightseeing tour of the city and then afterwards at a quaint little tea shop. Caroline completely ignored her, chatting away about people Alice had never met, while Alice sat next to her sister feeling invisible. She remembers making her way methodically through several stodgy scones that tasted of ash; she's never liked them since. Alice was too intimidated to object to Caroline's constant presence, and Vivi seemed oblivious to her sister's unhappiness.

'You're right, I believe I was.' Alice bares her teeth at Caroline. 'That was the same weekend that girl was found, wasn't it?' She wrinkles her forehead, trying to remember. 'Didn't you both know her?'

'Eliza Benson. She was in the year below us.' The smile has been wiped from Caroline's face.

'Did they ever find out what happened?' Alice asks.

'Overdose. Choked on her own vomit.'

'Oh God.' Alice feels slightly nauseous herself right now as they career around a bend and grapevines flash by in a blur of green. She swallows, then turns back from the window in time to see her sister and Caroline exchange a look. 'What? What aren't you telling me?'

Vivi speaks first. 'It was all a terrible misunderstanding.'

'In what way?' Alice asks.

Caroline bites her lip and looks out of the other window, her hands clasped in her lap.

'Come on, Caro. It's ancient history, surely,' Vivi says, a rare note of uncertainty in her voice.

'So why did you have to bring it up, then?' Caro glares at Vivi.

'You brought up that weekend, actually,' Alice says.

You could cut the tension between them with a wire.

Caroline sighs. 'I got a suspended sentence for possession thanks to a bloody good lawyer and the fact that I only had a few grams on me. They couldn't prove I was supplying, or that any money had been involved, which would have been an almost certain custodial sentence. And I got slammed with a fine, which Vivi and Will helped me pay, and for which I am eternally grateful.'

Vivi stares straight ahead, not a flicker of a reaction. It's almost as if she wishes she were anywhere else.

Alice feels the hairs on the back of her neck rise. Caro had the death of a fellow student on her conscience? Why had Vivi never mentioned this?

'But guess what, Alice? I never told them about Vivi, that she was the one who gave me the drugs in the first place, who suggested we share them with Eliza. Did I, Vee?' Caroline swallows. 'Never told a soul.'

Vivi? Her perfect sister, who never put a foot wrong, involved in drugs *and* stood by letting someone else take the blame? Alice can hardly absorb the information. She turns to her sister. 'Is this true?'

It's as though Vivi hasn't even heard her. She is staring out at the view, but Alice is pretty sure she's not taking it in.

'Yes, of course it's true,' Caro says when Vivi fails to answer.

'Is that why you never graduated?' Alice asks. For the first time, she pities Caroline. Funny how your whole future can dissolve before your eyes. One bad decision, one slip-up and things can never get back on track. No wonder Vivi's always been so defensive of Caro; she must be riddled with guilt that her friend took the blame. That she didn't speak up.

'No, of course not. I couldn't manage to juggle work and study.' Caroline sets her jaw. 'Some of us didn't have rich parents.'

With searing clarity, Alice realises that everything she once thought about her sister is wrong. She's always looked up to her, believed that everything she touched turned to gold, but now … Now she doesn't know what to think.

It occurs to her that she's judged Caro unfairly, has spent too long resenting a woman who has been nothing but loyal, some would say undeservedly so. Caroline's life has turned out so differently from Vivi's, and she has watched her friend's success without saying a word to threaten it. No wonder she left the country.

Although Alice doesn't often consider herself on the side of the have-nots, she has often felt perilously close to the boundary, especially since her divorce. She has two beautiful, smart daughters who are growing into fine young women, a roof over her head, a satisfying, creative career that mostly pays the bills, her health … Caroline has no one – no partner, no parents, no siblings, no job, few friends. She does her best to hide it, but quiet desperation comes off Caroline like a sea fog rolling into shore. At least now Alice can understand why.

'*Mi dispiace.*' It's one of the few Italian phrases Alice knows, and that's only because Isla repeated it so often when she was practising. Alice is sorry about a lot of things, but right at this moment she's sorry that she's been so dismissive of Caroline, even if she is still sometimes irritating beyond belief.

Caroline simply shrugs. 'Yeah, well, it was a long time ago.'

Vivi has still not said anything.

'We're nearly there,' Pete shouts before Alice has a chance to quiz the two women further.

He and Nick haven't heard a word of their conversation.

They drive through the centre of the village, which is almost completely deserted save for two old men leaning on their walking canes who look up as they pass. Moments later, Pete pulls into a parking spot in front of an ancient stone church at the top of the village. 'Delfina said the winemakers' collective is a little way down the road, but we're not due there until five, so I thought we could check out the church first. If that suits you, ladies?'

Caroline's phone beeps with a message and she pauses to check it while the others clamber out of the car.

It's blissfully cool inside the church and the sun streams though an enormous stained-glass window at the southern end. They're the only people there.

Nick wanders off to the back of the nave, followed shortly afterwards by Caroline.

Numerous paintings of Madonna and Child adorn the walls, but Alice takes her time viewing the statues of Mary, for there are several, including one of her at the foot of Christ on the cross. 'They go in for the full bloody depiction, don't they?' Pete says, coming to stand next to her.

'Sure do.'

They both turn at a noise that comes from a set of pews to their left. It sounds to Alice like a heavy sack thrown to the ground.

'Oh Christ!' Alice is oblivious to the irony in her words. 'It's Vivi.' She races to her sister with Pete close behind.

Vivi is sprawled on the floor, legs akimbo, mouth slack, eyes blank.

Alice drops to her knees and takes her sister's face in her hands, patting her cheeks, trying to rouse her. 'Vivi! Wake up!' When Vivi doesn't respond, Alice checks her breathing, hearing it faint and shallow.

'Vivi!' Alice says again, but still her sister does not respond.

They move her onto her side, into the recovery position. Nick joins them, checking her pulse. 'It's rapid, that's good. It'll be okay, she probably just fainted.'

'It is *not* okay.' Alice feels a bit wobbly herself and sinks onto a nearby pew.

Caroline's phone rings again.

'Jeez, can you turn that thing off?' Alice asks, her concern for Vivi turning to annoyance.

'Sorry, sorry. I've got to answer this.' Caroline disappears outside.

What the fuck is so important that she has to take a call when her friend has just fainted, possibly cracked her skull?

Nick is loosening the buttons of Vivi's blouse when she stirs, blinks, and the light returns to her eyes. 'Wh …?'

'You had a turn, but you're fine,' Alice reassures her, drawing closer again.

'A turn? I'm not ninety, for chrissake.' Vivi tries to sit up, but Nick restrains her.

'Take it easy, hey? You fainted – is that better? You might have hit your head. Is it sore anywhere?'

'Low blood sugar. Woozy,' Vivi mumbles, sitting up.

Alice reaches into her handbag and pulls out a tin. 'Have one of these,' she offers.

Vivi takes it, examining the raspberry candy before popping it in her mouth.

'You gave us quite a shock there.' Nick wets a handkerchief with water from his bottle and applies it to her forehead where a lump has already begun to swell. 'Give yourself a minute to recover,' he counsels.

'I'm not dead yet. Help me up, I'm fine now.' She struggles to her feet, with Nick on one side and Alice on the other, Pete ready on standby should she fall again. 'Please don't fuss.'

'Stress,' Nick mouths to Pete, who nods in acknowledgement.

'She's been working far too hard. Hasn't let up, despite everything,' says Alice. 'Perhaps you should take a seat,' she suggests.

Vivi nods, and they help her to a nearby pew. After a minute or two she stands up again. 'I'm fine now, really. Much better. We should still go on to the wine co-operative.'

'Are you sure?' Alice asks.

'Of course,' Vivi insists.

When they emerge from the church a little while later, blinking at the sudden brightness of the afternoon sunshine, Caroline is sitting on a bench outside.

'You look almost as bad as Vivi,' Alice says, only partially joking.

'Are you okay?' Vivi asks, sitting next to her.

Alice, realising that it might be best to leave them alone for a while, waits at a slight distance, pretending to be absorbed in the gravestones.

Pete and Nick decide to walk around the outside of the church. 'We'll only be a minute and then we'll head over to the co-op,' Pete promises before they round the corner.

'I can never apologise enough, can I, Caro?' Vivi asks, looking her friend in the eye. 'I live with the regret of my actions every day, you must know that. But we were *children*, barely out of our teens. We knew nothing. Haven't you made terrible mistakes in your life, done things you wish you could take back?'

Caroline makes a noncommittal sound in the back of her throat. 'That doesn't get you off the hook.'

'If I could change things I would, but it's far too late now,' Vivi says.

'I let you walk all over me. Why was that?'

Vivi reaches for Caroline's hand, but she flicks it away. 'Can you forgive me, after all this time? What will it take? Just tell me, Caro, please.'

Alice doesn't hear Caroline's mumbled reply.

CHAPTER THIRTY-ONE

'Everything okay?' Nick asks as they go upstairs to change for dinner. He's a step behind Pete, kneading his shoulders, and it feels good. 'You were pretty quiet on the ride home.'

'Yeah, just tired, I guess. Day drinking always makes me sleepy.' The best thing you could say about the wines they'd tried was that they were rustic, but although there was a spittoon provided, they hadn't bothered to use it. They'd bought a few bottles out of politeness to the winemaker, who insisted they try almost everything he had. Pete couldn't help wondering if the man's enthusiasm was because he thought they were rich foreigners, then berated himself for his cynicism. Everyone has to make a buck the best way they can, something he knows all too well.

'Shame we don't have time for a nap, huh?' Nick says, checking his watch as they enter their room. 'You want the shower first?'

'Nah, you go.' Pete kicks off his shoes and flops down on the bed with a sigh. Sometimes he gets too much in his own head. Nick has always gently teased Pete about this, saying he overthinks things to the point of paralysis.

What feels like mere seconds later, he opens his eyes to the sight of Nick drying himself with a towel, another wrapped around his waist. Pete takes a moment to appreciate his good fortune.

'It's all yours.'

Pete flicks his eyes up and down Nick's body. 'It is?'

Nick flicks a towel at Pete, grinning. 'Get your butt in the shower or we'll be late for dinner.'

'Sure, gimme a minute.'

'Hey, Pete?' Nick sits down on the edge of the bed.

'Yeah?'

'Something you said yesterday.' He looks serious. 'About not believing you'd be a good father. Why do you think that?' He runs a hand through his hair, sending it into little damp spikes.

Pete takes a deep breath. Now is not the time. He leans forward and kisses his husband, silencing him. 'Oh, you know,' he says, when they come up for air, 'there are so many other families out there, families with a mother and a father … I'm not sure I deserve to be one.'

Nick kisses him again. 'You're going to have to try harder than that, you know. I get that you might not *want* to be a father, but telling me you don't deserve it? That hetero couples are the only way to be a family? I'm literally *astonished* that you would think that. Anyway, give yourself a little more credit. You'd make an incredible parent.'

'Let's hold that thought for the time being,' Pete says, reluctantly getting up from the bed and shucking off his T-shirt. 'I gotta go clean up.'

When Pete emerges from the shower, there's no sign of Nick. Pete figures he must have already gone downstairs for an aperitivo.

Nick has left his phone on the bedside table, and it vibrates with a notification.

Pete can't stop himself from checking the screen.

It's a message from Riccardo suggesting a 'private'. Jesus. The guy is already in Nick's contacts. He's signed off with a yellow heart and an Italian flag emoji. What the hell does that mean?

***

'Another spectacular evening,' Alice says as Pete joins them downstairs, still shaken by the text he saw. Delfina hands him a flute of prosecco and he makes his way towards the others, who have gathered in a loose group near the edge of the terrace. The wine they had at the co-op wasn't a patch on the stuff that Marco pours.

'Sorry I'm late,' Pete says, kissing Vivi on the cheek. 'Are you feeling better? You look fabulous, by the way.' Vivi has on a white jumpsuit, and the sun (or perhaps judicious use of bronzer) has given her skin a healthy glow. He ignores Nick.

'Thank you, yes. Completely recovered.' She fingers a sore spot at her temple. 'Though this might look none too pretty by morning.'

'Glad to hear it. We can't have you under the weather for your birthday, that would be simply too cruel.'

Marco appears from the kitchen with a sharpening steel in one hand and a huge knife in the other.

'Steady on, there,' says Alice lightly. 'Anyone would think you were about to disembowel something.'

'I came to see how you would like the beef cooked,' Marco says, acknowledging her joke with a sideways glance. 'I will roast it over coals and it is served rare, but I thought I would check.'

'I'm sure you know best.' Pete comes over to get a better look at the knife.

'That okay with everyone else?' Vivi asks.

'The bloodier the better, huh?' Nick puts an arm around Pete's shoulders and it's all he can do not to shake it off. 'This man has always liked it raw.' Pete musters a smile and wordlessly hands Nick his phone.

'I was wondering where I put that.' He slips it into his pocket without bothering to check it.

'How about you, girls?'

'Sure,' Mia says, smiling sweetly at her aunt.

'Jade?'

'Oh, don't worry about me, I'm perfectly fine to have a plate of vegetables.'

'There will be a risotto as well,' Marco says. 'Vegetarian.'

'Thanks, Marco. That sounds wonderful. I'm sure it will be delicious, like everything else you've made for us.' Vivi beams at him.

Marco returns to the kitchen, his knife held loosely in his palm.

'Jesus, he's so hot he's smoking,' Alice says to Nick.

'I hadn't noticed,' he replies, but the corners of his mouth twitch.

Pete's heart twists painfully. This is what he gets for marrying someone much younger and better-looking than him.

The group drifts over to a pair of outdoor sofas underneath a large pergola covered with vines. Vivi takes a seat between her two nieces and proceeds to gently question them about their skincare routine and make-up preferences.

Jade lingers nearby, her head angled towards the trio, apparently also hanging on Mia's every word. Pete wouldn't be surprised if she whipped out a tape recorder – all the better to preserve the conversation for her boss. 'She never switches off, does she?' Pete says to Alice. He's always envied Vivi's genius for marketing. In the company's first year, she had the brilliant idea to give away a full set of the Vivid Natural Beauty line to some of the country's best make-up artists. Demand subsequently skyrocketed. Two years later, she launched a haircare line, Velvet by Vivid, helped in no small part by the fact that her own hair is enviably lustrous.

Right from the outset, Vivi insisted they base the company's marketing on an 'if you know, you know' premise, creating a community of customers who felt like they were in on a secret. It was a stroke of genius, one that has since been copied by others in the segment, some even more successfully than Vivi herself. Pete wonders what she might be dreaming up now – despite recent events, he has no doubt she's got any number of ideas brewing. He listens to her conversation with Mia with one ear while still talking to Alice.

'She was like this even when we were little – hyperfocused on what was important to her. It's like she doesn't see anything else.'

'Useful trait for an entrepreneur, though.'

'I wish I had some of it – but maybe that's the difference when you've got kids. Balancing making art and running around after the girls, as a single parent most of the time, is exhausting, not to mention shit for my concentration.'

'Sounds like you really needed this vacation,' says Nick. 'What do you do to balance your stress levels on a day-to-day basis? How much exercise do you get, what's your diet like, alcohol consumption, how many hours' sleep on average, that kind of thing?'

'Don't mind him, he's passionate about raising people's energy levels,' says Pete, an edge to his voice. 'He'll give you the third degree if you let him.'

'No one likes you,' says Nick, putting down his glass and whipping his head away in mock irritation.

Alice seems more than willing to get into it with him, happily ticking off her bad habits on her fingers.

Overhearing her, Mia snorts, collapsing against the arm of one of the sofas. 'Mum exercise? Get real.'

'Honestly, I know you're right,' Alice says to Nick. 'I definitely should get more exercise.'

'*Any* exercise,' says Mia.

'I didn't notice your presence on our hike the other day, darling daughter,' says Alice, an edge to her words.

'Talking of exercise,' Vivi joins them, 'I've been toying with the idea of hiring a personal trainer. Not just for me but for all the staff. God knows those kinds of perks are almost a given these days.' She casts a sly look at Pete. 'Staff retention is always a challenge, and I think a company-wide wellness program might really make a difference.'

Pete gives her an almost imperceptible shake of his head. He hasn't spoken to Nick about the offer yet.

'It could definitely help to reduce absences,' says Nick, oblivious to the swirling undercurrents.

'Don't think I hadn't thought of that.' She looks across to her assistant. 'What do you think, Jade? Would the staff appreciate it?'

'Appreciate what?'

She sounds apprehensive, Pete thinks. She must be nervous around her boss, even in this off-duty situation. It is a little odd, her being here, but then Vivi never did have clear boundaries between work and her personal life, and the girl clearly worships her. It might not be a bad idea for him to spend a little time with Jade, Pete thinks, though she's loyal as a labrador, and he doubts even getting her drunk will yield much.

'I was just saying how important staff retention is. How much I value *all* my staff.' She crinkles her eyes at Jade. 'Especially those who have shown their devotion to the company. That perhaps an in-house PT might be appreciated.'

Jade's gaze shifts from Vivi to Alice to Pete, as if she's deciding how best to reply. 'Um, yes, I guess. Though I wonder if people would feel uncomfortable getting sweaty alongside their colleagues.'

'Good point,' Vivi replies, and Jade looks relieved to have said the right thing.

'Some people might be really self-conscious,' Isla adds, twisting a strand of hair through her fingers. 'And they might worry that they're not as fit as everyone else. It'd be like school sport all over again.'

'Maybe we could offer one-on-one sessions,' Vivi muses. 'Though I'm not sure how efficient that would be.'

'And wouldn't some people feel obligated to participate?' Mia asks.

'I suppose it's all in the way it's framed. Anyway, it's a discussion for another day.' Vivi leans against the cushions, closing her eyes. She looks more exhausted than she's letting on – Pete is used to her being full of pep.

'Yes, remember that you're on holiday,' Pete says, raising his glass to the landscape. 'In this glorious place.'

Vivi gives him a wry smile. 'Old habits die hard.'

The morning after

As Delfina emerges from the shade, the sun is warm on her shoulders, though she barely notices. She can't stop shivering.

She goes first to the renovated outbuildings, for they are closer, sprinting along the corridor, banging on each door in turn, yelling for someone to come, someone to help. When she's tried every room and received no reply, she turns back and runs barefoot along the path to the palazzo. She doesn't feel the sharp stones cutting into her feet.

It is Stella who appears first as Delfina is halfway along the path, an apparition in black. For a split-second, Delfina thinks Stella is death, come for the newly deceased's spirit. Her mind spirals, flying off at hysterical tangents, and she's terrified she might be losing her grip on reality.

She reaches Stella, babbling nonsense. Her words are a torrent as she tries to explain what she's seen, what she's tried to do, that it has nothing to do with her.

Stella is calm, her voice rasping. 'Slow down, *ragazza*. Tell me again from the beginning what has happened.'

Delfina starts again and, in as few words as possible, recounts what she has just discovered.

Stella listens carefully. When Delfina has finished, she speaks. 'Go. Go back. Find Marco.' She pushes Delfina towards the palazzo. 'He will know what to do.'

CHAPTER THIRTY-TWO

One day earlier

It's early, and the mountains frame the palazzo like the painted backdrop of a film set, seemingly not quite real, but the pool, glassy and inviting, beckons, and Caroline sits on the edge, her legs in the water, idly swishing them back and forth. The movement against her skin is soothing and the sounds coming from the kitchen are far off and muted. It's a tiny sliver of peace amid several days that have been light on solitude.

She's not alone for long. Stella appears, a stooped figure in black wielding an incongruously large leaf skimmer. Caroline gets to her feet, concerned that if the old woman loses her balance – and it seems like she might – she could easily tumble into the water. 'Can I get that for you?' she asks in Italian, reaching for the pole. 'Honestly, I don't mind.'

Stella pays no attention, and for a moment they grapple over the skimmer until, feeling faintly ridiculous, Caroline lets it go. The old woman is stronger than she looks. 'Okay then. I guess you've got this.'

Stella says nothing, her eyes a silent reproach, then shuffles down the length of the pool, dragging the pole behind her.

Caroline tugs at a thought like a loose thread and has the first hint that there may be a story here waiting to be told. She has seen the photo in the hallway, and now, reminded of it, resolves to ask Marco what else he knows about his grandmother's early life. She will wait before asking Stella outright — it could be a sensitive subject. Besides, Stella is clearly not in the mood for conversation this morning. Caroline doesn't know why she hasn't thought of something like it before: she can't conjure any stories of her own, but she might be able to help other people tell theirs.

When she gets to the outdoor table on the terrace, Vivi is there.

Just in time, Caroline remembers it's her birthday and leans in to give her a kiss on both cheeks. 'I've got a gift too, but I left it upstairs.' It had seemed like a good idea when she saw the ad as she was scrolling her social media feed, a mix of humour and practicality. A token, really. Now, however, she's not so sure it will hit the right note.

'Oh, darling, that's so sweet of you,' Vivi says. 'But you shouldn't have. I honestly don't understand what the fuss is about turning forty — I don't feel any different than I did yesterday. Somehow I thought it might be more momentous.' She smiles, a beat too late. 'And there's no rush. I'm looking forward to a relaxing day. I've turned my phone off and left it upstairs — the only people I want to hear from are all here anyway.' She tips her head back to the cloudless sky. 'It looks like it'll be a perfect day.'

'You don't look a minute over thirty. No, I mean it,' Caroline insists as Vivi dismisses the compliment.

Delfina appears and places a teapot and a jug of milk next to them. She shyly wishes Vivi a happy birthday, asking what she would like for breakfast.

'I'll sit on this for the time being,' Vivi replies, indicating the pot. 'I'm in no rush.'

Delfina nods and returns to the kitchen.

Soon, everyone drifts down for breakfast. They're all in a celebratory mood, extravagantly toasting the birthday girl —

'*Alla vita!* To life!' – and bearing gifts. Caroline is relieved that they're all focused on Vivi and not the fact that she's failed to bring a present.

Alice gives her a beautifully wrapped miniature painting of the twins. 'Happiest of happys, darling Queen Vee!' she cries, hugging her. Vivi is thrilled by it.

Isla has crocheted her a blanket in the Vivid brand colours, burnt orange and cream. 'It's a bit lame,' she says, embarrassed. 'Honestly, it's nothing.'

'It's not nothing, sweetheart,' says Vivi. 'It's incredibly special. And it's going straight on my favourite armchair when I get home. I love that you made something so beautiful for me.' She leans across and drops a kiss on the top of Isla's head.

Mia has handmade a pop-up card, the white paper intricately carved in the shape of a snowflake. 'Because snowflakes are unique, just like you, Auntie Vee.'

'Aww, sweetheart.' Vivi blinks rapidly and looks for a moment like she might cry. 'It's exquisite. You both have your mother's artistic talent.' The girls have also given her an embossed sign that says 'I'm not bossy: I am the boss', which causes Vivi to explode into delighted laughter, wiping her eyes now. And finally, Mia brings out a child's friendship bracelet with the word 'HUSTLE' spelled out in plastic letters and fastens it around her aunt's wrist. 'Top marks, girls.' Vivi grins.

Pete, looking immaculately smart-resort casual in a navy polo shirt and crisp bone-coloured shorts, holds out a small, square turquoise box tied with a white ribbon.

He and Nick have bought her a delicate silver Tiffany bangle. 'Elsa Peretti. My favourite. You remembered!' she cries, unwrapping it. 'Thank you, boys. You shouldn't have.' She kisses them both then slides it along her other forearm, where it flashes in the sunlight. Caroline thinks of her gift: why does she always get it so wrong? She recently splurged on a special, cloth-bound, thirtieth anniversary edition of

The Secret History, an indulgent treat for herself that she's yet to crack the spine of. Vivi might appreciate it far more than Caro's original choice of a comedy mug, but she should at least find something to wrap it in first.

Jade appears to be on edge, picking at a fruit salad and saying little, but perhaps Caroline is reading too much into her quiet demeanour, projecting her own discomfort, or maybe she feels out of place in this moment that's meant for close friends and family.

Caroline pours herself another cup of tea and picks up her phone as Delfina begins to clear their empty plates. Thank Christ there are no more messages from Gabriele. She checks a few news websites and then turns to *The Times* online. Reading the English newspapers is a habit she's never shaken, despite the years living in Italy.

She thumbs past the general news – there's never anything particularly uplifting there – and scrolls down to the lifestyle section. She pauses at the financial news as the name Vivid Formulations jumps out at her.

She presses a finger to her lips. This might make things easier for her, but still, there's no sense in letting Vivi know she's seen it, not until the time is right.

thetimes.co.uk
28 July 2023
Annelise Jones, business reporter

Takeover Rumours at Vivid Formulations

Milan-based chemical conglomerate J&K today gave its strongest indication yet that it has prestige beauty industry darling Vivid Formulations in its sights. J&K has been on a UK acquisition spree in recent months with the purchase of the WeLove and Elleo brands, but sources close to the company say it is expected that Vivid Formulations will be the jewel in its crown should the purchase go ahead. Brazilian giant Copera Cosmetics is also said to be interested in acquiring a majority stake in Vivid, where the company would join its suite of international brands, including Reckon+Ganza and The Workshop.

Recently bereaved creative director of Vivid Vivienne Savidge is on leave and was unavailable for comment at the time of going to press. Sources within the company insist that she is not ready to walk away from the company she founded seventeen years ago.

CHAPTER THIRTY-THREE

'Marco, I swear your food has brought me back to life.' Alice has come to the kitchen primarily in search of Stella but also secretly hoping she might steal a few moments with Marco.

'*Grazie mille*,' he says, glancing up from the pasta dough on the kitchen bench. 'That makes me very happy.' He dusts off his hands and moves towards her.

'Your grandmother,' she says, locking her eyes on his and not looking away.

'Oh no.' He claps a floury hand to his forehead, stricken. 'She has been causing trouble again?'

'No, no, not at all,' she reassures him. 'I would simply like to sketch her. Now, if she has time?'

Relief clears his expression. 'I think she went to the olive grove. You know where that is?'

Alice nods but is in no rush to leave. 'What are you making?' she asks, seeing that he is rolling squares filled with a light-coloured paste into triangles and then small circles.

'*Tortellini*. They are said to resemble Venus's bellybutton,' he says, holding one up on the tip of his little finger.

'Nice.' Why is it that everything he says seems like innuendo? Is it him or is it her? She gathers her thoughts lest they stray somewhere dangerous. 'Is everything okay for dinner tonight? For Vivi's birthday celebration?'

'Of course. It is all under control. It will be wonderful, I promise. You have a good family, no? Time together is important.'

'Especially after the last few years,' Alice agrees.

'I think the palazzo is a good place for that.'

'Definitely.' She moves towards him and they're close now, inches apart, so close, in fact, that she can see the flecks of gold in his irises, the tiny lines that fan out from his eyes. He looks like a man who knows how to laugh, even when life throws its worst at you, and she can respect that.

'Here, try this.' He has put the pasta down and is offering her a morsel of something white from a nearby plate.

'You sure?' she looks at it dubiously, unable to identify it.

'Of course. It is *torrone*. Sweet.'

'Okay.' She takes it from him and pops it in her mouth. He is right, it is chewy, nutty and delicious.

'You like it?' He speaks quietly.

'Uh-huh.' She swallows as he leans towards her.

As if sleepwalking, she meets him halfway, not stopping to think of the consequences. Up close, he smells of coffee and cinnamon.

Her pulse thrums in her ears.

There's a terrifying moment when she thinks she's made a huge mistake, that she's misread the signals, but then his lips are soft on hers and she sinks into the sensation, blissfully oblivious to anything else. It's even more delicious than the *torrone*.

Eventually, she pulls away. 'Oh God, sorry, I shouldn't have ... Too much wine ... too much sun.' She can't look at him now, suddenly ridiculously self-conscious, as shy as a schoolgirl.

'Don't be. Sorry, I mean.' He takes a step towards her again, but she turns and flees the kitchen, leaving apologies in her wake.

* * *

It takes Alice a while to get over her embarrassment. She reminds herself sternly that she is a grown woman, all while cursing herself for running away like an embarrassed teenager.

She slips on a sundress, grabs her sketchpad and a pencil and goes in search of Stella, eventually finding her just where Marco said she would be, among the olive trees beyond the swimming pool.

Through clumsy gestures, she manages to convey to Stella that she'd like to draw her, holding up the pad and her pencil until Stella gives a brief nod. She makes a quick sketch of the old woman standing among the trees. Then she does a portrait study, just an outline, but as she examines it, she thinks it could be the start of something worthwhile. Stella has a fascinating face; there's a depth to her hollowed eyes that Alice doesn't often find in her younger subjects.

Stella stands completely still during the process, which takes around fifteen minutes. By then, Alice is dripping with sweat and has to stop as her hands are damp on the paper. 'Thank you, thank you,' she says, showing Stella the drawings.

Stella mutters something in gruff Italian and flashes Alice a smile that is more gum than teeth.

Alice returns to her room, drops off her sketchpad and shimmies into her swimsuit. When she gets to the pool, Vivi, Mia and Isla are there, sprawled side-by-side on loungers. Alice wastes no time slipping into the water, sighing at the relief of immersing herself in its cool depths.

She surfaces, admiring the contrast of her suit against the watery squiggles and aqua tiles and wondering idly if she should use those colours in her next painting. She's doing her best not to think about what happened with Marco, but the memory has been playing on repeat, interrupting her thoughts delightfully, even while she was drawing Stella.

A phone beeps with a message from somewhere in the girls' direction. Honestly, she thought they might take a break from all that, being so far from home, but of course social media isn't constrained by geography or time zones, not when there's wi-fi, albeit patchy.

'Yo, mamma!' Mia lowers her sunglasses.

When did her daughter start speaking like that? 'What is it, darling?' she asks, squeezing water from her hair and twisting it into a knot.

'Is it okay if Eleni comes over this afternoon? We might go and explore the valley.'

'I suppose so.' She can't face an extended argument with Mia, not while they're on holiday, and especially not today when they're supposed to be celebrating.

'Cool, thanks.' Mia gives her a sunshiny smile and picks up her phone, her thumbs flying over the screen as she types a reply.

'Do I have to go too?' Isla asks, not looking up from her book. 'I'd like to finish this.'

'Have you done your schoolwork, Mia?' Alice asks.

'Course,' Mia replies, not taking her eyes off her phone, which has beeped again with a reply.

'I'm not going to force you to go with them, Isla darling,' Alice says, then breaststrokes to the other end of the pool, enjoying the feel of her muscles stretching and loosening. *Be like water*, she reminds herself, *flow around obstacles*.

Pete and Nick return from a walk an hour or so later, scarlet-faced and grumbling about sore feet and the heat, shucking off their hiking boots and socks and cooling their feet in the shallow end of the pool. Unless Alice is mistaken, there's a tension between them that she hasn't noticed before.

'How was the massage, birthday girl?' Pete asks.

Vivi opens one eye. 'So good. I think everyone should have one on their birthday. I feel like a new woman. Though the therapist was a little strange.'

'How so?'

'She told me that my energy was "*agitata*". And then afterwards she said that the colour yellow surrounds me, that it will bring trouble.' She laughs it off. 'Not that I'm one for magical thinking, but, honestly, she could have found something more positive to say to me.'

'How bizarre.'

'Yes, it was rather.'

'Speaking of which …' Alice teases as Caroline appears along the path. Her earlier sympathy for the woman was short-lived. She doesn't relinquish a grudge easily.

Vivi shoots her a stern look, shutting Alice up.

Caroline is wearing that tatty yellow robe again, and drops it at the edge of the pool to reveal a modest black swimsuit. She dives in, stroking almost the entire length underwater before re-emerging with a gasp.

Pete picks up the robe and shrugs it over his broad shoulders, making a mincing impression of Caroline.

Alice stifles a giggle and Vivi shoots her a warning look.

'Hey, take that off!' Caroline is furious. 'You'll tear it.'

'Sorry, darling,' he says, sounding anything but. 'Keep your bloody hair on,' he mutters as Alice nearly explodes trying not to laugh.

Alice is distracted by the appearance of Marco, who brings out a bucket filled with ice and a bottle of prosecco. Stella follows with a precariously balanced tray of flutes. Alice holds her breath, concerned that the old woman might drop them, but she keeps up a steady shuffle and completes the task without mishap. 'Lovely, thank you,' she says, swimming to the shallow end and taking the glass that Marco is holding out to her.

He winks back. 'Sorry, they are plastic,' he says. 'Safety first. I'd hate for anyone to cut their feet, or glass to get in the pool. It happened once and it was not good.'

'Of course. Thanks for looking out for us.' She grins up at him, reddening slightly as she thinks again of their earlier encounter. He, however, looks as cool as a cucumber. 'Now, who else is going to join me for a proper drink? Vivi, it's your birthday, you can't say no.'

There's a splash as Nick dive-bombs into the pool, then another as Pete goes in after him. Isla puts down her book and joins them in the water, and even Mia looks up from her phone and watches Nick, Pete and Isla trying to duck each other under the water while shrieking with laughter.

'I want you to have an appetite for the dinner.' Marco returns with platters of ciabatta rolls stuffed with salami, tomatoes, buffalo mozzarella and basil, placing them on a side table. 'But hopefully this will keep the hungry wolf away until then.'

'Wonderful!' Vivi says as Delfina brings out another plate piled with figs, thin slices of pear, prosciutto and blue cheese. 'This is amazing, thank you.'

'He works hard, you've got to give him that,' Alice says when they've both disappeared. 'And I love how he manages to anticipate our needs.' She waves her glass in the air, spilling some between her cleavage. 'I feel like a glass of prosecco and, what do you know, it appears. I feel like lunch, there it is.' She licks spilled wine from the outside of her glass.

'You want him to anticipate all of your needs, little sis?' Vivi teases, but quietly, so the girls don't hear.

'Stop it!' Alice blushes.

The others haul themselves out of the pool and fall upon the food. They soon finish the prosecco.

'Who's that?' Pete asks, as the drone of a car engine reaches them. Mia is already on her feet, flying along the path that leads to the palazzo.

The insistent beep of a horn is followed by deep-voiced laughter, growing louder.

Minutes later, Mia returns to the pool with a tall young man in tow – a boy, really, with a crown of tumbling brown curls and liquid eyes.

'Mum, Auntie Vee, everyone,' Mia calls, 'this is Luca.'

He smiles broadly as he walks towards them. '*Ciao*!'

Alice is assaulted by pungent aftershave as the visitor swoops in and kisses her on both cheeks.

'Thank you for the invitation,' he says in charmingly accented English. 'I hope I am not intruding.'

'I thought you said Eleni was coming over?' Alice asks, puzzled.

'She wasn't feeling well,' Mia says. 'Luca is her cousin, so he came instead. It's not a problem, is it?'

'I suppose not.'

'So it's okay if we go for a drive?' Mia asks her mother.

'The Val Pellice is beautiful, especially in summer,' Luca says.

'Are you sure you don't want to go with them, Isla?' Alice asks, wondering for a moment whether it is entirely wise to let Mia go off with this boy on her own, but Isla shakes her head and holds up her book, and Alice is too relaxed to insist she accompany her sister.

Alice turns to Mia. 'Alright then, but don't be gone for too long.'

'We'll be back before dinner,' Mia promises.

'Don't forget a hat, darling,' Alice calls out.

'Yes, Mum,' Mia replies, sounding mildly exasperated.

'They grow up so fast, don't they?' Alice says fondly once Mia is out of earshot. She glances at Caroline, who looks stricken. 'Are you feeling alright, Caro? Had too much sun?'

CHAPTER THIRTY-FOUR

'Is Mia back yet?' Pete asks when they wake from an afternoon siesta. He still hasn't had the guts to confront Nick about the text message from Riccardo. It was on his mind the whole time they were hiking earlier, but he couldn't bring himself to spoil the beautiful morning, afraid of what he might hear.

Nick opens one eye, rolling onto his side. 'I think that was a car engine backfiring, so possibly yes.'

Pete raises his arm and checks his watch. 'It's nearly four.'

'Fancy a game of tennis? I promised Isla we'd play.'

Pete groans. 'Are you kidding? I'm still wiped out from this morning.'

'Come on. A good sweat will do us both the world of good.' Nick sits up, yawns and stretches, rolling out his neck.

'You promise?'

'Marco said he'd leave the racquets and some cans of balls in the shed next to the court.'

'Where is it exactly? I haven't seen any sign of a tennis court.'

'Behind the walled vegetable garden, the other end of the property from the olive grove.'

'I should do something before dinner, I guess. Promise you'll go easy on me.'

'Never.' Nick is already pulling on a pair of sneakers. 'I'll go see where Isla is. Maybe Luca and Mia too,' Nick says, ready to leave the room now. 'We can play round robin doubles if you like.'

'Sure, just give me a minute.'

Nick is impatient to be gone. 'See you on the court.'

* * *

The earlier heat has dissipated slightly, and Pete is relieved to see that the tennis court is shaded by a line of cypress trees. By the time he gets there, Nick, Isla, Luca and Mia are having a warm-up hit, their groundstrokes rhythmic and even. The girls have the edge, their shots for the most part accurate, although they lack the power of Nick's blistering returns. Luca appears to be completely outclassed, with Isla standing back to cover when he swings wildly and misses. Isla is a good sport about it, though, calling out encouragement or commiserations and trying not to laugh. Luca doesn't seem to mind either, taking it all in good humour.

'Want me to umpire?' Pete offers, seeing an opportunity to take it easy.

'We can swap in if you like,' Nick says, bouncing up and down on his toes. 'Best of five games and then we'll switch?'

'Sure.' There's an old metal chair outside the court and Pete pulls it level with the net. 'Players ready,' he says in his best Wimbledon accent, tipping his visor to see better and settling in. Nick has a competitive streak a mile wide, and even Luca seems focused as they toss a coin for first serve.

Nick throws the ball skywards and slams his racquet down to meet it, swearing as the ball goes long and a smidge wide.

'Second service.'

He tries again.

'Out!' Pete yells, starting to enjoy himself. 'Love-fifteen.'

'Patience, grasshopper,' Mia says.

Nick swings his racquet wildly through the air as he moves to the other side of the court.

He gets the next serve in, and thanks to Mia's follow-up groundstroke, they win the point.

Nick serves again and it clips the net but lands in.

'First service!' Pete calls.

He hits it perfectly the next time, and by some miracle Luca returns it, sending it sailing back across the court just past Nick.

Nick is grim-faced as he prepares to serve again.

What Luca lacks in skill he makes up for in enthusiasm, racing for impossible shots and sometimes managing to get them, shouting what sound like choice Italian expletives as he does so and making them all collapse with laughter.

'I need a break,' Mia says, red-faced, when Luca and Isla have won five games in a row.

'I think Nick does too,' Pete agrees as his husband storms off the court, reaching for a water bottle. 'Let's swap it out, hey?'

'Whatever.' Nick always was a sore loser.

Nick umpires next, and Pete and Mia manage to win the first game, Pete slamming a winner right down the line. 'Nice work,' Mia says, high-fiving him.

They're halfway through the next game when a woman appears, watching them from some way away. For a second Pete can't tell if it is Jade or Caroline — they have a similar build and hair colour, and though of course Jade is younger, it's not obvious at a distance. Pete waves, recognising the figure as Caroline when she gets closer to where Nick is sitting.

Luca double-faults the next serve and from then on is off his game, slow to get to the ball and looking as if he's lost in a daydream half the time.

'Everything okay?' Pete asks as they swap sides. He and Mia have got this in the bag.

Luca nods and crouches down, shaking his head and blinking as though trying to regain his focus.

Pete and Mia win the remaining games easily.

'Okay, let's switch it up. Me and Isla versus Nick and Mia,' Pete suggests.

'Fine by me,' says Luca, wiping his hair off his forehead as he comes off the court. 'I need some water anyway.' He goes over to Caroline.

Pete watches them for a moment. Caroline's body language could not be more hostile: her arms are wrapped around herself, and her expression is drawn into a scowl. She could try to be a little nicer to the boy, for heaven's sake.

'Are we playing?' Nick asks, sounding impatient, and Pete returns his attention to the court. The next time he has a chance to look over at Caroline and Luca, there's no longer any sign of either of them.

The new foursome is more evenly balanced, Pete's skill a match for Nick's fitness, Isla's well-placed, powerful groundstrokes often finding the edge of the court.

Pete hits a blistering serve to Nick, who is forced to duck to avoid being hit in the face.

'Jeez, what did I do to upset you?' Nick asks, shaking his head.

'All's fair …' Pete taunts.

The games go with serve, and a little while later, they change ends. Strolling across the court, Pete sees that Vivi and Jade have come over to spectate and raises his racquet in acknowledgement. Both are inscrutable behind their almost identical sunglasses.

'Care to join us?' Nick calls.

Vivi shakes her head. 'No talent for tennis, I'm afraid. Besides, after my fainting spell yesterday, I think I should take it easy.'

'Fair enough. Jade? I'll swap out with you if you like.'

'I'm fine, thanks anyway. Not really dressed for it.' She indicates her flimsy sandals. 'Besides, I didn't go to the kind of school that had tennis courts.' She offers him a self-deprecating smile.

'Oh, that doesn't matter,' Nick says. 'We can wait if you want to change?'

'Leave the poor woman alone,' Pete says. 'Come on, let's play. I'm going to beat you if it's the last thing I do.'

CHAPTER THIRTY-FIVE

'I think it's time we had a proper talk, don't you?' Vivi says, as she and Jade leave the tennis court. 'Why don't we take a seat?' She indicates two chairs at the edge of the terrace.

Her assistant does as she's asked, pulling out a notepad and pen, ready to do Vivi's bidding. 'Is everything all right for your birthday?'

'I'm not angry with you,' Vivi begins, deliberately keeping her voice calm. It's the truth; she's not angry.

No. She's icily furious, her rage underpinned by sickening dread of what would happen if the truth were to come out.

Jade's tongue flicks around her lips, a nervous tell.

'You've been with Vivid, and me more specifically, for how many years now?'

'Three years and four months.'

'And you've always been treated well? Nothing to complain about? Additional leave days, an annual bonus …'

Jade nods.

'And then I receive an email,' Vivi pauses, 'from a small London solicitors' firm. The ones I asked you to research, though I think now that you already knew who they were. An email, while I am on holiday, still mourning the loss of my husband, threatening to reveal a secret that would destroy me. I think you know what I'm referring to.'

Jade's fingers worry at the frayed edge of a cushion, and she won't meet Vivi's eyes. 'I … I'm sorry, I don't understand …'

Vivi deliberately makes her voice calm. 'Come now, really?'

Jade seems bewildered.

As the sun dips behind the mountains, cicadas begin their evening click-rasp-click chorus, and for a moment, Vivi thinks that Jade will not crack as easily as she first imagined. 'I know it was you, Jade, so do me the courtesy of not denying it. Very few people know the truth of how Will died; you happen to be one of them.'

'I didn't …' She swallows, lifting her gaze. 'I have no idea what you're talking about, Vivi.'

'Come on, Jade, do you think I was born yesterday? I must admit, I was shocked. I *never* expected something like this from you.' Vivi lets her words hang in the air, tilting her head to one side, pretending she has all the time in the world, is as calm and untroubled as the cloudless sky above them.

Jade hangs her head.

'Of course, having a boyfriend who is a solicitor no doubt made things even easier. Perhaps he knows this Gary Birdwhistle, perhaps he's using his email address? Did you cook up the plan between you? Did he, in fact, put you up to this?'

Jade, on the verge of tears now, swallowing and blinking rapidly, buries her face in her hands, but Vivi isn't buying her act anymore.

'I have noticed you've been rather distracted these past weeks. Forgetting to pay the balance of this holiday,' Vivi gestures to indicate their surroundings, 'was most unlike you. Perhaps you have been preoccupied with other matters?'

Jade cannot look at her, doesn't respond, instead shaking her head and burying her hands in her hair, raking her fingernails across her scalp.

'Like figuring out the best way to extort a large sum of money from your boss?'

Jade jerks her head upwards at this, a look of utter shock and disbelief on her face.

Vivi pauses for a second. Jade's a better actress than she gives her credit for.

'What? I promise, I would never ...' Her voice slips into her native West Country accent, very different from her usual modulated vowels. 'No!'

'How about we look at things from a different angle?' Vivi suggests, aware she needs to tread carefully, that Jade has information with the potential to ruin her. 'I could sack you for this, but then I'd have to explain it to HR, and that could get messy.' She gives an exaggerated sigh. 'There are so many protocols these days. And I think I can understand why you've done what you have – an aspirational lifestyle is an expensive one, isn't it? How did it happen? Bit by bit, the expenses of a new flat, bills getting out of control ...'

'What do you mean?' Jade's fingers have stilled.

'I think you deserve consideration. After all, you have worked extra hard in recent months. So here's what I'm thinking: a bursary. A company scholarship, if you will, awarded at the discretion of the directors. To enable the recipient to travel to several of our international offices, spend a week or two observing operations, helping them to expand their experience and advance their career. A generous travel allowance will, I imagine, be a part of that. I've already raised it with the board,' Vivi lies. She can argue for it as staff development and training if it comes to it. 'Wouldn't that be an elegant solution to our dilemma?' She hopes this suggestion will buy her some time, lulling Jade into a false sense of security until Vivi is in possession of the full facts, until she has irrefutable proof that her assistant has been blackmailing her.

Jade's face falls. 'I still don't understand.'

Vivi can't believe she's continuing to play dumb. 'Have a think about it, won't you? I expect you'll find it a pleasing prospect.' Vivi rubs her temples. Despite her outward calm, a headache is building, and the dizziness is threatening to return. The last thing she wants is to faint again. 'Now that we've got that all sorted, I'd better go and change for dinner,' she says lightly, getting to her feet. This is the last thing she wanted to deal with while on holiday, but she smiles as though the matter is settled, as though neither of them have a care in the world.

CHAPTER THIRTY-SIX

Alice ducks under the water and pushes off the edge of the pool. When she was younger – around the girls' age – she swam in squads four times a week and had the broad shoulders and voracious appetite to show for it. She wants to see if she can make a whole length without coming up for air. It's not a small pool – close to twenty-five metres – and she doesn't swim much at all these days, so she can't be sure she'll make it. She bends her body and wiggles her hips, dolphining her way along the bottom until she can feel the familiar pressure in her ears. Her lungs tighten, and the urge to come to the surface grows stronger until she can no longer bear it.

Her fingers graze the far end and she surfaces, gasping for breath. Water streams from her body and she wipes her hands across her face, blinking as she refocuses. A voice floats towards her. From her position, only a head is visible above the low wall that separates the kitchen garden from the pool. It's Caroline, speaking rapid Italian. Alice doesn't understand a word of what she's saying but catches the agitation in her voice, shrill and tight.

Then, another voice. Lower. Luca's curly hair comes into view. He sounds like he's gasping, crying. Crying? No, not crying, Alice thinks, but pleading. What have the two of them got to say to each other? As far as Alice is aware, they've never even met before. Turin isn't that small a city, surely?

'Gabriele. *Finito*. This has to stop. Do you understand me? It is over.' Caroline is speaking mainly in English now, and her voice is clear, determined. 'You should not be here. I can't believe that you somehow managed to contact Mia, to make her your friend. How did you know she was staying here with me? How did you manage to do these things? And *why,* for chrissake?'

'She tagged you on an Instagram post.' He shrugs, holding both hands open as if he has nothing to hide. 'I used a different profile and sent her a DM offering to show her around the city. I said I wanted to practise my English and that I knew you from the language school. It wasn't hard to convince her to meet me, to get her to invite me here. You refuse to see me, Caroline, what am I supposed to do?'

Caroline says some more, reverting to Italian again, but Alice has got the gist of it. Luca – or Gabriele, as Caroline called him – isn't Eleni's cousin. He knows Caroline. And they obviously have, or had, some kind of relationship. From the sound of it, Caroline's furious that he's here now, frantic even.

Alice's first reaction is to go in search of Mia and give both girls a serve for lying to her. But as she thinks about it some more, she decides to wait. Nothing can be allowed to jeopardise Vivi's special day. She's going to make sure her sister has the birthday she deserves, that she feels wrapped in the love and affection of her family and friends. After all, if the last few years and months have taught them anything it's that you can never take such things for granted. She will swallow her annoyance with the twins for the time being. They'll keep.

The conversation stops, and Alice is about to duck under the water again when a slap rings out, followed by a stifled shout. Shocked, she hauls herself out of the pool and runs over to the wall. She's about to call out but Caroline is too far away now, beyond the gate and running towards the olive grove. She scans the area. There is no sign of Luca, or Gabriele, or whatever his name is.

CHAPTER THIRTY-SEVEN

'Have you seen my aftershave?' Pete peers around the door of their en suite. He has worn Penhaligon's The Inimitable William since he was in his twenties and treats himself to a new bottle whenever he's in London. Nick teases him about it, calling it 'Old Bill' and asking, 'What does inimitable even mean?'

'Have you?' he asks again when Nick doesn't answer.

They left the tennis match separately, Nick staying to chat with Luca who had returned to the court, Pete going on ahead of him to grab a shower.

'What?' Nick looks at him blankly, sits down on the edge of the bed to peel off his socks.

'My Penhaligon's? I swore it was on the counter this morning. Do you think the maid might have moved it?' His voice has an edge to it; he can't stop thinking about the text on Nick's phone. He can't let it go but also can't bring himself to ask Nick about it directly, afraid of the answer he might hear.

Nick shrugs.

'Hey?' Pete comes into the bedroom now, one towel wrapped around his waist, using another to dry his hair. 'Everything okay?'

'You tell me,' Nick says. 'There's a lot you've been keeping from me apparently.'

'There is?' Pete's mind scrambles as he tries to work out what Nick is referring to.

'I'm not an idiot, you know.'

Pete sits down next to Nick, who moves a fraction away from him, his gaze directed to the open window. Pete takes a deep breath. 'To be honest, it's rather blindsided me, and I'm still trying to figure out how to handle it,' he stalls. 'I wanted to work out how I felt about it before discussing it with you.'

Nick gets up, pulls off his T-shirt and goes into the bathroom, closing the door, something he rarely does. The shower is turned on.

Sighing, Pete gets up, goes to the wardrobe and selects a pair of black formal trousers and a collarless white shirt made from cotton so fine it feels like silk. It was a gift from Nick, and he hopes that by wearing it, he might lessen the tension between them, even slightly.

The hiss of the shower ceases and a moment later Nick emerges from the bathroom, rubbing his face with a towel. He spots the shirt but says nothing. 'I'll tell you what does absolutely kill me,' Nick says eventually. 'It's that I had to find out from someone else.'

'I'm sorry,' Pete says. 'It's a lot, I know. Who told you?' He's still stalling, not sure what exactly Nick is referring to.

Nick doesn't answer, beginning to flip through the clothes hanging on his side of the wardrobe. After a few days of sun, his skin is the colour of honey, and despite everything, lust begins to curl through Pete's body.

'When were *you* going to tell me? Your *husband*?' Nick blows air through his lips in exasperation before pulling on boxer shorts followed by a pair of white jeans. He takes a black shirt off a hanger. The two of them will look like mirror images of each other, Pete realises. Nick turns to look at him now, shirt hanging open over his magnificent abs. 'When were you going to tell me about London?'

Relief washes over Pete. That's what the problem is. 'I haven't entirely figured it out yet. I certainly haven't committed to anything.'

'And what about me?' Nick glares at him, and Pete wants to tell him that his collar is askew but thinks better of it.

'Well, you'd come too. Obviously.'

'I've only just got the gym up and running again; you know I signed a five-year lease. And I'm working on my fitness app.' Nick shakes his head. 'I thought we were happy in Boston, that we were settled there. We have plans – remodelling the apartment … This makes no sense to me.'

'Look, I am fully aware it is a discussion we need to have, that it is a joint decision, but I thought you might be up for it. It's an incredible career opportunity for me, and I thought you *loved* London.' This is the first time Pete's had to consider anyone else when making major life decisions, and it's proving harder than expected.

'To visit, not to *live*.' There's a look of horror on Nick's face.

'Okay, okay.' Now is not the time to bring up the message from Riccardo; it'll only make things worse. 'You've made your point.'

'Don't patronise me.' Nick storms out of the room, his shoes clattering on the stone stairs.

CHAPTER THIRTY-EIGHT

'Can you make me look like Cleopatra, Auntie Vee?' Isla asks, picking up a bottle of liquid eyeliner from the box that sits splayed like a concertina on the dresser.

'Isn't that cultural appropriation?' Mia asks slyly, reaching for a bottle of nail polish and indicating to Isla that she will do her nails for her.

'Who made you the *polizia*?' Isla replies, raising a swift finger at her sister. 'Sorry,' she says, turning to Vivi, 'sometimes she gets on my nerves.'

Vivi laughs, reminded of her teenage exchanges with Alice and pleased to see that Isla does sometimes bite back. 'Of course, darling, that sounds like fun.'

'Thanks, Auntie Vee. Just the eye make-up – winged eyeliner, like you do yours. And like Jade does it too.'

'Does she?' Vivi muses. 'Yes, I suppose she does sometimes.'

'She even dresses like you, Auntie Vee,' Mia points out. 'And speaks like you.' She mimics her aunt's precise accent. 'It seems like she wants to *be* you. You must have noticed.'

'I love that frock,' Vivi says, changing the subject and pointing to a sequinned yellow mini-dress hanging on the wardrobe door. 'Is that yours?' She's always thought the fact that Jade sometimes wore similar clothes was simply the result of them spending so much time together. Truth be told, she was even a little flattered. Now, however, it feels like an invasion of privacy.

Mia nodded. 'I picked it up at a little vintage store when we were in Turin the other day.'

The two sisters exchange a look.

'Oh, clever you, you have got a good eye. I bet it will look amazing.' Vivi dabs foundation onto a sponge and picks up a fat brush.

'I think Isla should wear it,' Mia says. 'You like it, right?'

'Sure.' Isla shrugs, seemingly unenthusiastic.

'Oh, you should!' Vivi cries. 'Now, come and sit over by the window, Mia – the light's better here – and we'll make a start. You can finish Isla's nails in a minute.' Vivi feels a surge of optimism. This is what she loves – seeing the transformation of a person, bringing out their natural beauty with a little subtle enhancement, making them feel better. As she works, she thinks about the two girls, concluding that it's probably easier to have nieces than daughters, much as she would have loved to have her own children. With nieces, it's all fun, little responsibility. Though she doesn't see them nearly enough. If losing Will has taught her anything it's that time is precious. She is going to be far more deliberate about how she spends hers in the future.

'Oh my God, she's a swan!' Vivi cries when she is finished with Mia. 'Go on, there's a mirror in the bathroom, take a look. Now come here, Cleopatra, you're next.'

Mia returns from the bathroom with shiny eyes. 'You're brilliant, Auntie Vee.' She raises her fingertips to her cheek, stopping when she sees Vivi's look of concern that she might touch the carefully applied make-up.

'My pleasure, darling girl.' It feels good to make someone happy for a change.

* * *

Vivi is late returning to her room after spending much longer on the girls' make-up than she had planned — she completely lost track of time. She's got about fifteen minutes before dinner, and so any thoughts of having a rest are dashed.

She goes to the bathroom to shower and instantly recoils in horror. Scrawled across the mirror in red lipstick is one word: 'LIAR'.

Her heart begins to thump uncomfortably in her chest and her breathing quickens. 'Jesus!' The thought that someone has been in her room — someone who clearly hates her, and who knows her darkest, deepest secrets — and is taunting her with them stops her dead in her tracks. Is this Jade's work? Did she do it before Vivi confronted her or after? She's got quite some nerve.

'Fuck you,' she says, swiping at the message with damp fingers, desperate to erase the letters. They end up smeared across the mirror, a gash of scarlet.

She rinses her hands, drying them on the towel and then using it to clean the mirror until the only sign of the threatening message is a faint red mark on the glass. At least she now knows the identity of her blackmailer and has a plan to deal with her.

She showers, blow-dries her hair with only a slightly shaky hand, and applies her make-up. Tonight, it feels like warpaint.

Though she'd been determined to ignore her phone all day, she can't resist quickly checking it now. She switches it on as she flips through her holiday wardrobe, absent-mindedly selecting a pleated champagne-coloured dress that wraps softly around her body. She examines herself in the mirror then adds leather sandals, hoop earrings and the silver bangle from Pete and Nick. She wishes she felt more like celebrating.

She's about to leave the room when her phone comes to life, the intermittent wi-fi connecting, and it starts beeping with messages. Seventeen missed calls. Three text messages. Two voicemails.

She flicks through the list. Some of the numbers are not ones she recognises, but eight of them are from Robert, Vivid's CFO. She checks her watch: it's nearly eight o'clock, seven in London, though it is a Saturday. Not bothering to listen to the messages, she calls him.

He answers on the first ring. 'Vivi, I've been trying to reach you.'

'And not just to wish me a happy birthday, I imagine,' she says drily. 'What's up?'

CHAPTER THIRTY-NINE

Vivi ends the call, promising Robert that she will speak to him again in the morning when she's had time to think things over. 'It's fine,' she says to her reflection before leaving her room. 'It's all going to be fine.'

'Oh, there you are.' It's Alice, standing in the corridor ahead of her wearing a ruffled orange dress that vaguely reminds Vivi of the cocktails Marco has been serving. 'I came to see what was keeping you. You look lovely.'

'Thank you. So do you.' Vivi forces herself to smile. 'That colour really suits you.'

'Is everything okay?' Alice asks, looking at her more closely.

Vivi takes a deep breath. 'Absolutely.'

* * *

The mountains have all but blacked out the sky, but fairy lights have been looped from the trees, and torches flame at intervals across the terrace and along the path that leads to the pool. A white linen cloth has been thrown over the rustic table and flowers and candles are placed at intervals along the centre. Vivi stops on the threshold, rendered speechless by the scene.

'The birthday girl!' Someone spots her. Someone else starts with a note, and then the rest of the assembled crowd begin to sing, raising their glasses in a toast. A glass of prosecco is thrust into her hand.

Embarrassed at the attention, Vivi doesn't know where to look first, but she meets their eyes in turn. Her gaze slides over Jade.

She puts the earlier phone conversation to the back of her mind, determined not to let it spoil the moment. A rapid gulp of prosecco helps. She hadn't expected this rush of emotion and it's almost overwhelming. It's been a big day.

Alice grabs her hand and squeezes it, and Caroline clasps the other. Marco, Stella and Delfina stand by the kitchen door and everyone begins clapping enthusiastically as the ragged singing subsides.

'Honestly, I wasn't … I wasn't prepared for this,' she says, dabbing at her eyes with a tissue. 'Just as well I applied waterproof mascara.' That gets a laugh, and the tension in the room subsides.

Stella brings out a tray of antipasti and weaves between the guests with surprising grace as Delfina tops up their glasses. 'What a gorgeous dress,' Vivi says to Caroline, who is wearing a low-backed gown in midnight blue silk. The last few days have erased the furrow between her eyebrows, though the whites of her eyes are suspiciously pink and her eyelids are slightly puffy. Vivi resists the urge to suggest a soothing eye balm.

'Can I talk to you?' Caroline says quietly, her eyes darting about the room. 'About G— Luca?'

There's an odd vibration in the air, a disturbance, as though Vivi's not the only one unable to give themselves over to such a beautiful evening.

'About Luca?'

Caroline nods.

She's about to speak when Pete comes and kisses Vivi on both cheeks. 'Looking fabulous, darling.'

Caroline reddens, biting her lip, and shakes her head at Vivi's questioning glance.

'Thanks, Pete,' Vivi replies. 'Sorry I was late.'

'Not at all. Everything okay?'

Vivi nods. She'll talk to Robert first thing in the morning and together they will work out a strategy. There's no way in hell she will sell Vivid to J&K. 'Over my dead body,' were her parting words to him on the phone.

It's her birthday, she reminds herself, and nothing is going to change overnight. 'Absolutely,' she lies. Putting on a brave face is something she is all too accustomed to doing.

'You like?' Marco asks, coming to refresh her glass.

Vivi smiles at him, inclining her head and surveying the scene. Isla looks fabulous in the shiny yellow frock, and beside her, Mia is in figure-hugging black, her top slashed to the waist. Everyone under the age of thirty, except for Nick and Luca (who is, she notes with interest, wearing a clean shirt, possibly one of Marco's), is wearing heels so ridiculously high that if they take just one misstep, they'll well and truly wreck their ankles.

She casts around for Jade, anxious to keep an eye on her.

She's at the other end of the terrace now, standing next to Luca, wearing green. She wears the shade, in variations from lime and apple to moss and forest, so often that everyone at work comments on it. Vivi almost can't bear to watch her relaxing and enjoying the evening. She could have told her to leave earlier in the day, could have put her on a flight straight back to London, but Jade knows too much. For the time being, Vivi will keep her enemies close.

Alice takes Vivi's arm, leading her a little way away from the others towards the table. 'You're doing really well,' she reassures her. 'The girls and I made place cards,' she adds. 'They're mostly Mia's work. Come and see.'

'She might be even more talented than her mother,' Vivi says, picking up a card drawn with an astonishingly accurate miniature portrait of Pete. 'She's captured his expression perfectly.' She studies the one of herself, smiling at the scarlet lipstick, blunt hairstyle and enormous sunglasses.

'I know – I wish I could convince her of that. But it's far too close to what I do, and heaven forbid she be anything like me.' Alice grimaces.

'Would it help if I told her?'

'I suppose it can't hurt.'

She spots Mia with Luca now, further along the path, and is about to go after them when Delfina announces that it is time to take their seats. She is relieved when the pair reappears a few moments later. Caroline never did share what she had to say about Luca.

Tiny, delicate plates of the most delicious and unexpected flavour combinations appear, all with a nod to the heritage of the region, accompanied by a suite of local wines. After the antipasti, there is hand-cut *tagliarini* with sage and shaved white truffle, grilled baby leeks, a palate-cleansing *sgroppino* with macerated strawberries, prosecco and lemon sorbet, *brasato al Barolo* – a rich beef and red wine stew served with polenta – then blushing peaches roasted in marsala. The meal finishes with hazelnut *torrone*, *baci di dama* and the ubiquitous glasses of grappa and limoncello.

Vivi isn't the only one impressed. Pete moans audibly as he takes the first bite of each course. 'This tastes like love,' Isla murmurs, spooning butter-soft peach into her mouth.

Everyone's plates, even Nick's, go back empty.

Alice has arranged the table so that Vivi is at the head, with herself and Caroline on either side, Pete and Nick down from each of them, then the twins, and Luca and Jade beyond them. Every so often Vivi glances towards the far end of the table and tries not to think how different things would be if Will were sitting there. The pain of his absence is like a phantom limb.

'It's astonishing that all of this has been produced by one man. He must have been slaving away for days,' Pete says, brushing biscuit crumbs from his fingers. 'And Stella, of course. I saw her in the kitchen with her sleeves rolled up earlier. I've eaten at some pretty good restaurants over the years, but Marco has elevated such simple ingredients to another level. Thank you, Vivi, for this. For all of this.'

Vivi inclines her head. 'You're most welcome.' After the unending monotony of weeks spent caring for Will, an evening like this should feel magical, but Vivi has too much on her mind to completely enjoy it.

While the others are caught up in conversation, Caroline, who appears to have got stuck into the prosecco early on, grasps Vivi's hand and leans in towards her. 'I want to say how sorry I am.'

'It's okay, I know. We all wish he was here now. He should be at the other end of the table, by rights.'

'I must talk to you,' she insists again, but Alice interrupts her.

'You always had a thing for Will, didn't you, Caro?' she asks. Alice has also had several glasses of wine by this stage and seemingly can't help herself. She goes on, a mischievous glint in her eye. 'It's probably for the best he's not here, Vee, given what happened at your last party ...' Her voice trails off, and she appears to realise she's said too much. 'You knew 'bout that, right, Vee? I'm sure he would have told you.'

'No. He didn't.' Vivi swallows. *Jesus. What now?* 'Caroline?'

Caroline glares at Alice.

'Tell me.' Vivi is steely, sensing a change in the air.

'It was a stupid drunk mistake.' A vein pulses in Caroline's forehead. 'Honestly. It was nothing.'

Alice is flustered now, her hands waving like butterflies, aware that she shouldn't have brought up the subject, that she has gone too far this time. 'Of course, not even worth mentioning. Don't mind me, too much wine. My bad.' She swallows. 'Forget I said anything.'

'I never meant ...' Caroline says in a whisper, her eyes wide, pupils dark with concern. 'You must believe that. I swear on my mother's grave.'

Vivi's headache has begun to pound against her temples, but she wants to get to the bottom of this. 'Do enlighten me.'

'Will was kind to me and I mistook it for more than that. But nothing happened. Honestly.' Caroline breaks off, rising from the table, her napkin clutched in her hand. 'The bathroom ...' she mutters, scraping her chair as she runs from the table.

Vivi turns her attention to her sister. 'Tell me,' she insists. 'What happened?'

'They had a little, well, I suppose you'd call it a hook-up,' Alice says. 'Not even that.' She's doing her best to minimalise it, but Vivi's not fooled for a second.

No one else, thankfully, is paying any attention to them.

'Are you fucking kidding me?' Vivi hisses.

'Honestly, no one even saw, only me, Pete and the attendant in the ladies' room. They were drunk.' Alice hiccups. 'Caroline always held a torch for Will, surely you knew that?'

'The ladies' room? Really?' Vivi is blindsided. She had no idea, absolutely no clue. And Alice? Alice had to bring this up now, at her birthday dinner? Christ, does she have a sense of timing? And Pete knew about it as well and never said anything?

She doesn't doubt for a minute that it is true, despite Caroline's denial.

The betrayal is utterly humiliating.

It suddenly strikes her that the score has now been settled; she no longer owes Caroline a thing. That thought is remarkably freeing.

'Sorry. You did ask,' Alice says. 'But I shouldn't have said anything in the first place.' She seems genuinely penitent.

Marco arrives to check on his guests, and Alice seizes the opportunity to thank him. Vivi is relieved at the shift in focus.

'Spectacular,' Alice says, getting to her feet with a slight wobble and raising her glass. 'You are a true genius.'

'Hear, hear,' says Pete.

'Absolutely,' chimes in Nick, who had mopped up every scrap of sauce on his plate *and* asked for extra bread.

'Stella made the *tagliarini* – she's got a far lighter touch than me,' Marco says, accepting their praise. 'Not to mention many years more experience.' After a modest protest, he accepts Pete's invitation to join them for a drink, pulling up a chair at the end of the wide table beside Alice.

Caroline returns, looking pale, and takes her seat. You've got to hand it to her: she's got guts. If Vivi was in her position, she wouldn't dare show her face again.

And that's when Alice retrieves a pad of yellow sticky notes and a pen from her clutch bag, suggesting a game.

CHAPTER FORTY

Mia and her sister are at the other end of the table with Luca, and Jade, who is stuck in a kind of no-man's-land, too old for their ridiculous conversation (which is, to be honest, mostly about the best way to twirl pasta and not get sauce up your nose or down your front) and too young to fit in with the others. Jade is knocking back the wine like it's a competitive sport, reaching for a nearby bottle and sloshing more into her glass, spilling some on the tablecloth in the process.

Mia knows she should draw her into their group, but she becomes caught up in a competition with Luca, rolling and lighting amaretti papers and watching them levitate skywards as they briefly flame. She forgets all about her aunt's assistant.

In a pause between courses, Luca slips away from the table and, curious to know what he is up to, Mia excuses herself, saying she forgot her phone. Isla is firing obscure facts about the Egyptian museum ('Did you know that ancient Egyptians worshipped more than two thousand deities and that the bakers sometimes used their feet to knead dough?') at Jade, who looks like she'd rather be anywhere else, and neither of them notice Mia take the path that leads to the pool rather than going back to the house. She finds Luca perched on a sun lounger. As she approaches, a small plastic bag slips from his fingers and lands on the paving. Mia reaches to pick it up.

'You can have one if you like.'

The bag contains a couple of multicoloured pills that look almost like the old-fashioned Love Hearts lollies she used to buy in primary school but smaller.

'Molly?' she whispers. 'E?'

Luca giggles.

'Cool.' Perhaps something exciting will happen to her this holiday after all. Mia's never had anything stronger than a few stolen sips of alcohol, but that doesn't stop her placing one of the tablets — a pink one — on her tongue without a second thought. She doesn't know whether to let it dissolve, crush it between her teeth or swallow it whole, but she won't embarrass herself by asking Luca what to do. In the end, with him looking on, she swallows it dry. 'How long?' she asks.

Luca shrugs. 'Maybe half an hour.' He smiles, and Mia's heartbeat quickens. It's done now. She nods briefly, pretending a sophistication she doesn't possess.

The noise from the table drifts towards them. 'We should go back, no?' Even she can see that their absence will be noticed if they're gone for much longer. Without waiting to see if he follows, she turns and walks back along the path, feeling disappointingly normal. She tugs her dress down where it has bunched up around her waist, wishing she hadn't lent the yellow one to her sister, though the thrill of stealing it was far better than the anticipation of wearing it.

It occurs to her that Luca might have been playing a trick on her, that he has given her fake pills that are, in fact, nothing more than lollies, or sweets as she and Isla used to call them before they moved to Australia. Either way, she decides to play it cool; no one will be able to tell whether she's having the trip of a lifetime or is as firmly part of the earth as the mountains in the distance. She realises that almost any of her friends would kill to be in her position, at a dreamy Italian palazzo with an equally dreamy Italian boy.

'Darling, there you are.' Her aunt reaches out to her and circles an arm around her waist. 'Are you having a nice time?'

'Of course, Auntie Vee,' she says, her gaze fixed on Luca as he returns to the table and takes his seat again. She sees a glance shoot between him and Caroline a few places away from him, and it suddenly strikes her as odd that they have barely exchanged two words. Didn't Luca say he knew her from the language school? She will ask Caro about it when she gets the chance.

Mia shivers at a cool wind that seems to gust directly from the mountains, and her aunt grips her waist more tightly.

'I'm glad you came,' Vivi says to her. 'It means so much to me.'

* * *

When it hits her, she leans into her aunt, for it feels like she might float away on the next breath of wind. A spreading warmth turns her bones liquid and suddenly she is in love with everyone at the table, even Jade, even creepy Caroline, and she's sorry for having been such a bitch, but she can't care about that right now because she just wants to go and dance her arse off. Even to the dreadful music that Marco's put on.

'Are you okay, darling?' Vivi asks, but Mia shimmies away from her and back to the other end of the table, towards Luca, waving her hands to let her aunt know that she is more than okay, that she is, possibly for the first time, fabulous.

CHAPTER FORTY-ONE

It's Alice's idea to play parlour games, but surely no one can blame her for what happens next.

'What are we, geriatrics?' Pete scoffs. 'Come on, we can do better than that, surely?'

'What's a parlour game?' Nick asks, puzzled. 'Is that a British thing?'

'It'll be fun,' Alice promises, hoping she can make up for her enormous faux pas earlier and get the evening back on track. She really should ease up on the alcohol; she can't believe she might have ruined her sister's night, especially after resolving to do everything she could to make it special for her.

They start with Celebrity Heads, which has even the teens enthusiastically calling out guesses, then move on to Charades, which Nick proves surprisingly adept at, acting out obscure movie titles with gusto and exaggerated facial expressions. And then Pete suggests playing Never Have I Ever. A couple of the others protest. 'Really? That's still a thing?' Caroline asks.

Vivi pleads tiredness. 'It's nearly midnight. And I need my beauty sleep more than ever now.' She throws her hair back with enough panache to show she's only kidding.

Luca and Mia are on their feet at the other end of the table, dancing to the music.

'It makes so much sense now that I think about it,' Vivi whispers to Alice. 'Will and I had a huge row that night about the business, though I can't remember the specifics anymore. I hardly saw him at the party; I was too busy being the perfect hostess. Worried about others at my own goddam party when clearly I should have been worrying about him and Caro.'

'I'm so sorry. I thought you knew how Caro felt about him.' Alice has sobered up a little now. 'I should never have brought it up. Foot in mouth courtesy of the Barolo.' She raises her empty glass.

'You've never liked her, have you?' Vivi asks. 'Caro, I mean? If I didn't know better, I might almost say you let that slip deliberately.'

Alice's denial is drowned out by the younger guests, who insist on playing the game, probably eager to shock the oldies or uncover their secrets. By then the eight adults have sunk more than a dozen bottles of wine, the grappa has come out, and Nick wins the doubters over. 'Come on, you know you want to,' he cajoles.

They are still at the long table on the terrace, surrounded by the remains of the birthday dinner, chairs pushed back, linen napkins crumpled, leftover bread going stale in the cooling night air. Behind them, the sheer granite face of the Alps is an ominous presence, but overhead, a sea of stars glimmers in the cloudless sky, the valley stretching out darkly below. There is no one else around for miles, no one to hear if they blast music at full volume, shriek or scream with laughter.

Marco sloshes an inch of grappa into a glass and lights a cigarette as they explain the rules to him and Luca. '*Salute!*' He raises his glass to them, knocking it back in one swift gulp and pouring himself another.

'Fabulous meal again, *grazie*,' Alice says, unable to tear her eyes away from him.

'*Prego*.' A lazy smile plays across his lips as he drags on his cigarette, as though he is smiling at a joke of his own making or, more likely, remembering their encounter in the kitchen that morning.

Nick begins. He clears this throat dramatically, as if about to make an important announcement, and everyone stops mid-conversation. 'Never have I ever ... been skinny-dipping.' It's a harmless statement, and Alice is grateful that he has eased them in. Isla translates for Luca, though he doesn't seem to have too much trouble understanding. She has also explained the rules to him: that you take a drink when you've done the thing that's named. Alice has been watching him over the course of the evening, wondering if she's the only one aware of his connection to Caroline. Luca, or Gabriele, or whatever his name is, seems utterly carefree, chatting easily with Mia, Isla and Jade, charming them all, but she's not buying his act. When she gets the chance, she will warn Mia and Isla, and suggest to Vivi that he be quietly asked to leave. Perhaps Marco can call him a taxi if there is such a thing to be had all the way out here. He's clearly in no fit state to drive, none of them are.

Everyone drinks, even Nick. 'Boring!' someone shouts from the far end of the table. 'And you're supposed to pick something you haven't done.'

'Oh, sorry, I didn't realise.' Nick winks.

'Come on, at least make it interesting,' Pete says.

Isla is next up. 'Never have I ever ... stolen something from a shop.' She looks pointedly at her sister, whose blood-orange soda remains untouched. A couple of the party, including eventually Mia, drink to jeers of derision and amusement from the others. Alice widens her eyes at her daughter, giving her a questioning look, but Mia just shrugs.

They move on to Vivi. 'Never have I ever ... had cosmetic surgery.'

'What, not even Botox?' Nick asks.

'That's a procedure, not surgery,' Vivi argues.

Alice points to her nose, leaving her glass untouched. 'Are you kidding?' she says. 'Do you think I'd still have this if I had?'

'Never have I ever broken a bone.' Mia's voice carries loudly down the table, but no one accuses her of picking an unexciting truth. Isla, Nick, Luca, Pete, Jade and Vivi all drink.

'Never have I ever lied about my age,' says Alice when it's her turn. Almost everyone except Isla drinks, smirking at each other in recognition.

'No, I really don't think I ever have,' Isla protests as the others regard her with disbelief.

'Never have I ever cheated on anyone.' It's Marco's turn and he scans the table, curious to see the effect of his statement. Alice winces as she remembers what's recently come to light, and Caroline stares stonily ahead, her glass untouched, refusing to take part.

Alice gamely lifts her glass. 'I was *seventeen*, darling,' she protests when Isla gives her a scandalised look. 'Everyone's allowed to do at least one regrettable thing at that age.'

Then Pete raises his glass. 'Never have I ever … performed in drag.' He and Nick both drink, and they raise their eyebrows at each other before Pete gets up, goes around the table and hugs his new husband. This wouldn't ordinarily be surprising, but it hasn't gone unnoticed, by Alice at least, that they've barely spoken all evening.

'No, Pete, you're not supposed to have done it,' Isla says when he returns to his seat. 'Haven't you been paying *any* attention?'

'It's just as much fun this way.' Pete shrugs. 'Lighten up, sweetheart.'

Luca goes next. He pauses before speaking. 'Never have I ever –' a wicked glint appears in his eye '– had *un cosa a tre*.'

Those with a limited understanding of Italian look momentarily bemused. Isla goes red.

'What?' Alice asks for clarification.

'Come on, I think even you can work it out,' Caroline says, drinking. Marco joins in, raising his glass and winking at Alice.

'Oh, I get it,' Alice says after Vivi translates for her. She erupts with laughter, reaches for her glass and then catches sight of her daughters, her hand stilling.

'That's hardly appropriate,' Vivi speaks up. 'Luca, in case you weren't aware, Mia and Isla are only sixteen.'

He slumps back against his chair looking sulky, muttering under his breath in Italian.

'Let's move this along, shall we?' Pete says. 'And try to keep it on the cleaner side. There are sensitive people present, me included.'

Nick takes another turn, thinking for several minutes before speaking. 'Never have I ever been in love with someone I shouldn't,' he declares eventually.

Caroline, who looks as though she is about to cry, takes a tiny sip; Marco a large one.

'That's pretty broad brush,' says Alice, reaching for her glass. 'But I'm sure I must have at some time or other.'

Jade goes last. She gets to her feet, clinking the side of her glass with a fork until she has everyone's attention. She waits until the table falls silent before speaking. 'Never have I ever … killed someone.' She slurs the final word, puts her hand to her mouth and sits down fast.

There's a stunned silence. 'Hey, come on now, that's going a bit far.'

'Hardly in the spirit of the game.'

'What's that about?'

'F-f-fucking ridiculous.'

'I don't think she meant it seriously.'

'Oh, I think she did.' This from Vivi at the head of the table, uttered in a low voice.

The atmosphere is suddenly thick and cloying, like the air just before a storm breaks. Alice can't quite keep up with the undercurrents swirling around the table. Luca is clearly still pissed off, and Marco grinds his cigarette out on a saucer and pushes back his chair, returning to the kitchen without a word. Vivi's face is drained of all colour, and Pete has a face like thunder.

'That was *not* appropriate,' says Alice softly, absent-mindedly taking a sip of her drink.

Caroline rises from the table, excusing herself, and flees towards the palazzo.

'What exactly do you mean by that, Jade?' Vivi asks, gripping the edge of the table.

But Jade is also on her feet and stumbling in the opposite direction, along the path to the pool.

CHAPTER FORTY-TWO

'Come on, guys, this is supposed to be a celebration,' Pete says into the awkward silence before taking a sip of his drink. He stops as soon as he realises what he's done, but it's too late. Everyone pretends they haven't noticed, looking anywhere but at him.

He's never told anyone, certainly not Nick. He lets out a breath, senses Nick tense up next to him. Pete is thinking of taking Nick aside right now and explaining everything when his phone, facedown next to him, vibrates with a notification. He ignores it at first, but then it vibrates a second time and he picks it up.

Alerts. Five of them, including several received during dinner. The phone reception here is, if nothing else, reliably unreliable.

Pete clicks on the first, a news report on the rumoured hostile takeover of Vivid by J&K. It's happening already. They haven't bothered waiting until after the meeting next week, the one that he packed a suit for.

Marco, who has returned with another bottle, raises his glass to the table. 'We have all done things we would rather forget.' He takes a drink. 'At the restaurant in New York. Tribeca. It was November and there was a rumour that it might snow that night. A customer informed the waitstaff of his allergy and they assured him that there would be no sesame or peanut products in his meal. I oversaw the brigade, but the message never reached me, or any of the kitchen staff for that matter. Our allergen procedure policy was outdated. The server responsible for his table insisted that she had included it when sending the order through, but due to a glitch in the computer system, no record could be found.' Marco puts his glass down. 'His name was Julian Andersen. He complained of feeling unwell while eating dessert and began to struggle to breathe. He had not brought his EpiPen, and the restaurant did not have one either.

'Mr Andersen died at the scene shortly afterwards, despite the best efforts of a doctor who also happened to be there that evening. A verdict of accidental death was recorded, but the gentleman's grieving family filed suit against the restaurant anyway.' Marco leans back in his seat, looking around the table. 'I was fired. The server, who happened to be the daughter of the restaurant owner, was not.'

'Oh, Marco,' Alice breathes. 'That's a lot.'

He shrugs and lights another cigarette, the slight tremble of his fingers the only sign that it still bothers him.

Stella, who has appeared from the shadows, rests a hand on his shoulder, and Marco says something to her in Italian. Pete catches a couple of words: Marco is explaining what they have been discussing.

Stella gestures towards the bottle.

Marco splashes grappa into an empty glass and hands it to her. 'Please, come and sit,' Vivi says, but Stella shakes her head. She raises her glass with one hand, presses the other to her breastbone. '*Molti, molti morti.*'

Of course, Pete thinks, their own troubles thrown into perspective for a moment. She is talking about the war.

CHAPTER FORTY-THREE

'Well, technically, we should drink as well,' Mia calls out, lifting her glass high in the air, her eyes glittering in the candlelight. She winces and nearly drops the glass, rubbing at her arm. 'Ouch, what was that?' She inspects her arm but apparently sees nothing.

She tries again, raising it higher still. 'Come on, Isla, you too.'

Her sister flashes her a confused look.

'What are you talking about, darling?' Ice runs down Alice's spine.

'Bella.'

'Bella?' Pete asks.

'Our other sister. We were triplets. Don't you ever wonder what she would have been like, Mum?'

Alice nods slowly. Of course she does. She's reminded of her lost child every time she looks at the two that lived. 'She wasn't strong enough to keep growing. We don't know why, lovely. It just happens like that sometimes. Neither of you are responsible.'

Mia's never brought this up before; Alice had no idea that it bothered her.

'That's not entirely true, Mum,' Isla interrupts. 'It's called vanishing twin syndrome, though it applies to all multiple births. One twin, or one triplet or quadruplet even, can starve their sibling of nutrients to ensure their own survival.'

'Oh, darling, none of that makes it your fault,' Vivi says.

'That doesn't mean it didn't happen,' Isla replies with irrefutable logic, turning to look at her mother.

The girls' words have knocked the breath out of her. Alice rises, muttering an excuse and hurrying down the stairs and along the path that leads from the terrace. She needs a moment to herself.

She reaches the vegetable garden before she slows down, then stops abruptly and leans against the wall, forcing her breathing to return to normal. She's always believed she was to blame for her third daughter not making it. It was because she didn't want triplets, couldn't have coped; the power of her own thoughts had caused the baby to die. She knows it's ridiculous, but that doesn't stop the voice from nagging her in her darkest moments, reminding her what an evil person she is deep down, under all the supposedly carefree, fun-loving layers that she has so determinedly shellacked over herself, like varnish on a painting to disguise its flaws. She never for a minute thought that the girls blamed themselves too.

She whips her head towards the sound of footsteps on the gravel path. 'Who ... who's there?' Is it her imagination or has it got even darker out here?

The sound of someone clearing their throat reaches her, and then Marco appears from the shadows. 'Alice! I was worried for you. Are you okay?'

'Yeah, really, I'm fine.' She pulls her hair off her face. 'I'm sorry you had to hear all that.'

He shrugs. 'I'm not sure I completely followed it, but I don't like to see you upset.'

'You're so kind.'

Marco steps forward and she needs no further invitation, letting herself sink into him, feeling his strong arms wrap themselves around her. His lips are warm on hers and the voices in her head are silenced. Only this moment, being held, matters for now.

Desire leaps within her and she kisses him back, matching his ferocity with her own. She rakes his hair with her fingers then pulls him to her, desperate to be even closer. He fumbles with her skirt, his hand tracing a searing path along her thighs. She is consumed with want, with overwhelming need.

'Alice,' Marco whispers, and she reaches for him again as his lips leave hers. 'Alice, someone is calling for you.'

'What? No, don't stop!'

'Alice! We have to go back.'

She doesn't register it at first, but eventually the sounds, coming to her as if down a long tunnel, begin to make sense. It is Pete. Shouting her name, over and over.

'Forget him,' she says, grabbing Marco's hand and trying to keep him close, but the moment is shattered. He is already pulling away, dragging her back to the palazzo, giving her no time to straighten her dress, to refasten the buttons as she staggers behind him.

They sprint up the steps to the terrace, brushing past a glowering Delfina.

CHAPTER FORTY-FOUR

'Oh my God! Mia!' Alice cries, rushing to her daughter and catching her as Mia grabs at her throat and slumps forward in her seat. 'Look at her, she's bright red. Mia ... Mia ... *Mia Madeleine*!' Her daughter's eyes have rolled away, only the whites showing, her head tilted to one side, her mouth slack. 'What's wrong with her? Is it something she ate? She hasn't been drinking, has she?'

Mia's lips are puffy, as if they've been injected with way too much filler.

Isla shakes her head, her expression taut with worry. 'Just soda as far as I know.'

Mia's head hangs at an awkward angle, and despite the low light, Alice notices a bare patch on her daughter's scalp. She cradles Mia's head, tracing the baldness with her fingers. How has she missed this? What does it even mean? There's no time to think about it now. Fear rockets through her, adrenaline tingling at her fingers, as Mia's eyes roll forward and then disappear again. 'Mia! What is it?'

Mia can only make strangled, gurgling noises.

'Give her some air,' Pete says as he and Alice lay her gently on the terrace floor. Nick puts two fingers to her throat. 'Her pulse is weak, rapid.' He moves his hand to her forehead. 'She's burning up.'

Isla begins to cry. 'She was fine five minutes ago, honestly, you would have thought she was having the best time, then all of a sudden, she just stopped in the middle of what she was saying, like she blanked out. Where *were* you, Mum?'

'What is it?' Concern furrows Marco's forehead and Alice is instantly sickened that she was about to have sex with a practical stranger in the garden while her daughter was on the point of collapse.

'It might be something she ate.' Alice can't keep the accusatory tone from her voice.

'No, no, that can't be,' Marco replies, his eyes darkening. 'Everyone else is okay, yes?'

'Caro wasn't looking too well earlier.' Alice casts around, realising that half of the party is now missing. There's no sign of Caro or Jade or Vivi. When did they leave?

'I'm fine,' Pete reassures them. 'And I ate it all, even the mushrooms.'

'Mushrooms?' Alice asks. 'There were mushrooms?'

'Chanterelles,' Marco replies. 'But almost everyone had them, I am sure of it. Is your daughter allergic to anything?'

'Not that I know of,' Alice replies. 'But then I don't think she's ever eaten chanterelles before.'

Marco's jaw sets. 'Then we must make her vomit.'

'We what?' Alice asks. 'Don't you think we should call an ambulance instead? Can you call them? Now?'

'There's no time for that.' Marco bends down and rests Mia against one shoulder like he's about to lift a side of beef. 'The nearest ambulance station is down in the valley, more than half an hour away. If she has food poisoning and it is serious, then we need to act now.'

'Where are you taking her?'

'To the bathroom. Come.' He braces himself, straightening up and lifting Mia over one shoulder.

Alice follows him into the palazzo and towards the downstairs powder room, her heart thumping painfully in her chest. Isla is close behind, reaching for her, trying to say something, but Alice shakes her off. 'Please. Let me help your sister. I'll talk to you later.'

Isla falls back, and Alice is left to concentrate on Mia.

The three of them go into the bathroom and close the door.

'Is she going to be okay?' Isla calls from the hallway.

Alice doesn't have time to reply, listening carefully to Marco's instructions.

No one notices the tiny bee doing a last, waggling dance under Mia's plate.

* * *

Isla is sitting on the floor, head bowed, when Alice comes out of the bathroom followed by Marco carrying Mia in his arms. 'He's going to take her upstairs and get some ice to cool her down. We managed to get her to throw up, and her breathing's steadier, but she's still barely conscious.'

Alice places a hand on Isla's back. 'She's going to be okay, darling.' Then she remembers something. 'Isla, is Mia going bald?'

'What?'

'Going bald,' she repeats, though she's sure Isla heard her the first time. 'I noticed a bare patch on her scalp. Do you think that's got anything to do with her collapsing?'

Isla bites her lip. 'I think it's a stress thing. She can't help it.'

'Jesus, how did I not know this?'

'Mum?' Isla looks up, her eyes large and round in the dim light.

'What is it? I need to go to her – she's not out of the woods yet.'

'I don't think it was the mushrooms that made her sick.'

'You what?'

Isla swallows, and Alice has never seen her so scared. 'Luca gave her something, I think. Before dinner. He had a plastic bag; there were some pills in it, coloured, like lollies. And Mia started acting really strange later; she was being super-nice to me, hugging me and telling me how much she loves me. She, like, never does that.'

'You think he gave her something?'

'She was behaving pretty suss, so I asked her if she'd taken anything, what it was, but she just smiled at me and put her finger to my lips and then danced away from me.' Isla's eyes fill with tears. 'She'll kill me for telling you this.'

'I'm glad you have. How fucking dare he? She's fifteen, for chrissake,' she fumes. That boy is nothing but trouble. She should have listened to her instincts, told Vivi straight away what she'd overheard and had him marched off the premises there and then. 'He has no idea who he's just messed with.'

'Sixteen, Mum.'

'Whatever. You know what I mean. Too young to be taking drugs anyway. Where are the others?'

'I don't know. Auntie Vivi is on the phone in one of the living rooms, I think. I've got no clue about anyone else.'

Alice glances up at the stairs and then back out towards the terrace, coming to a decision. 'Can you go and help look after your sister? I'm going to try to call an ambulance.'

On the way out, Alice comes across Caroline, who has changed into that awful yellow silk robe and is swaying like a sapling in a light breeze. 'Is everything okay?' Caroline asks, ricocheting off one of the walls. 'It's still so hot, I thought I'd take a dip and try to cool down.'

Something ignites in Alice, the worry and fear of the last half hour, the shame that she wasn't there, all coalescing into a tight ball of fury. 'How the hell can you even think of swimming right now?'

'What do you mean? What's happened?'

'Mia's collapsed,' Alice seethes. 'It's all your fault. If you hadn't been involved with Luca – or Gabriele, as you seem to know him – he wouldn't even be here.'

'Hang on a minute, what on earth are you talking about? What's he got to do with Mia being ill?'

'Isla thinks he gave Mia drugs. And you said nothing to any of us when he turned up. *Nothing* about your relationship with him.'

'Oh my God, is she okay?' Caroline recoils. 'Drugs? Are you sure?' Her hands fly to her mouth and her face drains of all colour. 'What can I do?'

'Can you call an ambulance? My Italian isn't up to it.'

'Of course.' Caroline gets out her phone.

'Is this how he normally behaves?' Alice asks while they wait for the call to connect. 'Giving drugs to underage girls?'

Caroline shakes her head. 'How did you find out that we knew each other?'

'I heard you both arguing earlier today. He teaches at your language school,' she insists. 'And you are, or were, in a relationship with him?'

Caroline ignores the question. 'He was a *student* at the school. And I tried to get him to leave, but he wouldn't listen.'

'I find that hard to believe,' Alice says.

The call connects before Caroline has a chance to respond to Alice, and she begins to speak in rapid, urgent Italian.

'Are they coming?' Alice asks after Caroline hangs up.

Caroline shakes her head. 'There is a long delay – there's been a big accident on the autostrada.'

'What? How long?'

'They couldn't tell me but they said all of their vehicles were busy with that.'

'Jesus! This fucking country!'

'Not helpful.'

'Being unable to get an ambulance is what's not helpful.' Alice swallows. 'You know, I wouldn't have agreed to Mia spending time with him if you'd given me even the slightest heads-up about your history.'

'You would have refused your daughter? I'm not stupid – even I can see that you never say no to her. You can't bear the thought of upsetting her,' Caroline bites back. 'No wonder she's out of control.'

'How *dare* you question my parenting?' A red mist clouds Alice's vision and the words spill out of her mouth in a stream, fear making her vicious. 'You wouldn't know a thing about it. You're nothing more than a sad, barren old crone. You'll never understand how hard it is to be a mother, how little control you really have.' All her earlier resolve to be kinder to Caroline vanishes in the face of her concern for Mia.

Caroline doesn't back down. 'I've been a teacher for fifteen years. I've disciplined hundreds of young people. Don't you dare tell me I don't know what I'm talking about. When it comes to teenage supervision, I know exactly what I'm doing. You, on the other hand …'

Alice takes a step towards her, arm raised as if about to strike, when Vivi appears and intercepts her, grabbing Alice's wrist and pulling her away. 'You two squabbling will not solve anything. Let's all calm down a second, shall we? I only just heard what's happened. How is Mia?'

Caroline pushes past them both, wrapping her robe tightly around herself. Her feet slap the floor, the sound echoing along the hallway, and her shoulders shake as if she is holding in a sob. As she reaches the path that leads to the pool, she breaks into a halting run.

'I know you're upset, but she's not to blame,' Vivi says, turning to Alice.

'You didn't hear what Isla said. She thinks Luca gave Mia

pills, some sort of party drug. That's why she was behaving strangely and why she passed out.'

'It's still a stretch to blame Caroline, don't you think? Listen, I'm sorry I wasn't here earlier; I had to take a call.'

'That was more important than this?' Alice glares at her. 'Besides, it *is* partly Caroline's fault. She knows Luca – or rather Gabriele, which is I gather is his real name. She used to be in a relationship with him, if you can call a teacher taking advantage of a student a *relationship*. It's sick if you ask me.'

'Wait, what? He was her student?'

'Uh-huh.'

'I don't understand; I thought he was Mia's friend's cousin.'

'Just wait until I catch up with him.'

'Oh Jesus.' Vivi rolls her eyes. 'Okay, let's focus on what's important. How is Mia doing?' Vivi places a hand on Alice's arm. 'Who's with her at the moment?'

'Isla's upstairs keeping an eye on her and she's stable, for now. Marco got her to vomit, so hopefully that's helped. But I think we should take her to the hospital now we know about the drugs. Apparently, there's no chance of getting an ambulance, Caroline tried.'

'So where is he? Luca or Gabriele or whatever the hell his name is? We need to find out exactly what he gave Mia. Poor darling girl. I'll never forgive myself if she's seriously ill.'

'Isla said it was a pill, so maybe molly? She's in danger of overheating if she's had too much. Or maybe it's laced with something? And what if she's been drinking too? Isla swears blind that they weren't, but I wouldn't be surprised if Mia snuck some anyway. If there's any lasting damage …' Alice can't complete the sentence, her voice rising to a hysterical pitch.

Marco reappears with a set of car keys in his hand. 'I can take you. To see a doctor in the valley.'

'I think we should go straight to a hospital,' Alice says.

'The doctor will be closer,' Marco replies. 'The nearest hospital is in Turin.'

'Okay.' Alice checks with Vivi. 'Will you come too?'

'Of course.'

Marco goes upstairs again to fetch Mia, and when they return, Alice tells Isla what's happening.

'But I want to come too,' she says, new tears springing into her eyes.

'Darling, there's not going to be room for us all in the car. But I promise I'll call as soon as she's been seen and we know more.' She gives Isla a quick, fierce hug, grabs her handbag and hurries towards the car.

CHAPTER FORTY-FIVE

At a loss for what to do after the others have left, Pete decides to head upstairs. Everyone else has vanished, the evening soured. 'I think we should prepare to leave first thing in the morning,' he tells Nick, staggering slightly. He can feel his head beginning to pound. 'We'll take the autostrada to Milan, see if we can move our hotel booking forward by a couple of days.' Nick, to his credit, doesn't object.

Perhaps he can salvage something from his contract with J&K. He's betting that they might be prepared to meet with him sooner if he can promise a first-hand update on the founder of the company they are so interested in. He needs the money too much to let it go now, and the job offer Vivi dangled in front of him is looking less and less likely to eventuate.

'*Fermati! Subito!*'

'What?' He turns around to see the old woman – Stella – coming towards them from the palazzo.

'Jesus Christ!' Nick grabs his wrist. 'She's got a gun.'

'Come on, don't be ridiculous.' Pete strains to see in the dim light, but all he can make out is that she's raised her arm towards them. 'She has not.'

'Er, I think she has.'

Pete takes a step towards her, holding up his hands even though he can't believe the old woman would dare threaten them. 'Stella. Stella. It's us. Your guests.'

With a low growl, she spews a torrent of rapid Italian that neither of them can follow. However, the gist of it is all too clear. She waves what he is now sure is a gun at them, directing them around the side of the palazzo.

'Do something,' he hisses at Nick.

'Dude, she's got a fucking weapon.'

He can't even risk calling out. There's no telling if the gun is loaded, and Pete knows of too many shootings in the US not to take the situation seriously. Nor can he risk trying to overpower her. He catches Nick's eye again and they stare, panicked, at each other. He can't believe what's happening.

She forces them down a set of stone stairs at the back of the palazzo and through an olive grove until they reach a ramshackle old farm building. There's a moment of confusion as they try to work out what she's asking them to do, but she demonstrates, the gun waving wildly, and they stand facing the wall, spreading their hands above them on the stone.

Pete steals a glance as she fumbles with a large iron key, unlocking a door he hadn't noticed until then.

There's a light of madness in her eyes. '*Traditore!*'

It's not the first time she's called them this, and he wonders briefly if this is some kind of bizarre ritual. 'What is she saying?' he asks Nick in a whisper, but she hears him and repeats the word again, pressing the barrel of the pistol between his shoulder blades now.

Nick begs her to stop, but she is unmoved by their distress. She kicks open the door and nudges them inside. It's dark and dank and stinks of cow shit. Pete gags at the smell, stumbling as his shins graze a metal trough. 'Fuck!'

She barks at him in Italian and he gathers she is telling him to shut up.

Before he even has time to catch his breath, she slams the door behind them, plunging them into total darkness.

CHAPTER FORTY-SIX

The doctor, who comes to the door in his dressing gown, seems unsurprised to be woken up, and when Marco explains the situation, he agrees to examine Mia.

She is awake now, but groggy. 'She's complaining about not being able to breathe,' Alice says.

He flicks a penlight in both of Mia's eyes, takes her pulse and blood pressure, and presses a wooden stick on her tongue to examine her throat. He then raises both arms and checks the lymph glands at her neck and armpits, muttering to himself when he sees the bare patches on her scalp. 'This is part of the problem,' he says eventually, pointing to a swelling on the tender inner skin of Mia's arm. 'An insect bite. Maybe a bee sting. Has she ever had a bad reaction?'

Alice shakes her head. 'Not that I know of. But, look, her lips are so puffy. Do you think that's what it is?'

He shrugs then unlocks a small cupboard and pulls out a hypodermic needle and a vial of clear liquid. 'If she was worse, I'd recommend epinephrine. Antihistamines should help. I wouldn't advise anything else, considering what she may have already taken.'

He plunges the needle into Mia's arm and then studies her carefully. 'She may be out of sorts for a day or two, but she will likely recover with no ill effects. The important thing is to keep an eye on her temperature and not let her overheat.

If it does spike again, you must take her immediately to hospital.'

'Oh, thank God.' Alice squeezes Vivi's hand. 'Thank you. And thank you too, Marco.' She practically accused him of poisoning her daughter and is now overcome with a wave of shame. 'And I'm so sorry … about earlier.' The apology is lame, but it's all she can manage.

'You are a mother concerned for her daughter,' he says, tension clipping his voice. 'I do not blame you.'

Alice has always thought the secret to parenting teenage girls is to give them plenty of rope and not call them out on the unimportant stuff. That way, everyone is happy, and not a single door is slammed. She has assumed the girls are unaffected by their parents' break-up, and of course they're doing brilliantly in school. They have polite friends and no tattoos and only the most socially acceptable piercings. Now she kicks herself for not being more observant, for not keeping them on a tighter rein.

'I'm glad we got her checked out,' says Vivi. 'I would never have forgiven myself if anything terrible happened. Thank you so much, Doctor, Marco.'

As they are about to leave, there is a discussion between the doctor and Marco that Alice can't follow, although it seems to be something about payment. Before she has a chance to ask, Marco has unhesitatingly pulled a handful of notes from his wallet.

Alice is mortified not to have any cash on her.

'We will pay you back,' Vivi assures him.

'Of course,' Alice promises.

'Let's just get her home,' he replies. 'I am glad she will be okay.'

* * *

It's nearly two in the morning when they make it back from the village. Everyone else appears to have gone to bed, so Alice and Vivi help Mia, who is now able to walk, upstairs. Vivi reassures Alice that Mia will be fine and that she's not a neglectful mother. 'Teenagers do this stuff, even if you're the most observant parent in the world.'

Isla wakes when they get to the girls' rooms, and once Mia is settled, she insists that she will stay and keep an eye on her. 'Honestly, Mum, get some rest. You can't stay up all night. I'll be right here, and I'll call you if I need you.'

'If you're sure. I'll be just down the corridor.' Alice agrees to go and lie down for a while. 'I've set my alarm for every two hours, so I'll be back at about four,' she says, kissing Isla and Mia on the forehead before leaving.

They stop outside Vivi's room. 'Can I come in and lie next to you for a bit?' Alice asks. 'I don't think I want to be alone right now.'

'Of course. But she's going to be fine, you know.'

'I know, but it's shaken me up. They're the most precious things in the world to me.'

They lie side by side on Vivi's bed and for a while neither of them speaks.

Alice squeezes her hand. 'Tell me what happened … you know, after …'

'After I got the medication?' Vivi swallows, her words coming fast and low, a monotone stripped of emotion. 'Will was going to do it himself, he promised he would, but in the end, he couldn't get the glass to his mouth without spilling it all down the front of his pyjamas, so I had to do it.'

Alice gathers Vivi to her, wrapping her tightly in her arms and rocking her like she used to do to her daughters when they were younger. 'Oh, Vee, you poor, poor thing.'

'I killed him, Alice.' Vivi's voice is a wail.

'No, you helped to end his suffering,' she says firmly. 'I can't imagine what you've been through.' Alice cradles Vivi's head. 'It's incredibly brave. You did the right thing; anyone would say that you did.'

'It wasn't brave; all I felt was relief when it was over. What kind of monster does that make me?'

'You know that in Australia, Canada, lots of other places too probably, assisted dying is perfectly legal.'

'Well, it's not in England. I could go to jail.'

'Don't beat yourself up. You *did* do the right thing. I know it sounds simple, but you have to make peace with it. Dignity in dying, isn't that a better way to look at it? Compassionate end-of-life care.'

'I thought at first one of the nurses who came to look after Will had somehow worked it out, that they could tell just by looking at me. But they were so kind to him, and they are good people, I am sure of it. They would never … and Jade's the only person other than Will and me who knew anything. She worked from the house those last few weeks. She signed for the delivery from the courier before I even realised it had arrived. I found the opened package on my desk along with the rest of the post. She must have worked out what it was. Later that day she stayed much later than usual, and I remember her asking me if I was sure I was doing the right thing. I brushed it off, pretended she was referring to me not taking any time off from work.'

'So you think she's the one trying to blackmail you? What a bloody nerve that girl has!' Alice is indignant. 'Are you sure?'

Vivi nods. 'You heard her at dinner, daring me.'

'So that's what all that was about.' Alice is thoughtful. 'Jesus, Vee. What are you going to do? If this reaches the media …'

'I know. But there's more. I was on the phone to my CFO when Mia collapsed. He told me he's been investigating some accounting anomalies, irregular payments going back three years. Invoices to a couple of companies that it turns out don't exist. All vouched for by Jade and signed off on by Will. Robert says there's nearly a hundred grand missing. Not something that can be easily overlooked.' She clenches and unclenches her fists, and Alice wonders if she's trying to release the tension inside her or getting ready to punch someone. 'I always wondered how she could afford the expensive clothes she wears. Whenever I commented on it, she made a point of telling me what a bargain she got, that she shops on second-hand designer clothes-swap and clothes-hire sites. Robert is going to speak to Jade as soon as we get back. He's got the Fraud Squad on standby. He thinks Will must have known about Jade but, judging by a note he found in one of the files, was trying to sort it out without anyone else finding out – even Robert. He was fond of her,' she says, sighing, 'in a kind of avuncular way, although now I don't know what to think. Anyway, apparently he wanted to give her a chance to make it right, and he knew I wouldn't have stood for it had I been aware what she was up to.'

'She was telling me about the apartment she just bought. In Hackney, or Highbury or somewhere.' There's a catch in Alice's voice. 'She said her parents helped her out. Oh God, Vivi, she's really been stealing from you, and now she's blackmailing you as well?'

'It's the only obvious answer.'

CHAPTER FORTY-SEVEN

Caroline chews on her lip, drawing blood but barely noticing. There's no way Gabriele would be anywhere near here if it wasn't for her. Why hadn't she spoken up when she first saw him, told him to leave immediately? She could have – should have – prevented this from happening.

He disappeared during the kerfuffle over Mia, slipping away at the first sign of trouble. She's scoured the palazzo but been unable to find him, although his car is still in the drive.

Since then, she's been sitting on the terrace, filching cigarettes from the packet that Marco left behind, sending Gabriele message after message, but he hasn't replied. She doesn't know what to do next.

She's still there when Vivi, Alice and Marco return, and she eavesdrops on their conversation, relief flooding through her when she sees Mia on her feet. She steps away as they approach the terrace, unable to face them, hurrying into the shadows and along the path that circles the palazzo.

She slows as she reaches the pool. Lights at the waterline beckon, and she is so hot. Sweat pools under her breasts and armpits, beads on her forehead and dampens her lip.

The water ripples gently, cool and enticing.

Deciding that a quick dip is what she needs, she shucks off her sandals, loosens the belt of her robe and lets it slither to the paving with a soft hiss. She lowers herself into the pool, inhaling sharply as the cool water reaches her waist, oblivious to the person standing a short distance away, concealed behind a cypress tree, watching her every move.

CHAPTER FORTY-EIGHT

Vivi lies next to her sister, recent events swirling in her mind. She's too wired to sleep, though Alice has been gently snoring for some time now.

Air. Fresh air. That might help. She needs to calm her brain, to walk off the adrenaline that's still fizzing her synapses. She eases herself off the mattress. 'Sorry,' she whispers, as Alice stirs at the movement.

She threads a pair of sandals through her fingers and creeps down the stairs, shoving her feet into them when she reaches the door. With no idea where she's going, she first circles the kitchen garden and the olive grove then finds herself drawn towards the pool, which flickers tantalisingly blue thanks to the glow of underwater lighting.

She's halfway along the path when she sees Caroline, her yellow robe fluttering in the faint breeze as she stands at the water's edge. Why is she still up? She vaguely remembers Caro talking about a late-night dip, and sure enough, as she watches, Caroline shucks off the robe, bends down and slides into the water.

'Mind if I join you?' Vivi asks when she reaches the edge of the pool. 'I can't sleep either.'

'Yeah, it's too damn hot,' Caroline replies, slicking water from her hair. 'I'm sorry. About earlier. About Gabriele – Luca – and Mia. I should have spoken up.'

'You should have told him to leave or told me about it.'

'I can explain …'

'Don't. It's too late for that. And you know what? About Will? I always suspected you had a thing for him, and on some level I've always been aware that you're jealous of me. But I didn't think you'd go as far as that. More fool me, huh?' She holds up a hand as Caroline goes to try to explain again. 'Were there other times?'

Caroline shakes her head. 'He loved you, Vivi. I was just a convenience, a way to soothe his ego when you were shining so much brighter. But did it ever occur to you that he sometimes wanted to be the important one?'

Vivi glares at her. 'So I was supposed to play smaller just to salve his ego?'

'That's not what I meant. Just that he must have found it hard playing second fiddle to you.'

'Now you're putting words into a dead man's mouth. Seriously, Caro.' Vivi puffs air from her cheeks, exasperated. 'I've never heard anything so ridiculous.'

'We talked. Not often, not in the early years at least, but later …'

Vivi is stunned. 'I had no idea.' It feels like another betrayal.

'So why did you kill him?' Caroline asks the question so quietly that at first Vivi isn't certain she's heard her correctly.

'I'm sorry, what?'

'Are you? Sorry that you were the one who ended your husband's life? Do you think you're God or something?' Caroline laughs bitterly. 'I know you think pretty highly of yourself, but honestly …'

'What …' Vivi grinds out, scarcely able to believe what she's hearing, 'do you know about that? Did Jade tell you?'

'She's the soul of discretion, that assistant of yours. She worships the ground you tread on, but you're too caught up in yourself to even notice.' Caroline hauls herself out of the water and reaches for a towel, forcing Vivi to take a step backwards. 'I think she even wants to *be* you when she grows up.'

'Who told you? About Will?' Vivi wants to shake her.

'You never knew, did you?' A flare of satisfaction lights up her eyes for a second. 'He called me. After his diagnosis, when it was clear it was serious. Every morning when you went out for a walk or were in a meeting, he called me. Sometimes he rambled, but most of the time he was clear. He told me he was afraid. That he wasn't ready to leave, that it was all over far too quickly, that he wished he had been given more time.'

'I don't believe a word of it.'

'Why would I bother to lie about this now?' Caroline shrugs. 'He said it was a strain trying to be strong for you. That he was doing his best to keep on fighting, but that all you spoke about was making him comfortable, wanting to take away his pain. That you kept talking about euthanasia.'

'Strong for me?' Vivi can't believe what she's hearing. 'He begged me. *Begged* me, Caro. *Desperate measures,* he insisted. *I can't go on. You have to help me.* Those were his first words every morning. He said no one would dare let a dog suffer like he was.'

'You killed him, Vivi.'

'He begged me for a way out.' She sets her chin. 'And I'd do it again if I had to.'

'But he had a chance,' Caroline insists. 'And you took that away from him. He didn't want that. He told me what you were planning.'

'He wanted it, I promise you. He was in agony. And despair. I was *there*, Caroline, and though you were apparently at the other end of a phone, that doesn't mean you had any idea what was really going on.'

'But that's not what he told me.'

'He wasn't in his right mind, Caro, not at the end. He was manic, incoherent, imagining all kinds of things …'

Caroline blunders on, as if she hasn't even heard what Vivi is trying to tell her. 'Then one morning he didn't call. I heard the news later that day from a mutual friend. I couldn't believe it. I couldn't believe you'd actually done it.'

Suddenly everything makes sense. 'So it's *you*? *You're* the one behind this? The threats, the vile messages, the awful flowers … And who the fuck is Gary Birdwhistle? Is he in on this too?'

Caro shakes her head, a bitter expression playing about her lips. 'Smoke and mirrors. I cloned his email. It's not hard if you know how.'

'But why? *Why*, Caro? I thought we were friends.'

'We were never friends, Vee. You felt guilty – guilty that I took the fall for Eliza Benson all those years ago. You wanted to make sure I never spilled the real story, so you stayed friends long after you'd outgrown me. And then you just felt sorry for me, guilty perhaps that you had so much when I had so little. Or perhaps you told yourself that by being my friend you were being kind, even though nothing could ever make up for what you'd done.'

'I've never seen it that way. You were the one who insisted there was no point in both of us being punished, that you should be the one to take the blame. You said it was better if I stayed quiet. After all, you'd been in on it too.'

Caroline's eyes widen. 'That's some kind of revisionist memory you've got: I never said such a thing.'

'But you did.'

'Everything you've touched has turned to gold. You've always had all I ever wanted – money, success, the man I loved.' Caroline glares at her. 'And what do I have? Not even a job anymore, as it turns out.'

'Hardly my fault.' Vivi had offered Caro a job once, several years ago, against her better judgement, but at Will's urging. He thought she would make a good copywriter. But the expression on Caro's face when Vivi suggested it was one of such abject dismay and horror that she never brought it up again. She had tried, in various ways over the years, to make up for what she'd done, but it had never been enough. She sees now that it was never going to be enough.

'You've always protected your reputation at any cost – after all, that's exactly what you did when it came to Eliza, wasn't it? It's what you've always done. It's your Achilles heel, the one flaw in your otherwise perfect existence.'

Vivi stares at her. 'I'm sorry.' She holds her hands wide. 'What more do you want from me?'

Caroline shrugs. 'I wanted to see you suffer, to have your reputation destroyed, to know what it's like to lose everything.'

'And you think two wrongs make a right?' Vivi laughs bitterly. 'Come on, Caro. Will that really solve things? And so what if I obtained the medication? That doesn't mean I administered it.'

Caroline narrows her eyes. 'Will told me you were trying to kill him.'

'He was a very ill, very confused man by the end. You really think you knew him better than me?' Vivi has had enough. She wants to smack the self-righteous expression from Caro's face. 'Anyway, that doesn't matter: you have no way of proving any of it.'

Caroline regards her slyly and Vivi wonders what she's hiding, feels a shiver of disquiet.

'I could easily have recorded those phone calls, you know.'

But Vivi isn't fooled – Caroline is lying, she is sure of it. There's an uncertain note in her voice, as though she's trying too hard to be convincing. 'I'm afraid that I simply don't believe you,' she says, icy calm now. 'I'm sorry we see things so differently, but I can assure you that Will was out of his mind, barely lucid, by the end. So you can go fuck yourself and your pathetic blackmail attempt.' She's betting that Caroline will never follow through on her threat to go to the media; she's not brave enough for that. Besides, Vivi already has a plan to get ahead of the story, to control the narrative, no matter the personal consequences. 'I never give in to bullies.' Vivi turns to face this woman she has tried so hard and for so long to atone to. 'Under the circumstances, I think it would be better if you were gone by the morning.'

Vivi leaves then, walking back along the path to the palazzo, her feet leaden, an ache like a stone in her chest. To have finally discovered the truth behind the ugly threats is a relief, but to have been betrayed by someone close is devastating.

What Caroline doesn't know is that Vivi would have given the money to her, even if not the entire fifty grand, certainly as much as she could spare.

Then it occurs to her.

Jade.

It in no way excuses the theft, but Vivi's accused the girl of blackmail. In error, as it turns out. No wonder Jade said what she did after dinner. Vivi must have pushed her to breaking point.

CHAPTER FORTY-NINE

'Fuuuuck!' Pete slams his hand against the door, barely registering the pain in his now-bruised palm. The air is stale and feral, like rodents have long made their home in this old barn or storeroom or whatever it is.

They've been yelling and shouting so long they're now hoarse, but no one has heard them, no one has come. Pete slumps, sinking to his knees and then slumping on the floor, past caring if he ruins his pants.

'Let's just calm down,' Nick says. 'How about we take a minute and try to figure this out?'

'When we get out of here, I'm going to sue the arse off that dickhead Marco. His food may be brilliant, but how the hell he thinks he can run a hotel with that old woman as a liability I don't know. When I'm finished with him, he'll never run another place again.'

'Hold up, man,' Nick says. 'Cut him a break. If my grandma was losing her marbles, I'd want people to be kind to her.'

'I'd say it's gone beyond that, wouldn't you?'

'Maybe. But let's focus on the best way to get out of here rather than thinking about bringing down the wrath of the law right now.'

Pete pauses, taken aback by how reasonable Nick is being. He hasn't seen this side of him before.

'Look, if worse comes to worst, Vivi will realise we're missing by breakfast and send out a search party. They'll find us in no time – there are only so many abandoned farm buildings on the property, right?'

'I'm pretty sure I'm going to need to take a piss well before then.'

'It is what it is. Just go to the far corner.'

'I'll need to feel my way over there.'

'Follow the wall,' Nick says patiently.

When Pete returns, having relieved himself onto a pile of already foul-smelling straw, Nick places a hand on his shoulder. 'Okay?'

'Better.'

'So why don't you tell me what's been biting your ass ever since we played tennis? Make that since we got here. You haven't been yourself for days.'

Pete sighs. 'I'm not sure where to start.'

'Try the beginning.'

'Okay, smartarse.' But there's something about the dark that feels confessional. 'My meeting in Milan next week?'

'Yeah.'

'It's with a company that wants to acquire Vivid.'

'Vivi's business?'

'Uh-huh. They contacted me a couple of months ago and asked me to prepare a report, an analysis of the business. I submitted it before I even knew Vivi wanted us to come here and stay with her. They are aware that I once worked at Vivid, but they don't know anything about my personal relationship with Vivi.'

'And I'm guessing she has no clue about this?'

'She wouldn't have offered me a job if she did.'

'You have to tell her. She's your friend, for godssake.' Nick lets go of his hand. 'You should have told her as soon as you got here.'

'I know.' Pete hangs his head. 'I stupidly thought I could keep the two things separate. And now it appears that the takeover bid's happening far sooner than expected.' He will only receive a final payment for the job after the meeting, and Nick doesn't know that he can't afford to jeopardise that.

'You still should tell her about your part in it; it's the right thing to do.'

'Ah, Nick, the voice of my conscience.' Pete makes a half-hearted joke and Nick takes his hand again, squeezing it. 'I was planning to, I promise, just as soon as the meeting was over.' He sighs. 'It all seemed okay when we were in Boston, but here, having to look Vivi in the eye, I feel like the biggest shit there is ...'

Pete wishes Nick would deny this, rush to make excuses for him, but he is silent.

Eventually, he speaks. 'Somehow, I'm not convinced that's all there is. Am I right?'

Pete hesitates.

'Out with it. There's no sense in us having secrets from each other.'

'I saw the text from Riccardo,' Pete says quietly.

'Ah.'

'Yes. Ah.'

'You, Peter Hatchett, are my husband. We made promises to each other, remember? Promises I fully intend to keep. Riccardo is a yoga teacher, that's all.'

'But I saw a text,' Pete confesses. 'I wasn't meaning to snoop, but you left your phone on the table and the message came up. He suggested a "*private*".'

'And here we are ...' Nick begins to laugh. 'Oh, my sweet Pete. A *private yoga lesson*. Nothing else, I swear.' He laughs again, the sound bouncing around the empty barn. 'Perhaps I was flirting. A little. But I *never* would have acted on it.'

'Oh.'

'Now I want you to tell me something.' Nick is serious. 'Why is it that you think you don't deserve to become a parent? And don't brush me off this time, okay? I won't let it go until you tell me what's behind that statement.'

There's no point in keeping the secret from him any longer. If Nick leaves him because of it, so be it. Pete takes a deep breath. 'Twenty-two years ago last May, I was driving to work in the rain past a junior school in North London. I'd been entertaining clients the night before and we ended up at this club in Mayfair until nearly two, so I was hungover and tired. I looked down at some paperwork on the passenger seat. Just for a second.' He swallows, reliving the memory. 'A second, I swear. I didn't see the little boy run out. He was only four years old. Too young to understand the dangers of traffic. I was drug and alcohol tested and was cleared, but I never told anyone the real story.' He stifles a sob. 'I killed a boy, Nick. A little boy. His family lost a son, a brother … I can never forgive myself for that.'

'Jesus. That's a lot to carry,' Nick says after a long pause. 'But it was an accident – it's not like you deliberately ran down a kid.'

Pete rests his head on Nick's shoulder and closes his eyes. It's a huge relief to have finally told him.

Exhausted now, they doze fitfully, Nick's arm around Pete, huddled against each other for comfort.

Some time later, they wake to an ear-splitting scream that tears through the silence.

CHAPTER FIFTY

As Caroline gets out of the pool and begins to dry off, she sees a flicker of movement at the other end near one of the cabanas. It's probably just the wind rustling the canvas curtains, but wanting to be certain, she walks towards it.

It's only when her nose is practically pressing up against the fabric that she sees the outline of a person.

'Jesus!' She rears backwards, nearly stumbling over a towel, then peers blindly into the shadows. 'Who's there?'

A hand pulls back the curtain and Caroline feels a zap of recognition. Despite the gloom, she'd know that profile, the curly hair, the slim boyish body, anywhere. 'I can't believe you're still here.' She is standing over Gabriele now, not caring that she's dripping water onto his trousers. 'After what you've done.'

'I had some wine …' he says, sheepish now. 'I couldn't drive. I fell asleep.'

Caroline wraps the towel more tightly around herself, feeling suddenly exposed, even though she's been naked with him plenty of times. She gulps down a breath. 'And the rest … You are a guest at a special birthday dinner, one you had no business attending in the first place, and you bring drugs, and give them to an underage girl. Are you a complete fucking idiot?'

Her argument with Vivi has fuelled her temper and she's so angry now, she could almost pick him up by the collar and throw him headfirst into the pool. Anything to wipe that dumb expression off his face. 'What exactly did you give Mia? Do you have any idea how serious this could be? You could have killed her.' The memory of her uni year comes racing back. She knows exactly how wrong things can go.

He does at least now appear slightly contrite. 'Nothing. Nothing bad. Mia asked for one. I didn't force her to take it.'

'What. Was. It?' Caroline uses her strictest teacher voice, the one that forces even the most difficult students to listen to her.

'A happy pill. E. I had one too, and, look, I'm fine.' He spreads his hands wide, gives her a nervous grin.

'Yes, well, Mia clearly wasn't. Was she drinking as well?'

He shrugs. 'Maybe a little. I don't know.' He is like a sulky little boy again, and Caroline wonders how on earth she could ever have found him so attractive.

'She'll be okay, right?' he asks, the seriousness of the situation finally appearing to dawn on him.

'She's resting now, but do you know how much trouble you will be in if anything happens to her? Her mother is out for your scalp. If you've any sense at all you'll get the hell out of here right now. You've completely outstayed your welcome.'

'Caro …' He is on his feet now, places a hand on her arm, his fingers tight around her wrist. 'I came to see you, to talk to you. That's all I've been trying to do … but you won't see me.'

Gabriele is a lot stronger and taller than her. They're out of earshot of the palazzo, which at this moment feels too far away.

Caroline shivers in her damp swimsuit, suddenly chilled.

'Why can't you understand how I feel about you?' He leans towards her, attempting to land a kiss, but she backs away from him, just out of reach, scared and disgusted at the same time. The drugs and alcohol have made him sloppily affectionate and it turns her stomach.

She shakes her arm, trying to free herself from his grip, but his hold on her is too tight. 'It's over, Gabriele. *Finito*. I don't know what else I can say to make you understand that.'

He finally releases her wrist and she rubs where he's bruised it, hoping that will be the worst of it. But there's a glazed, intoxicated look in his eyes, and before she has the chance to back off, his hands are pressed around her neck so tightly that she can feel her windpipe begin to close over.

Panicking, she brings her hands up to his and claws at them. She kicks out, connecting with a shin, and his fingers loosen for a fraction of a second but then grip her even tighter. She hears a clunk of something falling to the ground, a solid sound, but can't make sense of it, is too terrified. She can't breathe. Her ears are buzzing and she chokes and splutters as she tries to loosen his grip on her neck. Tears spring from her eyes and starbursts form at the edges of her vision.

Everything around her fades to black.

Then, abruptly, he releases her, and she is so shocked that all she can do is gulp down air, her entire body shaking. She falls to her knees with the shock of it all. 'You fucking strangled me,' she gasps when she's finally able to talk. 'What part of you thinks that is okay?' Any remaining shreds of fear have hardened to white-hot rage, and she gives no thought for her own safety. The prudent thing to do right now would be to run to the palazzo as fast as she can, but instead she stands her ground, aware that she's close to the edge of the pool now. 'You can't do this to me, not *ever*, not to anyone, do you hear me? Do. You. Hear. Me?'

He looks away, mumbles something, and she is shocked to see tears glitter on his cheeks.

'I can't …' he says thickly. 'I can't let you go. I've tried, but I just can't. Besides, we can be together now, why can't you see that?'

'I lost my job over this, Gabriele.' She swallows and it feels like razorblades have lodged in her throat. 'I have no idea when or how I will get another one. Do you understand how serious that is for me?'

'That doesn't matter. I have a job now.' He brightens, pride restored for a moment. 'I start in two weeks. At the butcher on the via Giuseppi Garibaldi.'

He reaches for her arms but she yanks them away, putting them behind her back in case he tries to grab her again.

'Congratulations,' she says wearily, her rage fading now, hoping that if she attempts to placate him he might be more willing to leave. 'That's good news.' She tries again, more gently this time. 'But it is over, you have to accept that. I've been trying to tell you for weeks, but you just don't seem to hear me.'

His mouth twists. 'I'm in love with you, Caro.' He says her name like a caress.

'Love?' she says bitterly. 'This is not love. Love is not sending me vile messages; it is not standing outside my apartment building for hours on end so that I'm too frightened to leave. Love,' she says, swallowing, 'is not attempting to strangle me because you don't want to hear what I'm saying.'

Gabriele looks like he wants to smash something. His hands clench into fists, although they remain by his sides. Caroline backs away, out of his reach. She's said too much, gone too far, though the message seems to finally sink in. 'This … this is not a good idea anymore; it's not good for either of us.' She wants to tell him that if he doesn't stop, she will go to the police, that she doesn't care what they think of her, but if she says these things, who knows what he will do. 'Please?' she begs instead, desperate now. 'It will all be okay, I promise, but you must go.' She wants to scream at him, to punch him, to claw at his smug face, to hurt him as much as he has hurt her, but she risks her own safety if she does so. She should have left as soon as she had the chance.

He sneers, his protestations made only seconds earlier transformed into dangerous contempt. 'You know what? You aren't as great as you think you are.' He spits on the ground, a glob of saliva landing on her bare toes. '*Puttana.*'

There's a movement from the low building at the other end of the pool, a window opening or a door shutting, and Gabriele turns towards it, distracted for a second.

Caroline seizes this second chance, sprinting for the path. He grabs at her, but his fingers only graze her shoulder. With the advantage of surprise, she takes off towards the palazzo.

She has no idea if he follows her or not, for all she can hear is her feet slapping the gravel and her blood thundering in her ears.

CHAPTER FIFTY-ONE

After leaving Caroline, Vivi walks another lap of the grounds, attempting to make sense of the night's events. Discovering that someone she considered a friend is behind the blackmail threats has upended everything.

She reaches the pool area again, hearing low, agitated voices. Keeping to the grass so as not to be seen, she rounds a corner. Caroline is at the pool's edge. She has her back to Vivi, is wearing her yellow robe again, her long hair caught up in a messy topknot.

Then Vivi sees the Italian boy standing behind her.

There's something about the scene that sends a prickle of apprehension down her spine, and for a moment she thinks about stepping in, ordering him off the premises, but then decides against getting involved. Caroline can look after herself, she's proven that. Besides, Vivi's had more than enough of her for one night.

She turns and heads towards the palazzo, not bothering to stop even when she hears a yell and a splash. Let them be – she wants no part of it anymore.

They are welcome to each other.

CHAPTER FIFTY-TWO

After making sure Mia is settled, Marco decides there's not much point in going to bed. Besides, he didn't finish the clean-up after dinner, and his training will not let him sleep when there's a dirty workspace. He goes to the kitchen and brews an espresso, revelling in the quiet of a house at peace once again. These guests are due to leave in a day's time and he'll be glad to see the back of them. They've not been the worst group this summer, but he could do without the drama of silly teenage girls and late-night dashes for medical help. It is lucky that Delfina's father is a retired doctor and was prepared to see them in the middle of the night.

He puts on his headphones, turns up the volume and, after the last of the innumerable pots, pans and dishes are scoured, dried and put away, he goes to the cupboard, getting out flour and sugar, then butter from the fridge. Selecting a paring knife and testing its sharpness, he begins to cut apples into wafer-thin slices. He'll make apple and cinnamon pastries for breakfast.

He's ferrying a large baking sheet to the oven when the kitchen door swings open and Stella slips in, a dark shadow at first, then emerging into the light.

'*Nonna!*' He drops the tray in surprise, and it falls onto the stovetop with a clatter. Pulling his headphones aside, he asks her why she is up so late – or is it early? It's not the first time he's seen her up and about at an hour when most people would be sleeping, but still, it must be past three in the morning, possibly closer to four.

She points to the espresso machine, but as she does so, he sees what she's holding with her other hand, partially hidden in the folds of her skirt.

'Nonna!' He is exasperated now. 'I have warned you. You cannot carry these things around like that. You will get us all into trouble.' It's another of the old pistols from the cellar; he's confiscated four so far. He thought he had placed them beyond her reach.

She mutters the word '*traditori*' over and over.

'There are no traitors here. That was a long time ago. There is no war, Nonna. Please. Give it to me.' He holds out a hand.

He's told her over and over that she's perfectly safe at the palazzo, even with so many strangers around, but she either doesn't believe him or is infernally stubborn. Probably both. He can't ride her too hard about it; she's witnessed atrocities far beyond his comprehension. Her older sister was murdered by a Nazi officer in the grounds of the palazzo; he can only imagine how such an event would affect the mind of a young girl. He must find a way to dispose of the remaining arsenal in the cellar.

She offers the pistol to him with a shaking hand. He double-checks it is not loaded then puts it on a high shelf in the walk-in pantry. 'Sit. Let me make you a coffee.'

CHAPTER FIFTY-THREE

Vivi wakes from a dream. She and Will were sitting by a river, dangling their feet in the fast-flowing water. When she opens her eyes, the feeling of peace, of him being so close that she can reach out and touch him, is for a moment supremely comforting.

Alice was no longer on her bed when Vivi returned from her walk, and she hadn't bothered to draw the curtains. The windows are flung open in the hope of catching a breeze.

It's only just light outside now, and as the previous night's events come back to her, Vivi bemoans the fact that she is awake so early. Surely she could have slept in at the very least?

Something has disturbed her, and as a thin, high scream reaches her ears, she jolts against the pillow, eyes wide. That was the sound that woke her.

Is it a bird or an injured animal?

Fully awake now, she goes to the window. The view in the half-light is as serene as ever: valley, vineyards, a road that winds away from the palazzo.

Then another scream shatters the serenity. It's louder this time and definitely human.

Throwing on a sundress, she hurries barefoot down the stairs, meeting Alice on the way. 'Did you hear that?' Alice asks. She's still wearing her clothes from the night before.

'Why else would I be up?' Vivi says as they hurry downstairs.

Vivi stops at the kitchen first, for there is a light coming from there, and the muffled, rhythmic sound of chopping, a sharp blade meeting wood.

'Marco!' His back is to them, and he has headphones on.

She taps him on the shoulder.

'*Merda!* Sorry, you startled me,' he says, turning around. 'Is everything okay?'

At that moment, Delfina appears in the doorway, fully clothed but barefoot and dripping water over the tiled floor. She is gasping and gesticulating and telling Marco something in rapid Italian.

His face contracts and he says something that sounds like a curse, dropping his knife with a clatter on the countertop. He sweeps past the women and begins to run along the path towards the pool, Delfina only steps behind him.

Alice and Vivi look at each other in puzzled alarm. 'Did you get that?'

'Uh-uh,' says Alice. 'Let's go and see.'

When they reach the pool, they come to a halt a few feet away, and for a second Vivi can't make any sense of the scene in front of her.

Delfina and Marco are at the far end. Delfina's head is buried in Marco's chest, her shoulders heaving. His arms are around her, his expression both shocked and bewildered.

Vivi approaches, seeing a body at the bottom of the pool, as improbable as a mannequin. Half-dressed in a yellow robe, the front torn open and exposing bare breasts. Long hair a tangled mess covering her face. 'Caroline?'

'No,' Alice cries in a strangled voice. 'No, it can't be.'

CHAPTER FIFTY-FOUR

While they wait for the *polizia* to arrive, Alice returns to the palazzo to check on the girls. Vivi and Marco cover the body with a towel. Weak at the knees, Vivi sits at one of the poolside tables, at a loss as to what else to do.

'I can't find them anywhere.' Alice has run all the way back to the pool judging by her flushed face and rapid breathing.

'Who? Mia and Isla?' Anxiety flares in Vivi's chest.

'No, they're fine. Sleeping like babies. They can't have heard a thing.' Alice pauses to catch her breath. 'Everyone is accounted for except Pete and Nick. Their room is empty, their bed hasn't been slept in.'

'What? When did you last see them?'

Alice frowns. 'At dinner last night. I'm afraid it's all a bit of a blur after that, what with having to look after Mia. I didn't see them after we got back, I'm sure of that. You don't think they have anything to do with this—' She indicates the body with a shaking hand, unable to look in the direction of the pool.

Vivi considers it for a moment. Her first thought on seeing the body was that it had been a terrible accident, a tragic drowning, but perhaps she is being naïve? 'Honestly, nothing would surprise me anymore. Did you check to see if their car is still here?'

'No, I didn't think to look,' Alice replies. 'I'll go now.' She takes off along the path again and returns a few moments later, shaking her head, too out of breath to speak at first. 'It's still there,' she gasps.

'And you're sure they weren't in their room? Do you think they went out for an early run? Somehow missed all this?' Vivi sweeps her hand around the pool area.

'Their bed wasn't slept in. And I don't think they would have gone out before dawn, not with the amount Pete drank last night.'

'Good point.' Vivi's about to ask Marco if he has seen either of the two men when slow, scuffing steps come from the direction of the olive grove.

'Stella?'

The old woman shuffles towards them, muttering to herself and shaking her head. Vivi is grateful that they have covered the body; Stella doesn't need to see that.

'*Tutto bene*?' Marco asks.

'Stella, have you seen two of the guests?' Vivi asks. 'The two men?'

Marco repeats the question, and she mutters a reply in rasping Italian, speaking too fast for Vivi to understand even half of what she is saying.

'*Che cosa*? What?' Marco asks. 'Stella, what have you done?'

Stella shuffles away from them, muttering, as Marco races off in the direction of the olive trees.

'What? What is it?' Alice asks Delfina. 'What the hell is going on?'

CHAPTER FIFTY-FIVE

It's not until later that morning, after the arrival of detectives and a forensic team, that Marco discovers the two men in one of the unused cowsheds. They're filthy and furious, hoarse from shouting for help and suffering the effects of a sleepless night, but otherwise none the worse for wear.

Hearing the disturbance, Vivi goes over to them. She isn't entirely upset when she learns of their plight. In fact, the notion has a kind of perverse justice, though she still thinks Pete deserves more than a night of discomfort. She struggles to keep a straight face when she sees the state of them, smears of what can only be cow dung on Pete's shirt and Nick's white jeans, straw in their usually immaculate hair. She reminds herself of Pete's betrayal and instantly sobers. 'Pete, I wonder if I might have a brief word,' she says.

'I'd really rather clean up first,' he replies. 'And a coffee …?' He stops when he sees the look on her face. 'Of course. Nick, you go up and I'll see you shortly.'

Before Pete finds out what has happened at the pool, Vivi wants to set him straight about a few things. 'I had a call from Robert last night,' she says. 'About J&K, among other matters.' She watches his reaction, but he seems more focused on the state of his nails. 'But you probably already know, don't you?'

His head snaps up and at last his eyes meet hers.

Vivi laughs, a tight, dry sound. 'I've decided not to fight it,' she lies. 'If the board votes to sell, I'll not stand in the way.'

Pete staggers backwards, nearly ending up in the prickly embrace of a cypress tree. 'What? But what about London?' he asks. 'The job offer? What does that mean now for me?'

Vivi laughs again, harshly this time. 'Oh, Pete, did you really think I'd overlook this kind of betrayal, especially from a supposedly close friend? Robert found out all about the report you prepared, your meeting in Milan next week. It seems you are ready to sell any info you could glean about me.'

He shakes his head, blinking as if he can't believe what she's saying. 'I was going to tell you, I swear. But I needed the money, and I accepted the job before I knew that I was coming here. I was going to give you a heads-up just as soon as I'd made my presentation. Doesn't our friendship count for anything?'

'Seemingly not, Pete.' She stares stonily at him. 'You've underestimated me. Now, you should really go and take that shower.' She wrinkles her nose. 'You stink to high heaven. And when you're done, I believe the police want a word.'

'What?'

She turns away. Let him sweat on the answer to that question.

* * *

If the police hadn't insisted Pete and Nick stay, Vivi would have seen them out as soon as they'd had time to gather their things. As it is, their night spent locked in the barn affords them a solid alibi.

Later, all the guests, except for Caroline, gather on the terrace. A shellshocked silence fills the air, everyone deep in their own thoughts, staring at their hands, up at the mountains, or down into the valley.

Marco brings out a bottle of grappa and pours a glass for those who can stomach it. 'Alice?' he offers, but she shakes her head.

'I'm so sorry.' Vivi takes a glass from him. 'Your beautiful palazzo, this awful thing … I feel responsible.' Vivi has called Robert already, briefly outlining the situation and instructing him to take the necessary next steps.

'Stop apologising. It isn't your fault.' Alice squeezes her sister's hand. 'It was a terrible accident.' She has refused a drink but is taking tiny bites from a now-stale apple pastry. None of them have really eaten much, but Vivi can't imagine sitting down to a meal right now, let alone expecting Marco to cook for them.

'Pretty intense, huh?' Mia, slumped in a chair at the end of the table, looks up. Aside from bloodshot eyes and a lingering lethargy, she doesn't seem to have suffered any ill-effects from her experience the night before and insisted she was well enough to get out of bed. Alice is yet to grill her about how exactly she met Gabriele, but she's promised Vivi she'll put the fear of God into her daughter just as soon as Mia has made a full recovery.

'So she hit her head? They think that's how she … drowned?' Isla asks. She's been extremely subdued all day, but then they all have.

Vivi nods. 'She wasn't a very good swimmer. She didn't go in the water the whole time we were here.'

'I still don't understand why Jade was wearing Caroline's robe,' Alice says, taking a desultory bite of pastry.

'Perhaps she was trying it on?' Isla suggests. 'She seemed like she wanted to copy you all the time, Auntie Vivi. Maybe she was pretending to be Caroline for a change?'

'I don't think it is that simple,' Marco says, for he has been able to glean a little information from the police. 'There were signs of a struggle. Jade's death is being treated as suspicious.'

CHAPTER FIFTY-SIX

'Can we go through this one more time?' The detective, the younger of the pair who have been questioning them all, flips through his notebook.

This can't be happening.

'I went to the pool in the early hours of this morning. It was hot and I couldn't sleep,' Caroline replies. She's exhausted, and it's an effort to keep her voice steady.

'Can you tell us exactly what time that was?'

'Maybe sometime between two-thirty and three am? I'm not exactly sure. I wasn't wearing a watch.' Caroline surreptitiously cups her hands to her neck, hoping there are no bruises showing. 'I ran into Gabriele – Signore Galosso – and we exchanged a few words, and then I left.'

The detective raises one eyebrow then makes a note and whispers something to his partner.

'And you say that Signorina Treacher – Jade – was wearing your robe?'

'As I've explained, I must have left it by the pool. I remember returning to my room with a towel wrapped around me. Maybe Jade came out later – her room is close to the pool, and she always got up ridiculously early, apparently. Vivi said she's been sending emails to her at four-thirty in the morning while we've been here, did she mention that?'

The officer makes a note. 'So she was not on holiday?'

'I think it was half holiday, half work. Vivi will be able to clarify that if it's important.'

'How about we decide what is important.' The other detective looks her up and down. 'How tall are you, Signora Fenning?'

'Five foot nine. A hundred and seventy-five centimetres.'

The detective looks through his notes. 'About the same height as the deceased?'

'Yes, I suppose we must be.'

'And you both have long brown hair.'

'Well, hers is a bit darker than mine, but, yes, I suppose we do ... er, did.'

The other detective squints at Caro, clicking his pen, but she doesn't have to wait long to find out what he's thinking. 'And you say Signore Galosso was there when you left the pool?'

Caroline nods.

He changes tack almost immediately. 'You argued with Signora Treacher?'

'What?'

'Signora Savidge's sister and the two young ladies all stated ...' he consults his notes again, 'that they overheard the two of you disagreeing about a book? That you told her she was an "idiot" to believe what was written there?'

'I wouldn't exactly call it an argument. More a minor disagreement,' she stresses. 'And from memory I said the book was idiotic, not her.'

The detective sucks in a breath, taps his pen on his notepad.

Caroline puts a hand to her mouth. 'Oh God. You don't think I had something to do with this?' She begins to laugh hysterically, low blood sugar and lack of sleep giving the entire situation a surreal feeling. How much longer is this going to last? She's hungry and thirsty, not to mention the kind of tired that makes her feel like she might pass out given half a chance. The past few weeks have shredded every last nerve she possesses.

As if reading her mind, the other detective begins to gather his papers, whispers something in his colleague's ear that Caroline does not catch. He turns to her. 'Perhaps you might accompany us to the station.'

It's not a suggestion.

A jolt of panic clears the thickness in her brain. Fuck. It wasn't supposed to go like this.

Caro swallows hard. 'Do I need a solicitor?'

'You are within your rights to request one if you wish.'

What the hell will Vivi and the others make of this development? Will they even care? They probably all, without exception, hate her. 'Am I the only one being asked to come with you?'

A brief nod from them both. 'For the time being.'

Caro reminds herself that there is no evidence, save for a flimsy gown that she fully admits to leaving by the pool, to connect her with Jade's death. But her hands shake as she gathers her sunglasses and jacket, and she's freezing now despite the oppressive heat. She never was especially brave. 'May I collect my belongings first?'

'We will arrange for them to be sent on tomorrow.'

'At least let me say goodbye,' she pleads. 'And I need my phone.'

The two detectives accompany her to the terrace where she beckons to Vivi and in a stilted whisper explains the situation, making it sound as innocuous as she possibly can. 'I expect it's only a precaution. And anyway, I should get back to the city. This way I don't have to beg a lift from anyone.'

Vivi looks at her hard then shakes her head. 'Call and keep me updated. I've got your back.'

Caroline almost drops her phone as Vivi hands it her. 'I don't deserve that.'

Vivi shrugs. 'We all deserve better, Caro. Contrary to what you might think, you and I, we're not bad people, and there's no way I believe you're a killer.'

'Neither are you.' She considers giving her old friend a swift, grateful hug but decides against it, walking away without a backwards glance.

CHAPTER FIFTY-SEVEN

The police take Caroline to a station near the university, ushering her into a small, stark room furnished with a plain table and three hard chairs. A fluorescent light flickers overhead and a headache immediately tightens her forehead. 'May I have some water?' she asks as she draws her jacket around her body. After the heat of the day, the air-conditioning is ferocious.

The younger of the two detectives leaves the room and returns with a plastic cup of lukewarm, metallic-tasting water. She drains it in two gulps as they begin to speak, informing her that the conversation is being recorded.

'Once again, Signora Fenning. Your movements from midnight onwards.'

Caroline braces herself but doesn't get the opportunity to answer. The door opens and a duty officer ushers in a slim, dark man wearing a sharp suit and a crisp white shirt. Caroline, who hasn't even had a chance to shower or brush her hair all day, folds in on herself even more tightly.

'Signora Fenning.' He extends a hand for her to shake and introduces himself.

A solicitor. Thank God. Vivi has come through. Waves of relief flood through her.

'If I might have a moment to confer with my client?' he asks, opening a leather folder and clicking the top of his pen.

The two detectives prop the door open behind them as they leave.

He quickly summarises the key points, reassuring her that he'll have her out of the station as soon as possible. 'Is there anything else that I should know?' he asks, his eyes darting towards hers. He's good, but then she would have expected little else from someone connected to Vivi.

She takes a deep breath and tells him about Gabriele, about running away from him after their confrontation at the pool. 'He was almost certainly the last one there, the last one to have seen Jade,' she finishes, a tremble in her voice. 'It's him they should be questioning, not me.'

The solicitor nods, goes to the corridor, and the two detectives return.

Half an hour later, Caroline is allowed to leave. As she and the solicitor are exiting the building into a sultry summer evening, a squad car pulls up and they are forced to swerve out of the way to avoid it.

Caroline glances into the car as they pass.

In the back seat, head bent over like a stringless puppet, is Gabriele.

She walks straight past him, her own head held high.

Quickening her steps, she only breathes out when she is long past the station.

vogue.co.uk
Arts and Lifestyle – Viewpoint
Amy Morrison
1 September 2023

'He deserved so much better'
Beauty boss spills all about her husband's tragic illness, weighing in on the charged debate over euthanasia

'It pushed him to the brink,' Vivi Savidge says, speaking from the Chelsea Mews home she once shared with her husband of fourteen years. 'This is why it is so important that the laws around assisted dying are amended, so that others in my husband's position don't have to suffer for so long.'

Subscribers click to continue.

CHAPTER FIFTY-EIGHT

The detectives don't call her in for questioning a second time.

Two days after leaving the police station in Turin, two days in which Caroline is too scared to leave her apartment, two days of nothing to eat but crackers and a couple of tins of beans, all while scouring the internet for news, she finally gets the call she's been waiting for. Vivi's solicitor rings, telling her that Gabriele Galosso has been charged with the murder of Jade Treacher.

'*Mille grazie*,' she says to him over and over.

'Although you will almost certainly be required to give evidence when it goes to trial.'

She swallows hard. 'Of course.' A final bridge to cross.

After she ends the call, she goes to the kitchen and pulls a dusty bottle of Barolo from a drawer. Scrabbling for a corkscrew, she opens it and pours herself a glass, inhaling the sweet perfume of summers long past.

Heading out onto her tiny balcony, she perches on a metal chair and raises her glass to the buildings opposite. *It's going to be okay.* This is what she wanted.

She seized her opportunity when, after running away from Gabriele, she returned to the pool some ten minutes later filled with righteous fury, a six-inch kitchen knife concealed in her skirts, determined to scare him as much as he had scared her.

Except she had been too late. She had arrived to see him

push a woman, a woman wearing her robe. The woman had her arms raised, trying to fight him off, attempting to turn around, but she didn't stand a chance, and with a splash she landed in the water, heavy as a fallen log.

Seconds later, Gabriele ran into the darkness.

Caro called out to him, but he can't have heard her.

She was the person he'd meant to hurt, she reasons, leaning on the balcony railing to watch the traffic below, dangling her glass over the edge. He must have thought it was her in the yellow robe.

Caroline sees it again now as if watching a movie: by the time she reached the pool, the woman was floundering, splashing her arms and legs frantically, raising her head and gasping for breath, bobbing on the surface like a corked bottle.

Jade, Vivi's odd young assistant.

Caroline takes another sip of her wine, remembering how as she'd stood there and watched Jade flail, an idea began to form. An idea so risky, so outrageous but so *right* that it left her as short of breath as the woman in the water. A chance to stick it to Gabriele and hurt Vivi in the process.

It was perfect.

She knelt at the edge of the deep end, grazing her knees on the rough stone, and called to Jade. 'Over here!'

The girl finally saw her and reached out, gasping desperately that she couldn't swim. Caroline managed to get hold of her hand and pulled her closer.

Jade was within reach of the edge when Caroline firmly planted her palms on top of the girl's head, fastened them into her hair and held her down. She turned her face to avoid the splashes and for a second feared she might end up in the water herself.

Weakened by her struggles, Jade didn't put up much of a fight. It felt like an age, time expanding in the darkness, but it was probably only a matter of moments before she was still. Lifeless. Floating.

Caroline coolly untangled her fingers from Jade's hair, wiped her wet hands on her towel, remembered to pick up the knife from the side of the pool, and left.

There have been so many days when she was sure she would be found out, that some vital piece of evidence might connect her to the scene, that someone might have witnessed her terrible act, but she has held her nerve, and she is at least proud of herself for that. Gabriele will be their only suspect; he has to be. Vivi is, as Caro predicted, devastated at the loss of her trusted assistant.

Draining her glass, she goes back inside and, with a steady hand, helps herself to another.

Nine months later, Palazzo Stellina

Delfina is skimming wind-blown quince blossom from the water when the car pulls up and the gates swing slowly open. It's her least favourite job, for she no longer enjoys being near the pool. She may never swim in it again, not after what happened.

She sets the net aside and hurries along the path back to the palazzo, leaning over the terrace to see who it might be. They aren't expecting guests this early in the season, and visitors have been limited to the plumber (more than once) and the police (less often now), but each time, their presence leaves Marco in a foul mood and it takes all her feminine powers of persuasion, usually involving them both getting naked, to put him in a better one. This isn't either of those, however. The car is a sleek black limousine that weaves its way through the vines, which after the bleak of winter are now vibrantly green with the first budburst.

'*Un visitatore?*' she asks Stella, who sweeps the terrace with painfully slow movements. Delfina and Marco have told her she doesn't need to do this, but still she persists. Delfina thinks that Stella perhaps does not know how to do nothing, and that maybe she fears stopping lest she lose the ability to start again.

Delfina scampers down the stone stairs to greet the new arrival, smoothing a stray strand of hair back into its long braid and then wiping her hands on her apron. Behind the tinted glass, she can make out the over-large sunglasses and bright red lipstick of a woman.

The car pulls to a stop and the passenger door opens. 'Signora Savidge. *Buongiorno.*' She recognises her immediately. Of course she does; this woman's stay last summer is the reason for the police visits, not to mention the paparazzi, who hung beyond the palazzo gates for days like jackals anticipating a feast.

'Delfina, how lovely to see you again. And it's Vivi, please.' She says it with warmth, but Delfina is wary. This woman and her friends brought so much trouble the last time they were here.

'Can I be of help to you?' she asks. Delfina has been practising her English with Marco, but she is still self-conscious about it.

'I hope so.' The *signora* looks lighter than she did in the summer, fresher, as if she is getting more sleep perhaps. 'Marco is expecting me, although I must confess, I am a little early. Is he about?'

'Please, come in. I shall tell him you are here. Would you like some tea?' She is surprised Marco has not come out himself as he would surely have heard the car from the kitchen, but then he does like to put on his headphones when he's absorbed in his work.

'How good of you to remember.' Vivi reaches into the car and pulls out a leather folder. 'Thank you, that would be nice.'

Delfina leads her up the stairs and invites her to take a seat at the table on the terrace, wondering why the woman has returned. If she were in the *signora*'s shoes, this is the last place she would come, but then it occurs to her that it is almost certainly something to do with the incident – she can't bring herself to refer to it as the murder. The nightmares about that morning have only recently stopped waking her, shuddering and sweating, in the middle of the night. What does Marco call them? Loose ends. Yes, perhaps that is why she is here.

Delfina is still thinking of loose ends, imagining them like long brown hair curling in water, when she arrives in the kitchen and finds Marco with, as she suspected, his headphones on. He has his back to her, and she goes up behind him, gently tapping him on the shoulder, mindful that he has a paring knife in his hand.

'*Che?*' He tugs one of the cans away from his ear and she can hear the tinny strings of the music he's listening to. He doesn't miss the opportunity to kiss her, wrapping an arm about her waist and drawing her close.

She leans against him for a moment, breathing in the smell of him, returning the kiss, but eventually breaks away. 'Signora Savidge is here. You are expecting her?' Why hasn't he mentioned this before? She thought that they talked about nearly everything, especially since he broke down one night after too much grappa and confessed that he isn't sure he can keep the business running for too much longer. Bookings are almost non-existent. News of the murder has been splashed across international media websites and scandal magazines, and it seems that only the ghoulish are prepared to stay at the scene of the crime. Few among them are the wealthy European and American clientele that the palazzo needs in order to survive.

'Yes, though she was unclear about the reason for her visit.' He goes to his phone, presses a few buttons then pulls off his headphones, abandoning them on the countertop.

'*Allora.* I will bring you both some tea. She is waiting on the terrace.'

Marco summons a smile. He looks so tired.

A few minutes later, as she carries a tray bearing a pot, cups, milk in a jug and a dish of the nubbly brown sugar chunks that so many of their guests like, she overhears the *signora* telling Marco about her friends. 'Pete and Nick are on an adoption waiting list, from what I understand. They will make terrific parents.' She flashes a tight-lipped smile and Delfina wonders how happy she really is for them.

'Alice has moved to London for the girls' last two years of school. Her ex-husband agreed when he realised they would be able to apply to Cambridge or Oxford for university and not have to pay overseas fees. He's a raging intellectual snob, and a complete tightwad, so that's worked in Alice's favour for once.' She rolls her eyes dramatically. 'They're living just around the corner from me as it happens. Alice is working on an exhibition of overlooked women – including her portrait of Stella. I think she sent you a photo of the finished piece. She's one hundred per cent focused on that, as well as her girls, of course.'

The *signora* colours, a flush rising from her collarbones, and Delfina is pleased that she hasn't brought her sister with her. She had been all too aware of Marco's interest in the woman. Delfina no longer worries about Marco's interest in anyone but her, but that doesn't mean she is anxious for her to return. 'Especially after what happened with Mia. I did offer to get the girls some professional help, but Alice says they're fine. "As resilient as a new tennis ball," she reassures me.' Vivi swallows. 'I'm still so grateful for your help that night.'

Marco shakes his head. 'Anyone would have done the same.'

Vivi and Marco chat some more, and Delfina withdraws, though she stays where she can observe them unnoticed. She understands English reasonably well now, certainly far better than she speaks it, the focus she once put into swimming now diverted to language lessons.

She overhears Signora Savidge ask Marco how things are at the palazzo. 'Seventy per cent vacancy. Multiple cancellations,' he says glumly. Delfina has heard these figures before, but she is curious why he is speaking of them now, and to this woman. He is a proud man, but with the *signora* he is an open book. 'The wolf is at the door.' He runs an exasperated hand through his hair and gulps down a mouthful of tea.

'I'm sorry. I did my best to keep the name of the palazzo out of the media, but …' the *signora* shrugs, then brings out a small tablet from her leather folder, 'you know how it is.' She taps away at the screen, pausing occasionally to jot something on a notepad to her right. It seems rude, but Marco doesn't appear to mind. 'We have so little control.'

Delfina also read in one of the British newspapers that the *signora* was suspected of hastening the death of her husband, that she had made enquiries of an organisation that helps people with such things, but no proof could be found and the story fizzled. Shortly afterwards, they published an apology, saying that they had insufficient evidence on which to base their allegations, and reached an agreement to donate an undisclosed sum of money to a cancer research charity.

Marco shrugs. 'It is what it is.'

Delfina lingers, anxious to hear more. Marco will probably tell her about it later, but he is sure to forget the details, and she wants to hear the conversation for herself firsthand. It is English practice, she justifies, despite knowing full well that it is outright curiosity.

'… a partnership. An initial investment of two hundred thousand euros, and in addition I will secure the services of one of our best PR firms and cover that cost. That should help with the roof at least. We will turn this around, Marco. I believe in what you're doing here.'

'And in return? What am I to give you?'

'A small share in the business. We can get the accountants to work out the finer details; I don't want to haggle over it. It's more important that you can continue to operate, to take the palazzo to where it deserves to be – as one of, no, *the* foremost luxury accommodation with the best food in this part of Italy.' She pauses, looking up from her screen. 'When I did the deal to sell Vivid to Copera, one of the conditions was that I had to sign a fifteen-year non-compete contract, so although I'll probably never create another cosmetics company, nor do I think I'll ever want to, I now have the opportunity to explore other interests, things that mean something to me personally.'

Marco drains the last of his cup and it rattles briefly on the saucer as he replaces it. 'Won't you miss it?'

Vivi shrugs. 'Cosmetics entrepreneurs are ten a penny these days, not like when I started. Everyone's in the game. It's time for something new. And besides, I feel responsible … for what happened here. You would not be in this position had I chosen to spend my birthday anywhere else, had I not agreed for a visitor to join us when I couldn't personally vouch for him.'

'That was hardly your fault.' He covers her hand with his.

'Nevertheless, I can help … and I believe the Palazzo Stellina has a brilliant future.' She smiles at the inadvertent pun. 'It will please me enormously to play a small part in that.' She fixes him with a no-nonsense expression, as if the matter is already agreed upon.

Delfina holds her breath. Will Marco accept her offer? Or will his stubborn pride prevent him from grasping the lifeline the *signora* is offering?

Marco shifts in his seat.

'It's going to be okay, you know.'

'I'm beginning to see that,' he replies, a long-absent smile lighting up his face. 'And for you too. It's going to be okay for you. There is always the sweetness of honey to be found, even though there is the sting.'

Delfina exhales.

She walks back onto the terrace in time to see them rise from their seats, Marco pulling Vivi's chair out of the way before folding her into his arms for an embrace. Delfina watches with narrowed eyes. She and Marco are a couple now, but he is a flirt. She finds herself counting the seconds, relaxing only when he releases the woman.

'Can I get you anything else?' Delfina asks.

Vivi shakes her head, and this time her smile encompasses them both. 'That was just what I needed, thank you, Delfina. So, Marco, we are agreed?'

He nods. 'Subject to the finer details.'

'Excellent. We'd best get to work then. There's a lot to look forward to.' A thought occurs to her. 'I will be in Turin next month for the trial. Perhaps I could book in here for the weekend if you have space? That might be nice. No additional guests this time, I promise. If you have any availability?'

Delfina holds her breath, waiting to hear what she might say next. The story of the alleged murder had made for lurid coverage in *La Stampa* and *Corriere della Sera*, *The Times* and *Daily Mail* in the UK, as well as online news sites. She has read everything she could find about the incident, telling herself she was reading the English sites for language practice. The press was vicious in its condemnation of the student, portraying him as a psychopath and painting Jade as a young woman *this close* to sainthood. The young British innocent, so tragically slain by the predatory Italian man. It felt as though it was an attack on Italy itself sometimes.

Journalists and paparazzi had camped out in the village and beyond the palazzo gates for weeks, and Delfina had come to appreciate Marco's concern for security. It had got so bad that she moved into the palazzo, Marco insisting she sleep in one of the guest rooms, until one cold night she stayed with him and has been there ever since.

According to Marco, who heard it from a friend in the local *polizia*, they initially suspected Caroline of being somehow involved because of her relationship with Gabriele, but that theory collapsed after the intervention of a lawyer engaged by Signora Savidge, who rightly pointed out that they had no grounds on which to detain her, let alone arrest her. Then DNA recovered from scrapings under Jade's fingernails matched to Gabriele, and the case was accelerated from suspected manslaughter to second-degree murder.

The police now allege that Gabriele grabbed Jade from behind, that he pushed her into the pool. He hasn't admitted to it, but the police will also allege that he held her down until she stopped breathing. Marco says the police have told him that the autopsy findings bear this theory out, with evidence of haemorrhaging and water in her lungs.

'Gabriele says he was only in the pool area because his phone had fallen out of his pocket and he went back to look for it,' Vivi says. 'He claims that he never saw her and certainly never drowned her, that he never touched her. It's not going to make much difference, though, because the evidence against him is damning. It seems likely he will be sent down for a long time.'

'Sent down?' Marco asks.

'To prison.'

'And *l'insegnante*? The teacher? Caroline? She is to give evidence too?'

The *signora* nods. 'I believe so. She will confirm that Gabriele was by the pool, that he was stalking her. She has his threatening text messages.'

Unsurprisingly, the newspapers had gone into a feeding frenzy over the relationship between the young student and the teacher. They tore her reputation apart.

'Apparently, she's writing a book about the whole thing.' Vivi arches an eyebrow. 'It seems as though she'll finally have her bestseller.'

ACKNOWLEDGMENTS

Boundless and heartfelt thanks to:

Stephanie Thwaites at Curtis Brown UK for seeing something in a tiny sample of a previous manuscript, for having the faith and belief in me as a writer and always pushing me to do more.

Pippa Masson at Curtis Brown Australia for her insight and acumen.

Carolyn Mays at Bedford Square for her wisdom and attention to detail, and for saving me from myself on more than one occasion.

Anna Valdinger for giving me a new home at HarperCollins in Australia, and especially for her enthusiasm for the characters and the story.

Vanessa Lanaway and Madeleine James, who have so deftly made my prose both sharper and smoother.

I'm incredibly fortunate to have such smart, generous women in my corner, and never for a minute do I forget that bringing a novel to publication is the work of many minds and hands.

About the Author

Image Credit © Jed Grace

Kayte Nunn is the internationally bestselling author of seven novels, most recently 2022's *The Only Child*. They are available worldwide in English, and have been translated into eleven languages.

She was brought up in England, lived in the US for a number of years as a child and now calls the Northern Rivers of NSW, Australia home.

📷 @kaytenunn2
kaytenunn.com

NO EXIT PRESS
More than just the usual suspects

— CWA DAGGER —
AWARDED BEST CRIME & MYSTERY PUBLISHER

'A very smart, independent publisher delivering the finest literary crime fiction' **Big Issue**

MEET NO EXIT PRESS, an award-winning crime imprint bringing you the best in crime and suspense fiction. From classic detective novels, to page-turning spy thrillers and literary writing that grabs the attention. Our books are carefully crafted by some of the world's finest writers and delivered to you by a small, but passionate, team.

In over 30 years of business, we have published award-winning fiction and non-fiction including the work of a Pulitzer Prize winner, the British Crime Book of the Year, numerous CWA Dagger Awards, a British million-copy bestselling author, the winner of the Canadian Governor General's Award for Fiction and the Scotiabank Giller Prize, to name but a few. We are the home of many crime and noir legends from the USA whose work includes iconic film adaptations and TV sensations. We pride ourselves in uncovering the most exciting new or undiscovered talents. New and not so new – you know who you are!

We are a proactive team committed to delivering the very best, both for our authors and our readers.

Want to join the conversation and find out more about what we do?

Catch us on social media or sign up to our newsletter for all the latest news from No Exit Press.

f fb.me/noexitpress   **X** @noexitpress

noexit.co.uk